Blazing Nights

A Night Games Novel
Book One: Kate

Linda Barlow

Linda Barlow Books
Boston, Massachusetts

Linda Barlow Books
www.lindabarlow.com

Publisher's Note: This is a work of fiction. Names, characters, places, and incidents are a product of the author's imagination. Locales and public names are sometimes used for atmospheric purposes. Any resemblance to actual people, living or dead, or to businesses, companies, events, institutions, or locales is completely coincidental.

Book Layout ©2013 BookDesignTemplates.com

Blazing Nights/ Linda Barlow. — 1st ed.
ISBN 978-0-9893070-3-1

TO MY READERS:

Welcome to my sexy contemporary romance series, *Night Games*. The series is about a group of college friends who have stayed in touch since graduation via an online game that one of them created.

The books are each complete and separate, but in some respects they build upon one another. Characters are introduced in the first novel, *Blazing Nights*, who appear again later in the series. While it's possible to read the stories in any order, readers will probably have the most fun if they read them sequentially.

Each of these books was published previously in some form, but they have been completely rewritten and bear little resemblance to the originals. All are considerably longer, with new characters and different events. In one case, I only kept the first chapter and threw out the rest, writing an entirely new book.

The first two books of the series are *Blazing Nights* (Kate's story) and *Wicked Nights* (Max's story). The others will follow.

Other recent releases by Linda Barlow: *Fires of Destiny*.

First Witch: When shall we three meet again
In thunder, lightning, or in rain?
Second Witch: When the hurlyburly's done,
When the battle's lost and won.

–William Shakespeare, MACBETH

She could feel his eyes on her. She'd been spooked by it all evening. For some reason she couldn't fathom, the hottest guy in the room had spent most of the evening staring at her, which was not the sort of thing that typically happened to her.

She tried to ignore him, but this was difficult. His stare— actually, it was more of a glare—was creating havoc in her body. Parts of her that had been numb for ages were tingling, and the warm, glowy feeling in her belly persisted even when she was doing her best to pretend Mr. Hot-As-Hell-But-Can't-Stop-Scowling didn't exist.

Most people circulated at parties, attempting to be social even if they weren't in the mood. This guy didn't bother. Keeping to the gloomy edges of the room, he seemed to be one with the shadows. He had shaggy black hair, a hard-molded jaw and wicked eyes. His clothes, too, were dark: He wore a long-sleeve black tee over a pair of black jeans, enhancing the monochromatic effect. Yet, in the rare moments when she permitted herself to meet his intense gaze, Kate felt flashes of color zing through her: vibrant crimson, angry orange. She had never experienced anything quite like this before.

"Scorpio," said a light, British-accented voice in her ear.

She looked up, finding her friend Graham Hamilton beside her, his mercurial mouth curved in a smile. He had returned to the table in the corner of the Beacon Hill apartment where he and Kate were serving as astrologer and psychic for the entertainment of thirty or forty guests.

Psychic—what a charade. She had agreed because Graham had pleaded with her to help him out tonight. His blind friend, Stephanie, the hostess of this evening's party, had promised her friends to have an astrologer and a fortune-teller present. It was for a worthy cause. The fees they were charging for "readings" were being donated to the National Foundation for the Blind.

The trouble was that Kate was no fortune-teller. Her mother was a famous psychic, but if Kate had inherited any of her powers, they had yet to manifest.

"Who's a Scorpio?" she asked Graham.

He lounged over the arm of her easy chair, handing her a glass of red wine. "Your brooding admirer." Graham flicked one hand in the direction of the man Kate was beginning to think of as her dark angel. "I'm betting that's his sun sign. Powerful physique, hawk-like features, heavy brows, intense eyes. Sexual magnetism, too; that goes without saying. Better watch out, luv. He could be trouble."

Kate didn't argue; she knew trouble when she saw it. "Who is he?"

"You're the mind reader. You tell me."

Kate rolled her eyes. "I haven't forgiven you for getting me into this." But she smiled as she waggled her fingers at him in as spooky a manner as she could manage. "I'm putting a spell on you the moment we get out of here. Madame Katrina indeed." She gestured toward the fortune-telling paraphernalia laid on the table in front of her: tarot cards, palmistry charts, I Ching sticks, and Graham's astrological tables. "About the only thing we don't have is a crystal ball."

Graham grinned. "Concentrate on him, luv." He nodded at the brooder. "Tell me the time and place of his birth."

"As if I could."

"If he does turn out to be Scorpio, you and he would be compatible. You're a water sign, too. Great empathy is possible, and the sex would be hot. You could use a little hot sex, couldn't you?"

Kate sighed. "I've gotten used to living without it."

"On the other hand," Graham went on, darting another glance at the stranger, "He would try to dominate you. A yielding little fish like you could be sucked in and swallowed."

She gently pushed away the arm Graham insisted on slinging around her shoulders. "You know I'm not the yielding type. Besides, I don't think I believe in astrology."

"Sacrilege! It's the one true path to enlightenment. And it has the virtue of being scientific as well."

"Ahem, scientific?"

"Okay, maybe not so much."

"There are many paths to enlightenment." Assuming there even was such a thing as enlightenment.

"I'm still waiting for one of those paths to lead you into my bedroom."

She grinned at him. "Didn't you once admit to me that our charts decree we'd be hopelessly incompatible in bed?"

"Did I? Stupid me. I'd better recast those charts."

Kate laughed, and then sobered as she cast another look at her tarot cards. Why had she ever agreed to this masquerade? Fortunately, the guests were fun loving and sophisticated, and no one was taking her too seriously.

"Do you really have a colleague named Madame Olivia who's down with a virus? And since when have you been teaming up with a psychic?"

"I only worked with her a couple times, actually. A strange lady. She not only has a sixth sense, but a seventh, eighth, and ninth as well."

"The only thing my sixth sense tells me is that I'm probably going to be denounced as a fraud."

"No way. You're an actress, and a damn good one. You can do this."

"I'd rather do Shakespeare. When can we leave?"

"Not for at least an hour. We've got four or five more readings after this break is over. Want some more wine?"

"Bring the bottle."

She and Graham were officially on one of the evening's breaks, during which they were supposed to be regenerating their psychic energy. Wine wasn't going to help, although it might relax her. Kate recalled her mother's confirmed belief in the mystical powers of herbal teas. She was glad her mother wasn't here to see her now. Mom had been encouraging her to develop her supposedly natural powers for years, as if ghost-whispering were something that could be passed down in one's DNA.

Playing idly with her tarot deck, Kate watched Graham return to mixing with the guests. His British charm, combined with his slender elegance and his blond good looks, always seemed to bring him ample success with the women. Like Kate, he was an actor, and he was accustomed to playing the role of the elegant Englishman charmed by American beauty and high spirits. He had snagged the lead role in more than one Noel Coward revival.

She snuck a quick glance in the direction where she'd last seen the hot-eyed stranger. Maybe he'd left? Nope. His tall, lean body was still casually propped against the opposite wall. She noted his lazy grace, the aura of dynamic physical power he radiated. He was not the most classically handsome man she had ever seen—his features were a little rough rather than perfectly molded—but there was an exciting earthiness about him. His hair was black and wavy, a trifle long over the collar. He had that been-in-bed-too-long and needs-a-shave look. Sexy, scruffy whiskers that one would hesitate to call a beard. She had a flash of what that rough stubble might feel like against her cheek, her throat, her breasts... Uh-oh. Lust alert.

Because of the way he was lounging against the wall, with one hand thrust aggressively into his hip pocket, Kate could see that his stomach was trim, his hips and thighs taut and free of extra flesh. She supposed he must hit the gym regularly to stay so fit. A line or two on his face suggested that he must be close to thirty.

He was certainly persistent. He was still glowering at her in a strange and rather malevolent manner. Deliberately she met his gaze and smiled. He didn't smile back, but she saw his eyes widen, as if in shock.

Maybe he was mentally deranged. Or high on the latest fashionable drug. Maybe he was some kind of freak who was engaging in a lurid fantasy about abducting and ravishing her. He looked like a ravisher, with that rugged jaw and those broody bedroom eyes. Unlike Graham, who slyly cajoled and gently seduced women, this man looked as if he would simply take what he wanted, and to hell with the consequences.

Looking away, she shuffled the tarot cards. He was making her nervous.

When Graham returned to their corner a couple of minutes later, he seemed a trifle subdued. He sat down beside her and scanned the guests. "Someone just told me that D. B. Haggarty's here tonight. You know, that investigative reporter turned web phenomenon who made a name for himself by rounding up and exposing fakes?"

"Fakes?" The word came out in a squeak.

"Everything from political corruption to falsely-labeled organic foods to sleazy hedge fund managers. He's a real crusader in the old muckraker tradition. His cable TV show has been a big hit, and his web broadcasts supposedly get YouTubed all over the world."

Kate's eyes flew to her black-clad nemesis. He was still propping up the wall, sipping a drink. It's him, she thought. It must be. No wonder he was glaring at her—he must have marked her out as a fraud right from the start. "I've heard of him. Didn't he run a piece about Myra Kelley, that medium who used to be a friend of my mother's?"

"Yeah, he did. I didn't see it myself, but I heard Haggarty's minions really slammed her. Said she faked readings and ripped off grieving widows. He's got a thing against psychics, particular those who claim to be able to contact the dear departed."

"He probably eats bogus fortune-tellers like me for supper." She shivered slightly. "I knew I shouldn't have agreed to this."

"I'm sorry for getting you involved. It's just that I'd promised Stephanie, and I couldn't bear to disappoint her." Graham was searching the room, examining each of the guests. "I don't see him. Maybe he won't notice us."

"What does he look like?" She glanced again toward the man she was starting to think of as her silent stalker. "Our Scorpio brooder has been contemplating my ruin all evening."

"Nah, Scorpio is too young. Haggarty's fiftyish and balding, if I remember correctly. He doesn't actually appear on his webcasts; he's the head writer and producer. But I did see a picture of him once. I've been trying to pick him out ever since I heard he was here."

Kate felt a little bit better to hear that the brooder was excluded.

"Besides, that guy is too busy contemplating your body. Smart man," Graham added, leaning over the side of her chair to run a finger around the neckline of her green silk top.

She removed his hand, exasperated. She'd known Graham too long to be overly offended. He was a good friend, but if he overindulged in wine or pharmaceuticals, he tended to sprout more hands than a Hindu goddess.

"The lady doesn't seem to want your attentions," said a deep voice from just above their heads. Kate looked up. The Scorpio brooder had proved himself capable of motion—startlingly swift motion, in fact. The latent aggression she had sensed in him had come to the fore; his fists were clenched, and he looked as if he were about to toss Graham across the room.

"Bloody hell, an old-fashioned chivalrous knight to the rescue," Graham gave the man a careless once-over, and then shot a mischievous look at her. Had he provoked him deliberately? "She doesn't require aid. I'm only a poor misguided astrologer, but she is a witch." Then he winked at Kate and rejoined the other guests.

Kate winced. Graham was such a meddler. He was referring to her upcoming role in the New Cambridge Repertory production of *Macbeth*. She was playing one of the three witches. But unless the Scorpio brooder was an aficionado of small Boston-area theater groups, he wouldn't understand the reference.

With some trepidation, she met the stranger's eyes. Once again, she felt the strange sensation of colors flashing: golds, scarlets, deep, arcing blues. What *was* that? And what was it about this guy that sent her imagination into such vivid flights of fancy?

"A witch? That I can well believe." His voice was a husky baritone. Up close, his eyes were actually blue, a dark velvety blue. His gaze flicked over her, taking in everything he had studied for so long from across the room. "They used to burn witches, didn't they? Tell me, witch," he spoke the word caressingly, "have you no fear of the flames?"

Feeling a little pensive, she answered as if under some sort of compulsion. "I do have a recurring dream of a fire that threatens me."

His eyes narrowed, and skepticism showed plainly on his face. Kate's trancelike feeling vanished. What a lame thing to say! What was wrong with her? This fortune-telling charade was really getting to her. She hardened her voice. "Who are you? Why have you been glaring at me all evening?"

"Have I?" His lips quirked mischievously. "I didn't mean to glare. I apologize."

Okay, she thought, a bit surprised. He didn't seem like the apologizing type. "It felt pretty hostile."

A rueful smile softened his features. "My bad. I thought I was being discreet."

She smiled back, warming to his faintly self-deprecatory tone. He had strong, high cheekbones, an aggressive nose, and a sulky, sensual mouth. His velvet eyes radiated masculine confidence. His tall body was both athletic and graceful, and he radiated a subtle impression of leashed power that brought sexy bedroom fantasies to her mind.

Down, girl.

"Are you here for a reading?" She pretended to consult her list, even though she knew he hadn't been one of the people who'd signed up. "What's your name?"

"Surely you can reach into my brain and pull out my name, like a rabbit from a hat. Go ahead, witch. Try."

"I'm not that gifted."

His heavy black eyebrows rose. "No? I am astonished."

His sarcastic tone declared that he was anything but. But his heated gaze felt as if it were melting the silk of her top. It didn't take any psychic ability to recognize the sensual intent in him. She wasn't quite sure how to deal with it. She wasn't accustomed to being hit on by mouth-watering strangers. "If you don't want to sit for a reading, perhaps you'd care to contribute something to the National Foundation for the Blind anyway?"

Surprising her, he lowered himself into the chair opposite her and placed his arm on the table between them, palm up but hidden in by his clenched fist. "I'd be happy to. Go ahead. Open my hand; open my heart."

Curiosity surged in her. She wanted to look into his palm. She even wanted to touch him. It had been so long since she had last touched a man. Too long, her friends were insisting. Her solitary life was not exactly normal, they all kept telling her. She was still young, and she couldn't mourn forever.

She did know something about palmistry. She could hardly grow up as the daughter of a famous crackpot psychic without learning the basics. She could lay out the tarot deck and interpret the cards, too. Without these minimal talents, she would never have agreed to help Graham out tonight.

She knew enough, surely, to play this game with him. After all, she was a professional actress. So why was her heart doing a kettledrum impression?

He was waiting, his fist still clenched on the table between them. "Do you want me to cross your palm with silver first?" He didn't bother to disguise the snarkiness in his voice.

As she looked down at his hand, she had a fuzzy mental image of the injured paw of a jungle beast. She felt a powerful need to stroke the injured paw and heal it. This odd impression was succeeded by a sense of the man across from her as fiercely predatory on the surface but tender deep inside—pierced by the same thorn of loneliness and sorrow that tormented her.

She shook her head, feeling a little dizzy. For a moment or two, the room seemed to tilt. Maybe she shouldn't have had that second glass of wine. "Your name is Daniel," she heard herself say. "First or last, I don't know, but one of your names is Daniel."

His eyes opened wider for an instant before the lids half closed, hiding his reaction. "Very clever. Although I don't know why I'm still so surprised when people recognize me. You're going to have to do better than that to impress me."

"You mean your name *is* Daniel?"

"Of course it is."

Dear heavens. Could it be that she...her mother had always said...no. Surely not. Get hold of yourself, Kate. It was a lucky guess, that's all.

Daniel. She liked the name.

"I'm Kate."

"I already know your name, Ms. Carter."

"I'm not a Ms., I'm a Mrs.," she corrected him, puzzled. Carter was her birth name, but she hadn't used it for years. Even on stage, she had always called herself by her married name, Kate Kingsley. "Have we met?"

The fist on the table between them seemed to tighten even more. "You're married?" He sounded so shocked at the idea that Kate was taken aback. She was tempted to lie, sensing that the sensual threat in this man would be reined in if he believed she was married. But she couldn't lie to him, at least, not any more than she was already doing by enacting this masquerade.

"I'm a widow."

"How long?"

"What?"

"How long have you been a widow?"

The usual response to her widowhood was a polite statement like, "I'm so sorry," or "How sad." Not that most new acquaintances felt any real sympathy, she reminded herself. How could they? They didn't know her, and they hadn't known Arthur. At least Daniel didn't pretend a sympathy that he couldn't possibly feel. "It's been nearly three years now."

"And you still say it so mournfully? Such devotion."

A seed of anger burst inside her. How dare he mock her grief? A sharp longing for Arthur rose, as it still so often did. Three years? Sometimes it felt more like three months, or even three weeks since she had lost him. Wasn't the pain ever going to go away?

"Look, I'm not here to be baited and snarled at. If you want a reading, fine; if you don't, kindly take yourself back to the same dark corner where you've spent the evening so far."

He shifted, looking abashed. "I'm sorry. I was just surprised. You look much too young to be a widow. Was your husband in the military? We've lost some fine, brave guys over there."

"No. It was a car accident."

"Again, I'm sorry to hear it." In a much friendlier tone he added, "Open my hand, Kate. Please."

Her anger faded, and her Arthur-yearning receded into its normal place, too. Those painful pulses of grief and desolation used to haunt her spirits constantly, but now, at last, they had receded somewhat. She was starting to feel alive again, finally. There were many things she took joy in, and she had wonderful, caring friends. She had even begun to notice attractive men, and to feel her body's urges to connect, indulge, and savor the pleasures a lover could offer her.

This man, combative though he was, held a certain appeal for her, if only because he was so unlike the affable, easy-going Arthur. Perhaps it would be easier if she connected with guys who didn't remind her of her dead husband.

His hand was right there, offered up to her. But still she hesitated. Again she felt that peculiar rush of blood to her head which seemed to spawn a riot of vibrant jungle colors, an earthly paradise of temptations and delights. Yet, somewhere in the midst of this profusion, she also sensed a hole gaping, as dark and deep as any pit. She was afraid to move, to take a step in any direction, and most of all, she was afraid to touch him.

His eyes had darkened to near black, compelling her. Get it together, Kate! Her fingers covered his. His fingers were still curled, but his hand looked less like a fist than an intriguing gift about to be opened. He was warm. His heat radiated through her like a sunburst. She felt herself flush, and hoped he wouldn't notice, but his eyes wouldn't release hers. There was magic in those dark-pool depths, a strong, hypnotizing pull on all her senses. Who was he? A real psychic? A sorcerer from another world?

Kate tore her gaze away, calling on all her inner reserves of calm. Her imagination was running away with her. She was tired and overly fanciful. She never should have allowed Graham to talk her into this. She ought to get up right this minute and leave.

But Daniel's flesh was firm and pliant beneath her fingertips, and she couldn't resist a look into his palm. Gently she pried open his fingers. Touching him felt a little forbidden, and very exciting. His hand was nicely shaped, firm and masculine, its palm richly covered with clearly defined lines.

"Your hand is ruled by fire, the most passionate of the four elements," she said as she compared the relative length of his fingers to his palm. Her mind had slipped into analysis mode.

"What's that supposed to mean?"

If there was anything to palmistry, it meant that he was emotional and intuitive. A man radiant with energy who lived life to the fullest. But she knew that already, simply from looking into his eyes.

Without answering, she turned his hand over and examined the shape of his nails, then turned it back to compare the individual fingers. He had a strong, forceful thumb. That was a good sign. The mount of Jupiter, from which sprang the index finger, governor of earthly ambitions, was particularly well developed.

"Well?" he drawled. "Are you estimating how many years I've got left on my lifeline?"

"I'm not even looking at the lines yet. The shape of the hand, the position of the fingers and their relative lengths, and the condition of the fleshy mounts beneath the fingers are at least as important as the lines."

"Is that so? What do these marvelous signposts of personality tell you about me?"

The sarcasm was back, but it was beginning to amuse her. She tried not to show that she was on the verge of laughing at him. He would probably be offended. But why should she care if he was? "You're dynamic, energetic, and determined to succeed in whatever you undertake. The strength of Jupiter—your index finger—confirms that you have the ability to be both a leader and an innovator, and the willpower to follow through." She tilted her head a little to one side as she added, "I would even go so far as to say that when you set your mind on something, you are driven to achieve it, no matter what the cost."

"That's true. But I don't believe you're getting it from my index finger."

Shrugging, she touched the fleshy mount of the moon, on the outside edge of his palm. "The shape of this part of your hand suggests that there's a conflict going on between reason and intuition, logic and imagination." She moved her fingertips inward. "Note the lines of the head and heart." She traced them on his palm, highly conscious of the heat of his skin beneath her fingertips. "Both lines are firm and deep, but the headline swings down into the mount of the moon—imagination—while the heart line moves upward toward Jupiter—practicality."

She raised her eyes to meet his. "A lot of conflict, Daniel. An interesting hand."

He raised his eyebrows and smiled. She had the impression that despite his skepticism, he was intrigued. Then his strong thumb curved down over her fingers and began softly massaging them. "Tell me about my love life, witch."

His touch was light and sensual, and her hormones responded with enthusiasm, sending crazy hot signals pulsing through her bloodstream. She probably ought to snatch her hand away. But something about him challenged her, daring her to take risks that would have seemed unthinkable only a few minutes ago.

Deliberately she ran her nails over the base of his thumb. She kept the touch delicate, but she could have sworn he shivered a little. The flesh there was warm and firm. She had another of those odd mental images—his hand stroking her flesh, slowly, with erotic expertise, and she shivered too.

Concentrate, girl!

The semicircular line known as the girdle of Venus showed clearly under his middle finger. That area was known in palmistry as the mount of Saturn. "You are an extremely sensual man. You have unruly passions. Sex is important to you. But the nature of fire is to burn brightly and consume, leaving ashes in its wake."

"So let my lovers beware? Is that what you're intimating?"

"Yes," she said, a tad irritated at the satisfaction he seemed to be deriving from this. Looking up, she smiled at him. "But I wouldn't get too smug if I were you. Your heart line is ragged at the beginning," she slid the tip of her finger slowly along the line in question, "but here, you see, it deepens into one smoothly flowing groove."

He seemed fixated on the sight of her finger stroking his palm. "What does that mean?"

"It suggests that you might end up channeling all your sensual energy into a single relationship someday."

"Ah, your first prediction. I'm going to meet a beautiful stranger, I suppose, and fall madly and permanently in love with her?"

She lifted her fingers away from his hand. Her fingers were not happy about this. They itched to keep touching him, stroking him, feeling the delicious friction of his flesh against hers. "Please don't put words into my mouth. I don't make predictions. You make your own future. It grows out of your character."

This was a slip, she knew—the actress of Shakespearean tragedy speaking, not the psychic. She hoped Daniel wouldn't catch it, but he immediately pounced.

"A fortune-teller who believes in free will? Now that is original."

"I'm not really a fortune-teller," she said, sick of the pretense. So what if he found her out? Somebody was bound to; she had known that from the start. She pushed his hand away. "The truth is, I'm an actress."

"All fortune-tellers are actresses, so don't waste your touching confessions on me. I'm not as gullible as the people who usually sit across the table from you."

Kate heard his words and laughed, a spontaneous burst of amusement. So much for being honest about her profession. He had drawn his own conclusions about her, and that was that. "You're much too self-assured to be gullible. You have strong opinions, and you make harsh judgments. Tolerance of other people's foibles is not your long suit, is it?"

His eyes met hers and he seemed to consider her words. After a couple of seconds, he smiled. It was a warm smile that made his eyes sparkle. "I don't believe in psychic abilities, but you're pretty perceptive. Yes, I'm opinionated, judgmental, and intolerant. I'm also aggressive and hot-tempered. But I have some good qualities, too."

"You admit your faults. That's a good quality."

"I'm honest. I'm constant. And I'm trustworthy. When I make a friend, the tie endures for life."

"And when you make an enemy?"

His blue eyes glimmered. "Chalk up a few more points on the negative side of the ledger. Let my enemies beware: I will hold a grudge for years and hound them relentlessly."

She shivered a little. She believed him.

"You're reluctant to make predictions for me," he said after a brief silence. "Let me give it a try." He raised his eyes to hers again. "I will leave this party with a dark, mysterious, and utterly feminine stranger." His fingers closed over hers, sending waves of heat radiating through her body. "I'll develop such an obsession with a certain beautiful witch that it's almost going to make me forget my intentions regarding her."

Kate wanted to look away, but he held her mesmerized.

"Almost," he repeated, his voice deceptively mild. "But, like a stern old Puritan, I know my duty. Witchcraft cannot be allowed to flourish. Obsession or no, I'm going to have to break all her spells."

She jerked her hand away as all the danger she'd felt in him coalesced. "Who are you?"

He smiled in a charming manner, but there was a steely undertone to his words as he said, "You're a witch, and I'm a witch-hunter. Daniel B. Haggarty is my name, and I intend to see that your tricks are discredited forever. I'm going to lead you to a very public stake, Witch Kate, and then I'm going to burn you."

CHAPTER TWO

Kate's immediate reaction to Daniel's threat was to stare round-eyed at him for a moment, then burst into peals of laughter. "You're making a big mistake." He looked so surprised to see her laughing that she giggled even more, bringing several of the guests wandering over in their direction, clearly wondering what was so funny.

"I'm damned if I see anything to be so riproaringly amused about," Daniel growled. But there was an affable glint in his eyes as he watched her laugh, and Kate sensed that on some deep level her refusal to take him seriously appealed to him.

"You will when I explain. You see, I'm here this evening only as a favor to a friend, and—"

"You don't usually perform at private parties? No, I imagine not. And for charity, too. I suppose you prefer to work in the privacy of your own home, where you can control the environment and manipulate the sound effects and the lighting?"

Her eyebrows rose in an exaggerated gesture of continuing mirth. He was determined not to alter his initial impression of her. She supposed she couldn't blame him: First she had billed herself as a psychic; then Graham had declared her a witch; and just now she'd charged right ahead, reading his palm and analyzing his character. If it was true that he hated psychics and made it his business to expose frauds, naturally he'd be out to get her.

She was seized with an irresistible desire to take the formidable D. B. Haggarty down a peg. He was going to feel foolish when he discovered the truth about her, and in the meantime, she could have a little fun with him. It would serve him right for glowering at her all evening.

"I'm only reading cards and palms. I'm not claiming to be a medium or anything like that."

"Fortune-tellers, witches, mediums—you're all in it together. Cheating people, preying on their superstitions. In some cases you cause grave psychological harm." He was glaring at her. "You with your sixth sense. You do realize that several of the guests here tonight don't even have a fifth sense? But you are 'sighted,' aren't you. You are 'gifted'—"

"Kate," Graham's voice interrupted. He had unobtrusively made his way to their side, and Kate looked up at him in amused relief. "I've just found out which one D. B. Haggarty is."

"So have I. You told me he was fiftyish and balding."

To her surprise, Daniel laughed at this description, a rich, full-bodied laugh not unlike her own. Kate shot him a reconsidering look from under her eyelashes. Until this moment she would have characterized him as fairly humorless, much like the dour Puritans he had compared himself to. "It must have been that photo in the *Globe*," he said. "Mislabeled. It should have said 'from right to left' instead of 'from left to right.' I was the tall, dark, and borderline handsome one."

"Opinionated, judgmental, intolerant, and borderline egotistical," said Kate. She smiled wryly at Graham. "You see what you got me into? He's threatening to burn me at the stake." She turned her gaze back to Daniel. "Burn Graham instead."

Haggarty was regarding her with the intent concentration a cat lavishes on an injured bird. "But it's you I'm after," he said, making the threat into a kind of sensual promise.

She laughed.

"You're not intimidated by me, are you?" He tilted his head to one side as he considered this apparently significant piece of information. "I like that."

"If I were what you think I am, I probably would be. As it is, I can afford to laugh at you, Mr. Haggarty."

"Daniel."

"Daniel," she agreed with a slight shrug of her shoulders. "What does the B stand for?"

"The B?"

"You said your name was Daniel B. Haggarty."

"Ah. Just a silly middle name. It's not important."

Before either of them could speak again, an elderly woman decked out in elaborate copper jewelry came to the table, pointing triumphantly at her watch. "This gentleman's time is up," she said, tapping Daniel on the shoulder. "I'm so excited, Madame Katrina. I just can't wait to hear whether or not Rudy is going to propose to me."

Kate smiled at the woman. "Mr. Haggarty was just leaving. Please take a seat."

Daniel shrugged and rose. He was about to move away when Kate touched his arm. He stopped, looking as electrified as she felt. "What?"

She pointed to the canister marked National Foundation for the Blind. "My fee."

If she expected annoyance, she was disappointed. He was gracious about opening his wallet and dropping a hundred-dollar bill into the slot.

"I'll get my money's worth later," he promised, and strolled away.

* * *

An hour later, Kate gathered up the tools of a fortuneteller's trade and looked around for Graham, who had offered her a ride home. She found him draped over the sofa in the living room with a beautiful blind redhead, who was guiding his hand as he ran his fingertips over her bare shoulders. When Kate signaled, pointing at the door and raising her eyebrows, he called over to her, "Wait a bit, luv. Marissa's teaching me braille."

She decided to take a taxi home.

As she collected her jacket and said good-bye to the hostess, who gushed over her spurious psychic abilities, Kate couldn't help noticing that there was no sign of Daniel B. Haggarty anywhere in the apartment. He must have left. She felt a flicker of regret. She suppressed it, reminding herself that she ought to be glad if she'd escaped the further attentions of the Scorpio brooder.

As she started down the narrow staircase of the old Beacon Hill town house, Kate ran their conversation through her mind. Why had he stared at her for so long before approaching her? How had he known her maiden name? And why had he left without making good on any of his threats? He didn't seem like the type who would back down without the confrontation he had promised her. Maybe he had a short attention span.

She wondered why he was so down on psychics. Many people were skeptical, but Daniel seemed to carry skepticism to an extreme. Something about the subject made him angry, almost fanatical. She disliked fanaticism of any kind.

But in spite of this, she couldn't exactly say she disliked Daniel. Not after that unexpectedly affable laugh of his. And there was the hotness factor to consider. He made unruly images of naked, entwined limbs and beds with rumpled sheets flash through her mind.

She flushed slightly. He was the first man she'd thought of that way since Arthur's death.

Once again, the memory of Arthur brought a sharp pang. She pictured the cheerful, good-natured face of the only man she'd ever loved—his chestnut hair, his warm brown eyes—and compared it with the dark, intense features of Daniel Haggarty. The two men couldn't be more different. "Oh, Arthur," she said out loud, "I miss you so much."

"Conversing with the spirit world?" said a sardonic voice at the bottom of the stairs.

Damn. Kate stepped down the final few stairs into the dingy, badly lit lobby of the old building. D. B. Haggarty was lounging on a bench under the mailboxes, his long legs stretched out in front of him, blocking the exit, his dark windbreaker open down the front and his hands tucked into its pockets.

"Did you think I'd gone off and left you? Impossible. Didn't you read your own cards tonight? I'm your fate."

"So far, you've done almost as much fortune-telling tonight as I have. I'm beginning to wonder if you're really the skeptic you claim to be."

He took his time about unstretching his legs and rising to his feet. He proved to be several inches taller than she was, and she was tall. She rarely had to look up to see a man's face. She tried to discount the pleasure this gave her. Ever since junior high school, when none of the boys had wanted to dance with her because she could rest her chin on the tops of their heads, Kate had appreciated tall males.

"I'm a skeptic all right," he assured her, his voice hardening. "I'm doing my best to rid the world of the idiocy you were spouting up there this evening."

"Yes, yes, I know. Don't keep scowling at me, please. It's aggressive and not in the least appealing."

Again he laughed. She liked the way it made his face change. He looked almost boyish, and his dark blue eyes sparkled. "Not the right approach with you, huh? Works with some women; you'd be surprised. But hey. I can be a gentleman if I really try."

"I'd prefer a gentleman to a self-styled witch-hunter."

"One gentleman, coming up." He bowed in a formal manner like someone at a Regency ball. "May I see you home, my lady?"

His arrogance irritated her, but it wasn't going to be easy to resist his charm. She curtsied with equal formality, saying, "thank you kindly, sir, but I can see myself home."

As she moved to step past him into the cool September night, D. B. Haggarty reached out, took her hand, and placed it on his arm. "Allow me, please. My carriage is waiting right outside."

Rapidly she considered her options. Struggling? Acting indignant? Treating his persistence as a joke? Or allowing the sensations his nearness engendered to sweep her away without protest?

"You're offering me a ride? How do you know I don't have my own—"she smiled "—equipage?"

"I did my research. It seems you came with your astrologer friend, but he has acquired another companion for the evening. Since I'm being strictly a gentleman, I'd better confess that I'm the one who introduced him to the lovely Marissa."

It figured. She threw him another dazzling smile and left her hand on his arm. As she spoke, she used her free hand to zip up her jacket and adjust the white silk scarf around her neck as nonchalantly as possible. When she had settled it to her satisfaction, she allowed her eyes to take his again. "Well-played. That luxury car at the curb is yours, I presume? Very nice, but I don't accept rides with strangers."

"A sensible policy, but how can I be a stranger to you when you've looked into my palm and analyzed my character?" He waited a beat before adding, "You'll be safe with me, I promise."

"You say that now, but you've already made that tiny little threat about burning me at the stake. Tell me, do I get a trial first? I can't wait to hear all the evidence against me."

His eyes glowed as he answered, "You're entitled to a chance to bewitch me into silence."

"Aren't you afraid my power might prove too much for you?"

"Nope," he said with astonishing confidence. "I doubt if your power—or that of your mother—will stand up to my scrutiny."

"Wait, what do you know about my mother?" She dropped his arm and retreated a step. She had been enjoying flirting with him, but the reference to her mother snapped her back to cold reality. The last thing she wanted was to have her mother exposed to a cable TV/web crusader's scrutiny. Ever since that debacle on a radio talk show a few years back when Iris Carter had announced to an audience of thousands that she was a female reincarnation of the Druidic priest who had come to be known in legend as Merlin, Kate had been careful to protect her flaky mother from the press.

"I know a good deal about her. I've been doing research for a program I'm planning on famous American mediums of the past fifty years. Your mother, naturally, is one of my subjects."

"Oh, no," Kate moaned.

"I've seen pictures of her taken when she was younger. The resemblance between the two of you is striking. I knew she lived in a suburb of Boston, and I remembered reading somewhere that she had a daughter named Kate. But I had to stare at you for a while before I made the connection."

Well, that explained his odd behavior and the fact that he knew her birth name.

"None of my research ever turned you up as a successor to her, though. You're barely even mentioned. I didn't know she had a psychic daughter."

His tone had put the verbal equivalent of air quotes around the word "psychic," but his misconceptions about her didn't alarm Kate anywhere near as much as his newly revealed intentions toward her mother. He couldn't put Iris on TV. Or the internet. Although she had never actually seen *Facts and Fantasies,* the program he produced, she had heard enough about it to understand how devastating it could be. D. B. Haggarty and his interviewers would make a laughingstock of her mother, even though she was not a fraud. Kate was convinced of the validity of her mother's powers, but she knew from experience that most people were not so willing to believe. They preferred to think Iris Carter was some sort of madwoman.

"My mother doesn't do interviews. She's getting on in years, and anyway, she's retired." She challenged him with her eyes as she added, "As for my being her successor, that's absurd. I can't do what she does."

"If that's true, you, at least, have nothing to fear from me."

But his revelation had rattled her. "Wait, let me get this straight. So it's not actually me, but my mother you're interested in? The reason you approached me was to try to gather more information about her?"

"No." He shook his head vigorously. "I was invited to the party this evening by Stephanie, the hostess, who's a friend of mine. Meeting you was pure serendipity." He had dropped the sardonic tone he had used when referring to her mom. For perhaps the first time this evening, he sounded serious, even earnest: "It is you I'm interested in. Sorry if the reference to my research on your mother upset you, but the truth is, I'm really not thinking about *Facts and Fantasies* right now." He reached out and took her hand lightly in his. He was wearing driving gloves, but she could the warmth of his fingers right through the thin leather. He nodded toward his waiting car. "Will you come? I'd like to see you home."

When she hesitated, he added, "Please don't tell me you'd prefer to ride your broomstick on such a windy night?"

She smiled. She really ought to clear up this misunderstanding now. She ought to tell him that in spite of her mother's profession, she was not a psychic, and that the closest she had ever come to dabbling in witchcraft was the role she was currently rehearsing at New Cambridge Rep. She ought to explain to him about Graham's psychic friend, whom she'd been replacing this evening. She ought not to get into that car with him.

But the magnetism in his eyes, combined with the incendiary pressure of his fingers on hers, scuttled her reason. So, instead of being sensible, she said, "I wasn't looking forward to searching for a taxi. It's not as if they're plentiful around here at this time of night."

"You would have conjured up a taxi easily. Skeptic though I am, I feel as if you've put a spell on me."

"And I feel as if I'm going to get burned."

He leaned closer and lowered his head. She could feel the warmth of his breath against her lips. He smelled delightful: fresh, spicy, and masculine. Her eyes drifted closed, and tingles shot through her body. Was he going to kiss her? An excitement she hadn't felt in years took hold of her. One of his arms slid around her shoulders as he closed the distance between them.

"Not burned," he murmured, his lips almost touching hers. She could feel his warmth. His sweet breath caressed her lips, making them soften as if ready to welcome him. "Singed a little, maybe. Heated, melted, fired up—"

A nameless anxiety shot through her at his words. She turned her face away before his mouth could take hers. What was she doing? He was a stranger. "Please, Daniel. I don't even know you."

"That can be remedied." He withdrew the threatened kiss and drew her gently in the direction of the car. "Come."

What the hell. It had been too long since she had last had an adventure of any kind. She went.

CHAPTER THREE

Daniel's fingers remained locked on hers as they walked to the low-slung car. The night air was unusually crisp and cold for September, and the sidewalk shone crystalline in the light from the old-fashioned streetlamps.

When he handed her into the sporty car, she stretched in the luxury of the soft seat, enjoying the smooth feel and the faint leathery scent. Sweet, she thought as he went around and let himself into the driver's seat. She didn't know a great deal about cars, but she thought it might be a Porsche. Graham drove a clattery old Honda.

"Where do you live?" he asked as he put the car in gear and glided away from the curb.

"In Salem, of course. Where else?"

"I don't know. Hogwarts?"

She laughed, pulling off her scarf and shaking her long brown hair free. Daniel glanced sideways and stared; she could feel the touch of his eyes. "Across the river, actually, in Cambridge. I have a small house near the Somerville line. Do you know your way around Cambridge?"

"Yep."

It was not in front of her small house that Daniel Haggarty stopped his car ten minutes later, however; he parked at a local Turkish restaurant just off Mass. Ave. that was famous for its food, its festive atmosphere, and its belly dancers.

"Are you hungry?" he asked. "There was hardly anything to eat at that party."

She was a little hungry, now that he mentioned it, and the restaurant was a favorite of hers. "Do you think they're still serving?"

"This place stays open late. I suppose you're on a perpetual diet, like all the other women I know?"

For some reason she resented this reference to "all the other women." She imagined them lining up, waiting their turn in his bedroom. "No, as a matter of fact, I'm not on a diet, and I adore Turkish food." And she was out the door before he could come around to open it for her.

The restaurant was crowded despite the late hour, and people were getting up and dancing to the exotic twang of the Middle Eastern music provided by tabor drums, a violin, and an oud. Kate and Daniel sat in a dark corner across from the band, at a tiny table for two. He apologized when his long legs bumped hers under the table, but he didn't move them.

"What do you want? A full-course meal?" she asked him.

"How about a selection of appetizers?"

"Sounds good. There's a good combo plate with eggplant salad, humus, cheese boreks and grapeleaf dolmas."

"Their humus is full of garlic," he warned.

"I don't mind if you don't."

His mouth curled. "Isn't garlic supposed to ward off evil spirits? I'll eat it to fortify myself."

"I'm a witch, Daniel, not a vampire."

"Vampires are all the rage, though, aren't they? I've never understood why women are so into the idea of being attacked by some guy who wants to suck out all their blood." His eyes sought a spot on her throat, and Kate felt her pulse scampering there, as fast and uneven as static.

"I think it's the thrill of being so desperately wanted and need-ed. And there's a powerful erotic element involved, too, of course. Do you ever play computer games?"

He blinked at the apparent change of subject. "Sure. Do you?"

"Yup. Have you ever played Hunt the Night City? It's my fa-vorite. I play it with some old friends of mine from college."

"Is that a World of Warcraft sort of thing?"

"Similar, yes. It's more of a futuristic dystopia than Warcraft, though. There are vampires, werewolves, witches, and other su-pernatural creatures."

"I haven't tried that one." He gave her one of his more endear-ing smiles. "You're a gamer as well as a witch? A serious gamer?"

"Serious enough. I'm pretty geeky, in some respects."

He looked impressed. "I honestly haven't met many serious girl gamers. Most of the women I know are into cell phone games, not MMOs." He grinned at her. "Things are looking up. I don't sup-pose you're a football fan, are you?"

"Sorry. Basketball. Celtics forever."

"Well, that goes without saying. But no love for the Patriots?"

"None."

"The Red Sox? I'll take you to a Celtics game if you'll go to Fenway Park with me sometime."

Whoa, she thought, aren't we getting a little ahead of our-selves? Wasn't baseball almost over for the season? "I like base-ball, but isn't this football season? There's no way you'd ever get me to a Patriots game. Why anybody would freeze their butt in an outdoor stadium during the cold weather to watch a bunch of grown men jump on each other all afternoon is beyond my comprehension."

"You do have a point." He glanced down at the menu. "Would you like some wine to go with the food?"

"I think I'll have a beer, thanks."

"The lady likes beer, computer games, and professional sports. You certainly know the way to a man's heart."

She screwed up her nose and laughed at him. "So beer-drinking sports fans don't get burned at the stake?"

Daniel reached across the table and grasped her hand. "Kate," was all he said, but a dozen other messages came through, heating her flesh and softening her bones. She thought she understood why he had brought her to the restaurant. He was hungry for more than just food, but the time in the car together hadn't been long enough for him to ensure that she wouldn't slam her door in his face. He wanted to get to know her a little better so it wouldn't seem so abrupt when he made his move.

She was about to tell him straightforwardly that he might as well forget it. Attractive though she found him, she didn't jump into bed with men she had known only a couple of hours. She didn't jump into bed with men, period. There had been no one since Arthur had died.

But before she could say anything, the waiter appeared at their side, and Daniel dropped her hand to order. Moments later the band launched into a loud, rhythmic pounding as a voluptuous belly dancer made her appearance in the dimly-lit room. "Ah, I like this part," he said, shifting his gaze to the vision in crimson and gold veils and sequins who danced out among them, tinkling her tiny brass zils between her fingertips.

"Great for the abs."

There were two more belly dancers before the beer was downed and the tasty appetizers consumed. There was also a pleasant exchange of easy, companionable conversation. They found they had plenty of things to chat about. Daniel was charming, witty, and intelligent. In spite of his hostility toward her supposed profession, he gave every indication of being just as pleased with her as she was with him.

"So why do you hate all the myriad practitioners of the occult?" she finally got up the nerve to ask.

"I told you: because they cheat people and prey on their gullible clients' superstitions."

"Not all psychics are frauds. Some have genuine powers."

He snorted into what was left of his beer.

"No, really. Don't you at least believe in ESP?" She was dabbing up the last of the humus with a bit of pita bread, making sure she got every last bit of the tasty dip out of the dish. Daniel watched her with a smile, obviously enjoying her hearty appetite. "Surely you don't think science has solved all the mysteries of the workings of the human brain?" she added, licking her lips.

"No," he admitted. His eyes were on her mouth, and his voice sounded abstracted. He cleared his throat. "There are still some things we don't know about the brain, but I'm confident that sooner or later neuroscientists will answer all those questions. Some 'practitioners of the occult' are just a helluva lot cleverer than others."

"So you claim to be a strict rationalist? What I saw in your hand contradicts that."

"Don't start with that palmistry garbage again. I only let you do it because I wanted the pleasure of your fingers against my palm."

She flushed, remembering that pleasure. He moved one hand across the table, threatening to repeat it. When she folded both her hands in her lap, he laughed at her and changed the subject.

They proved to have quite a bit in common: They liked several of the same books and movies, they shared political opinions, and they both enjoyed outdoor activities. "You cross-country ski?" she said. "I love to cross-country ski. But I haven't done it in years." Arthur hadn't been particularly athletic, she recalled sadly.

"Whoever heard of a witch on skis?" he teased.

She decided to attack his profession for a change. "How come you're not on TV yourself, Haggarty? I'll bet it would give the ratings a boost if you roasted your victims yourself instead of making your underlings do it."

"Maybe I'll take you up on that the day I do a segment on you."

The beer had made her reckless. "Any time," she said cheerfully. "How about you forget my mother and put me on your program instead? It would do wonders for my career. I could use all the publicity I can get."

"You don't know what you're talking about." His voice had turned harsh. "That kind of publicity could destroy you."

"Really?" She grinned at him. It had been on the tip of her tongue several times to tell him the truth about her profession, but he was so smug on the subject that she couldn't take pity on him yet. "Then I suppose I should be afraid of you, shouldn't I? But, Daniel, you seem so nice."

He scowled. She could tell he was having second thoughts about "burning" her, a fact that gave her immense satisfaction.

At one point, Kate got up to use the bathroom. When she returned to the table, the waiter had cleared away the used dishes and her cell phone was sitting on the table beside her napkin.

Daniel nodded to it as she sat down, saying, "Your pocket was chiming. I didn't want the other guests to be disturbed, so I found your phone and muted it."

"Thanks." That had been careless, leaving her phone in her jacket. She couldn't really fault him for seeking it out to stop its ringing, but the idea of D. B. Haggarty going through her pockets made her uneasy.

She glanced at the screen as she put the phone into her purse. The incoming call had been from Jeff Slayton, an old friend. "You didn't answer it, did you?"

"Nope. Who's Jeff?"

Jeff's name and his picture would have popped up on the screen while the phone was ringing. "He's one of my friends."

"A close friend?"

Jeff was in fact a close friend, although not in the sense that Daniel was insinuating. She had known him since college, and it had been Jeff who had sparked her interest in computer gaming in an effort to draw her out of the black hole she'd fallen into after Arthur's death. "Pretty close, yes. I've known him for years. We game together. He's probably wondering why I haven't logged on this evening."

Daniel looked slightly relieved. Was he assessing what he imagined to be the competition? It was probably not a good idea to let him know he didn't have any competition. He already seemed to be taking too much for granted.

By the time the last belly dancer of the evening performed, Kate was clapping and swaying her own body to the sensuous music. "I love it! I think I'm going to take exotic dance lessons myself."

Daniel hadn't been watching the belly dancer for some time. His eyes were fixed on Kate's green silk top. "I'll be happy to poke ten dollar bills into your hopefully very scanty dancing costume."

"Ten dollar bills! Is that all? How about hundreds?"

He met her mischievous gaze. "You already know I think you're worth at least that." His glance darted briefly toward "Zenobia," then returned to Kate. "You're a much higher class witch than she is." He signaled the waiter for the check. "Shall we go?"

Her smile vanished abruptly. Go where? Home, to her house, to her bed? A higher class witch. Why did she have the feeling that the word *witch* was synonymous with *easy hookup*? She remembered some of his earlier remarks, and she wondered what she was doing here, at midnight, laughing merrily with a black-hearted stranger who probably regarded her as a sure thing.

Kate knew from her wretched experiences with a couple of men who had made unwelcome advances to her since her husband's death that she gave the impression of being more free-spirited than she actually was. Her instinctive manner with people was warm and friendly, and she enjoyed a true zest for life. So far this evening she had joked around with Daniel, and—she might as well admit it—flirted with him, too. But that was as far as it was going to go.

If, like those other guys, he saw her engaging behavior as a come-on, she'd better set him straight right here in the restaurant. Otherwise, the evening would end in a tussle on her front porch.

"I'm not going to have sex with you, you know."

His eyes widened slightly. "Reading my mind again?" he drawled.

She stuffed her hand into her purse and extracted her wallet. "I insist on paying my half," she added, dropping a twenty on the saucer the waiter presented.

Daniel was unexpectedly emotional, glaring at her money as if it had insulted him. "Are you afraid that if I pay for your supper, I'll expect sex in return?"

"Look, Daniel, let's not complicate things. I've enjoyed this evening—I don't get out very often—and I've even enjoyed sparring with you. But that's as far as it goes. I don't sleep with men."

There was a brittle silence before Daniel asked, "Who do you sleep with?"

She realized what he was thinking and smothered a laugh. "I don't sleep with anybody. Well, except Chester. My cat."

"You sleep with a cat?"

"Not always. I try to kick him out, but sometimes the monster waits till I'm asleep, and then cuddles up beside me."

"Dear God, the witch keeps a familiar," Daniel growled. "I'm allergic to cats. Whenever I'm in the same room with one I start sneezing with all the force of an erupting volcano."

"That settles it," she said with a sigh of mock relief. "You'll have a hard time making unscrupulous advances if you're busy sneezing."

"Don't count on it. I'll take an antihistamine."

* * *

Sitting beside him in the dark car, she watched his hands moving on the gearshift and the steering wheel. He was wearing his leather driving gloves—black, like the rest of his attire. She had a brief mental image of his gloved hands sliding over her naked flesh. Idiot, she chided herself. Save the fantasies for when you're alone, safely locked away from this exciting and dangerous man.

They didn't speak except to give and acknowledge the directions to her house, which was located on a quiet residential street two blocks from the noise and traffic of Cambridge's Massachusetts Avenue. When he pulled up under the huge elm in front of her house, she murmured a goodnight, which he ignored. He was out of the car and around to her side before she could get her door open.

"You don't have to see me to the door," she protested as he leaned down to help her.

He didn't bother to argue. He took her arm and marched her up the walk to the front porch of the old Victorian house. He hovered over her while she fumbled for her house key, and she wondered whether he was going to try to push past her. Forcible entry was the only way he'd get in. Daniel Haggarty was not the sort of man you could offer a coffee to and then dismiss.

She found the key and inserted it, then turned to him with her back against the door. "Thank you for a pleasant..." she began, but her words died as she was trapped in the smoldering blaze of his deep blue eyes. He was standing close, and while she waited helplessly, her fingers clenched around the keys, he moved closer still, pressing her against the solid oak door. She gasped as she realized that the first contact between them was not to be a kiss at all, but the exciting surge of his hard, sexy body against her own.

Oh. My. God. There was a rustle of cloth as he slowly moved his hips against hers. She could feel his arousal and, even more unnerving, she could feel her own body yielding, softening, and welcoming him. Her hands went to his shoulders, meaning to push him away, but instead her fingers clung to him, feeling firm bone and muscle under the fabric of his jacket. "Daniel," she protested as he repeated the motion, stoking the heat that was rising inside her.

His forehead touched hers; his gloved hands speared into her hair and cradled her head. His lips were so close she could feel his warm breath on hers as he whispered, "I'm sorry, Kate. I don't mean to be offensive. I just want you to know how much I need you, how much I've burned for you all evening. I've never felt like this, acted like this. Don't be angry."

"I'm not," she whispered back, wondering why she wasn't.

"You're so warm, so sweet, so full of life." His tongue touched her lips, stroking lightly over the sensitive contours, probing the corners provocatively. She shuddered and slipped her arms around him, her fingers now exploring his firm muscled back. She was still clutching her house key in her right hand, and he must have felt the metal edge of it scraping him as she pulled him closer, but he didn't seem to mind. Colors were flashing in front of her eyes again in bright, triumphant, rainbow bursts. She, too, was burning.

His hands urged her face closer. His kiss was gentle. At first his lips did nothing more than mold hers, seeming to try their shape, enjoy their taste. He pressed lightly enough to tempt her with the sweet warmth of his breath and the sensual current that seemed to leap from his mouth to hers. Then he drew back, leaving her so bereft that she exerted pressure with her fingers on the back of his neck to bring their mouths together again. She felt him sigh and heard him mutter something unintelligible in the instant before his control evaporated and his kiss turned fierce.

Kate arched against him as his tongue drove into her mouth. She was no longer put off by the latent aggression in him; it had unleashed a similar fever in her. As his lips and tongue explored her, she responded with some ardent exploration of her own. His lips were soft, but the planes of his body were muscular and hard, and she reveled in the sensuous, masculine feel of this stranger's body molded so tightly against her own. Her mouth opened fully to him as a knot tightened in her pelvic region. It was a soul-wrenching kiss, a sorcerer's kiss, a kiss that both asked for and promised satisfaction. And all the things it promised had been denied to her for so damn long. I want him, she thought. I want, want, *want* him.

"You're amazing," he said, pulling his head back for an instant. "I don't think I've ever been so captivated by a kiss." One of his leather-encased fingers slid down over her face, touched her lips, and then moved to the pounding pulse in her throat. He dropped two feather-light kisses on her tingling lips. "Invite me in."

"I can't."

"You can." His mouth took the place of his finger on her throat, and she felt the exquisite sensation of his tongue chafing her skin while her blood beat just beneath it. Liquid warmth blossomed in her, and there were spasms all through her, everywhere. He let her feel a hint of teeth. "Let me teach you all manner of dark, sensual delights."

She laughed. "I'm not that foolish. You creatures of the night only have to be invited in once; after that you can enter at will."

"I'll remember that," he vowed, raising his lips to seize her mouth in an unchecked, passionate attack that was duplicated by the erotic rocking of his hips. She could feel the tension in all those lovely hard muscles of his body, and she felt herself weakening. Damn. This was so difficult! Her body had a very different objective than her brain.

Somehow she managed to free her lips. "No more, Daniel. I'm sorry. I did warn you."

Frustration flashed in his eyes for only an instant before rueful acceptance took its place. He expelled his breath heavily, and she could feel the taut tendons in his arms vibrating slightly. "You warned me. You don't have sex with men you've just met."

"I don't have sex at all."

"I can't believe that. You're beautiful, sensual, and there's not a hint of coldness about you." His eyes turned speculative. "There's someone else? That guy who called you in the restaurant? Jeff?"

"No. Jeff and I are friends from college. There's no one else. I just don't want that sort of complication at present. I'm content with my life the way it is."

"You're attracted to me," he pointed out, moving provocatively against her once again, making her insides melt.

"Stop." This time she twisted away, half turning toward the door. "I'm going inside. Good night."

"Wait. Can't we talk about this?"

"It's after midnight. I have to get up early to get to the pool."

"Please don't tell me you mean some sort of divining pool."

She smiled. "Swimming pool. I swim every morning for exercise."

"I like a woman who keeps in shape." He brushed his lips against hers. Her cheeks were flushed from the roughness of his whiskers, but it felt good. "Kiss me again."

The temptation to do so was almost too great to resist. But she had just begun to explore the possibility of dating again. She had signed up for a couple of internet dating services, but she hadn't actually corresponded yet with any of the men whose profiles had been emailed to her. She was determined to take it slowly. She had only ever made love with one man in her life, and he was dead. Getting back into the whole sex thing was going to take some time. She needed patience from a prospective lover, not incendiary passion. And she wasn't going to be some hot stranger's one-night hookup.

So instead of surrendering to her desire to kiss him again she said, "It would never work. Don't forget that you disapprove of my, um, profession."

The reminder made his jaw tighten, and there was a flare of hostility in his eyes. "I do keep forgetting. I think you really are a witch."

"You desire me, so I'm a witch? You sound like some sort of Puritan throwback."

He took a step back and thrust his hands into the pockets of his jacket. "I was under the impression that the attraction between us was mutual."

Her gaze dropped beneath his relentless stare. "Maybe so, but I'd be an idiot to surrender to a man who's already declared his intention to burn me."

"It was just a metaphor."

"Yes, but its connotations are cruel."

"I'm not going to hurt you, Kate." He moved closer to her again, but he kept his hands in his pockets, as if to prove his good faith. "When can I see you again?"

"I really don't think—"

"When?" His voice was a sexy growl. "Tomorrow night? Dinner?"

"So we can have this same debate all over again? No. I'm not going to get involved with you."

"You are." He pulled his gloved hands from his pockets and held her face softly. "You've no free will in this matter, Lady Kate. I'm your fate, and you're mine." He kissed her again, far more tenderly than she'd expected, stealing her breath, enchanting her body. Then he drew back, ran one hand through her loose hair, and turned to leave.

When he reached his car, he stopped and looked back. "Go inside. I won't leave until I know you're safely ensconced in your fortress."

Kate bit her lip, wishing with all her heart that it could have been different, wishing she had the courage, the freedom, the easygoing attitude about casual sex that so many women her age seemed to possess. "Good-bye," she said as she opened her door.

"Until next time," he corrected, lounging in all his masculine glory against the side of his car. "I won't give up."

CHAPTER FOUR

Despite the lateness of the hour, Kate couldn't get to sleep. She kept reliving her meeting with D. B. Haggarty and the whole crazy rest of the evening. It felt as if her world had shifted under her feet. She had gone to the party with Graham at the beginning of the evening without the slightest hint that she was about to tumble down the rabbit hole.

After tossing and turning for a while, she realized she wasn't going to slip peacefully into sleep. Rising, she went to the taller and more masculine of the two dressers that still remained in her bedroom, which she had once shared with Arthur. The dresser had contained all his clothes. She had donated most of them after his death, and slowly filled the drawers with her own shirts and sweaters, but a few things of his remained. There was a particularly cuddly fleece that he'd loved to wear. Whenever she looked at the garment, she could picture him in it. She pulled it out now and buried her face in the soft fabric. It still seemed to carry Arthur's scent, although she was pretty sure that was impossible after all this time.

Memories slid back slowly through her mind. Happy ones, mostly—the sturdy little boy who lived down the street, sometimes friendly, sometimes shy, sometimes mischievous, but always kind to anyone who was scared, beleaguered, or in trouble. He had loved every kind of animal, and had once dreamed of growing up to be a vet. Instead, he had become a social worker, counseling underprivileged kids.

He had been very good at his job, and the number of young people who had turned up, weeping, at his memorial service had been huge. For someone who had died so young, Arthur had touched the lives of a great many people. He'd had a rare gentle quality that had not in any way softened his masculinity. He knew how to make people feel at ease, and his manner had conveyed what Kate knew to be sincere empathy. He had had an impish streak, too, and a dry, deadpan sense of humor that always made her laugh.

With his fleece in hand, she wandered downstairs to the room that had been Arthur's office, sat in front of the computer table and switched on her monitor. Her screensaver featured a huge picture of happier days: herself in a silly group pose in her first apartment with Arthur, before they were married, and their roommates Jeff Slayton, Stephen Silkwood, and Nick Gabriel. She was sitting on Arthur's lap, her head thrown back, laughing, while Stephen was down on one knee in front of them as if begging a boon from the king and queen. Jeff and Nick, both fair-haired and handsome, were facing off with wooden swords purloined from the Drama Club prop room, pretending to be ferocious but unable to hide their grins. They had been rehearsing a college play, she recalled; she, Arthur, and Stephen had acted together in several productions at the school, and they were forever trying to get the others to join them.

How young they all looked! She had fallen in love with Arthur in high school. They had gone to the same college, and it was there that they'd come to know the guys, their fellow students. Some kind of magic must have been at work back then, because the bonds forged among them had survived college, her marriage, and the boys' various tumultuous relationships and jobs. Kate regarded Jeff, Stephen, and Nick as the brothers she had never had. When she had been lost and broken in the aftermath of Arthur's death, they had all been there for her, supporting and pulling her through the darkest days. Jeff, in particular, had been her rock.

Jeff Slayton was one of those stand-up guys who are always there when you need them. He was the hub of the wheel that held her and her oldest friends together—solid and immoveable, warm and dependable while everyone else's lives spun haphazardly around him. Jeff was the one who stayed in touch with everyone, organized get-togethers, kept tabs on who went where, who had fallen in love with whom, and who needed to be pulled back into the circle when they began drifting away.

They were all spread out in different cities now, but the guys still hung out together via computer gaming. After Arthur's death, Jeff had dragged Kate, kicking and screaming, into their geeky online world.

"Since you refuse to go out of your house except to do errands and go to work, you might as well game with us," Jeff had said when, six months after Arthur's death, she had still been unable to rouse herself or find delight in anything.

"I'm not interested in computer games," she had insisted.

"Tough. We're going to teach you to play, and then we're gonna kick your ass."

"Nobody kicks my ass."

"That sounds more like the Kate we all know and love."

"If it has dwarves and elves you can forget it. I'm not playing any game where my avatar has stubby little legs or long pointy ears."

"It's not that sort of game."

Hunt the Night City had turned out to be set in a dark and rather grim dystopia that had suited her own black mood. Initially she had been skeptical, but the game had turned out to be curiously addictive.

Her friends all played, although their in-game hours varied depending on what else was going on in their lives. The guys had all been technology geeks in school, a little shy around girls and more comfortable hacking than hanging out, but that had changed over the years. They had gone on to successful careers in the real world. Jeff was a history professor at one of the colleges in the three-college area in Massachusetts where they had all met; Stephen was a mystery novelist whose books were now hitting the bestseller lists; and Nick was an archaeologist whose work took him to all sorts of exotic places.

Unlike her friends, Kate hadn't played many computer games while growing up. She was clumsy at first, but as she leveled up and learned to play her character, her confidence grew. Jeff and Stephen had been the ones to spend the most time with her while she was learning, but she also learned a lot from an old friend of Jeff's whom she hadn't known in college. Nekrotic, as they called him, played a vampire in the game. His real name was Max, but Kate didn't know much about his life outside the game. Max protected his privacy fiercely. He was some sort of computer genius, and very good at Hunt the Night City. If she ever found a bug in the software, all she had to do was tell him about it, and the problem would disappear.

"He's some kind of super hacker, isn't he?" she had asked Jeff, who knew Max's profession but had been sworn to silence.

"Something like that," Jeff had admitted.

Kate grew to love Hunt the Night City. When she played, she tended to get so immersed in the game world that she was able to forget her real life problems. She turned out to be a good healer, and her friends began to seek her out to heal their group through some of the more difficult content. When she proved she could handle it, they invited her to do multi-group raids with them.

It was after one a.m. tonight when she logged on, but there were always people online. Gamers from all over the world played. Despite the late hour, Jeff, Stephen, and Max were hanging out in a trio together. It was a little unusual for Jeff to be up so late during the week, since he usually had to teach a class in the morning. As a writer, though, Stephen could make his own hours. As for Max, he was always on at odd hours. "He never sleeps," Stephen had said. "We think he really is a vampire."

Kate joined their channel and started typing: "Hey guys."

There was a chorus of welcomes from Jeff, Stephen and Max, who told her to boot up her voice chat program so they could talk instead of type at one another. When she did so, Stephen's and Jeff's faces came up in small rectangles on the upper corner of her screen, broadcast live from their computer cams. Max's face didn't appear, which was typical. Kate had heard his voice many times, but she'd never actually seen Max's face.

Jeff was wearing headphones with a small microphone hovering at his lips. Stephen's set-up was similar. Kate didn't find headphones comfortable so she just played the sound through her computer's speakers and used a desktop mike when she spoke. No one knew what Max's equipment looked like, but Kate was sure it was top of the line. She figured he was either a sophisticated hacker or an NSA agent.

"You're up late," Stephen said, grinning at her via the video link. Stephen was almost always grinning. Even though he wrote dark, bloody mystery novels, he was one of the most light-hearted men she had ever known. "Can't sleep?"

"Nope. Agitated mind. I thought I might sign on and kill some monsters to make myself feel better."

"That almost always works," Jeff agreed. "Digital stress relief."

"What are you doing up, Jeff? Don't you have class tomorrow?"

"Not in the morning, no. Just an afternoon seminar, so I can sleep in."

"I saw that you called me earlier. I thought it was too late to call back."

"No problem. It wasn't important. I was just being sociable."

"I'm not even going to ask why you're not asleep, Max."

"Very wise," said Max in the deep, husky voice that had inspired some delicious fantasies over the past couple of years. He even sounded like a sexy vampire. "What shall we kill? We won't have a full group, though. No other friends are online. Haven't seen Nick for a while."

"Nick's on a dig in central Turkey," Jeff said. "His internet connection sucks, so he won't be around much for a few weeks."

"I probably won't stay on for long anyway," Kate said. "I just wanted to say hi to you guys."

Jeff was staring at her through his screen. He was a nice-looking man, light-haired with unusual violet eyes. You'd never guess from looking at his chiseled cheekbones that back in college he'd been a few pounds overweight and out of shape. After one of his romances had gone south, he had gone on a hit-the-gym and get-healthy kick, started lifting, taken up fencing and meditation, and replaced any excess fat with hard, sculpted muscles. His healthy habits had stuck, and he was pretty damn sexy now. But Kate had known him for so long that she rarely noticed it. Nick and Stephen were good-looking too, but she'd regarded them as brother figures for so many years that none of them ever stirred her hormones.

Okay, maybe that wasn't strictly true where Stephen was concerned, but that little flirtation had happened many years in the past, when she and Arthur had broken up for a while. It hadn't amounted to much—a single drunken make-out session that had left them both mortified when they'd sobered up. She was pretty sure that Stephen had never mentioned their brief encounter to anyone; she certainly hadn't.

As for Max, all she had to go on was his seductive voice. He sounded yummy, but given how insistent he was that nobody ever see him, she figured he was probably 100 pounds overweight and butt ugly. The guys were all around her age and single, so it was too bad, in a way, that the thought of getting romantic with any of them now seemed so unlikely. They were friends, and good ones, but none of them would ever replace Arthur in her life.

Neither, she vowed, would Mr. Daniel Witch-hunter Haggarty.

"You look odd, Kate," said Jeff. "You're not at your mom's house, are you?"

"No, I'm at my own place. See?" She moved slightly so the camera could record the familiar furniture around her. They all knew that her computer was in the room that had once been Arthur's study. Many of his things were still in there. "Why do you ask?"

"You're glowing. I figured there must be a ghost or two hovering around you."

"Shut up," she said, laughing. Her friends loved to tease her about her mother's ghosts. But unlike Daniel, they did it in a genial, lighthearted manner. "I can't be glowing. What would I have to glow about?"

"Bzzt. The subject is lying," said Stephen. "I can always tell. Spill, girl. Otherwise I may have to break out my protagonist's special interrogation skills."

Since the hero of Stephen's novels, Bartholomew Giles, was prone to using extremely violent forms of medieval torture on his victims, Kate rounded her eyes and pretended to shudder. "No, please, Master Giles," she begged, making him laugh.

"You know, I think he's right. You're blushing, babe," said Jeff. "What's up?"

"Jeez, I can't keep anything from you meddlers. It must be hormones or pheromones or something. I went to a party tonight."

"And?"

"And I sort of met someone."

Loud whoops erupted from her speakers. The guys had all been urging her to get back out there. It had been Jeff who had vetted online dating sites for her and recommended the best ones, while Stephen had ordained that she wasn't going to accept so much as a coffee with anybody unless she shared his info in advance. Max had assured her that he could run security checks on anybody, and use all the tools at his command to digitally eviscerate them if they ever treated her badly. Kate had laughed at all of them and told them to mind their own business, but in truth, she was touched by their caring.

"Who is he?" Jeff asked. "Were you with him tonight? Is that why you didn't take my call?"

"Did you finally get some lovin'?" Stephen wanted to know.

"Yes, I was with him, but no, nothing happened." Not entirely true, she thought, remembering Daniel's kisses. "We went out for some food after the party, and then he dropped me off at home. That's it. I didn't invite him in, and I don't plan on seeing him again."

"Which explains the glowing...how?"

Kate laughed. "Dammit, I am not glowing."

"You so are."

"Well, he is pretty hot. It's the first time I've thought anyone was hot in, like, years. But that doesn't mean I'm going to do anything about it."

"Why not?" asked Stephen. "What's wrong with him?"

"He came on a little strong, considering I had just met him. And he thinks my mother is a fake."

"How does he even know about your mother?" asked Jeff. Having been her friends for many years, they knew that she didn't go around blabbing about her eccentric mother to people she'd just met.

"It's actually my mother he's interested in." She explained the circumstances of her meeting with D. B. Haggarty. "Graham told him I was a witch, referring to the play, but Daniel concluded I was some sort of Wicca chick. I tried to explain, but he wouldn't listen. I think he was half-expecting me to pull out my wand and challenge him to a death duel."

All three of her friends were chortling.

"You're going to have to see him again so you can tease him some more," said Max.

"Yeah, like you tease us with your vampire shtick?"

"Hey, don't mock. I'm 400 years older than you, young padawan."

"Dude, you're mixing your metaphors," Stephen objected. "Unless you were turned undead long, long ago on a planet far, far away?"

"Trust a writer to object to my metaphors," groused Max.

"Bringing us back to the subject at hand," said Jeff, "if this guy is so good at searching out the truth and exposing deceivers, how could he make such a mistake about you? I don't think I like him. Maybe you should follow your initial impulse and refuse to see him again."

Kate decided not to confess that her initial impulse had been more along the lines of stretching out with Daniel on the nearest bed.

"Well, I think she should fuck his brains out," Stephen said. "She's glowing, and we all know what that means."

"I am not glowing."

"Girl, you are so ready. Ignore what Jeff says. You know we'll all be cheering you on. Have some fun with the guy, and then dump his ass if he continues to be a jerk."

"I think I'd rather just hang out with you guys instead."

"You do need to get back out there," Jeff agreed, if a little reluctantly. "This is the first guy you've shown even a flicker of interest in. There was chemistry?"

"That would be a yes. Blow up the lab sort of chemistry."

"Are we talking hookup, or friend with benefits, or oh my god I think I'm in love?" Max asked.

"A quick, easy hookup is probably all he's interested in."

"Would you be down for that?"

"Not so much, but it does seem to be the way these things are done nowadays, doesn't it? I guess I need to start living in the present."

"Not everybody wants a quick, easy hookup," said Jeff.

The other two laughed at him. "Name me one guy who doesn't," said Stephen. "And don't name yourself, or I'll tell her what you did last weekend."

Jeff was laughing now, too. "Fine. But Kate's got higher standards than we do, don't you, Kate?"

"Well, I don't know about that, but I don't think I'm Hook-up Girl. I wish I were, but the idea of getting all naked and sweaty with someone I've just met seems icky to me. I guess guys don't have that problem?"

"Nope," said Stephen.

"Getting naked is what we live for," said Max.

"Men are sluts," agreed Jeff.

"I can fantasize about having crazy hot sex with a stranger," Kate said, "but that's different from actually doing it."

"How about having crazy hot sex with a vampire?" suggested Max in that soft, erotic voice of his.

She laughed. "I don't know why that's appealing, but it kinda is. Weird, since you vampire dudes are allegedly cold to the touch, not to mention dead, but the fantasy is hot."

"Sometimes," said Jeff wryly, "I really don't get women."

They chatted for a few more minutes about this and other things before Max had some work-related emergency and made his apologies. Stephen declared that he'd had an inspiration for his current book and logged off, too. Before saying goodnight, Jeff gave her one more piece of advice: "If you're resisting the attraction to this guy, it's probably because you're feeling disloyal to Arthur. Am I right?"

"I guess. I know I have to go on with my life, and that Arthur would want me to. But I don't know quite how to do that."

"Maybe it's a good thing you've met someone who lights you up, even if it's not going to lead anywhere. That chemistry could be a gift. It'll make everything easier. Go with it and enjoy, then lose him if it doesn't feel right. You'll have gotten the big 'oh my God, I can't do this with anybody except Arthur' over with, and when someone really good comes along, you'll be ready."

She smiled at his image on her computer screen. "You know, that makes a twisted sort of sense."

"But?"

"I don't know. I have the feeling that if I get involved with him, it won't be easy to extricate myself. He's very intense."

"If you're getting negative vibes from him, steer clear. Last thing you need is some stalker type."

"Not negative, exactly. I guess I'm afraid I'll get hurt. Emotionally, I mean."

"You can call me anytime, you know. You've always got a shoulder to cry on."

"Thank you. I love you, Jeff."

"I love you, too, babe."

It was true that D. B Haggarty didn't give up, Kate learned in the course of the next few days. He was nothing if not persistent, and he was gradually wearing her down.

The first time he called her, she was surprised to hear from him. "How did you get this number?"

"I kinda lifted it off your phone the other night when you went to the bathroom."

"That's kinda an invasion of my privacy."

"I know. I'm sorry. I didn't look at anything else on your device, in case you're wondering. But, in my defense, I could probably have found your phone number easily enough on the web."

That was true, she supposed. Nothing was private anymore.

"I'm an investigative journalist by profession. It's my job to go looking for information."

"So what have you discovered about me?" If he'd sought her out on the internet, he must have learned by now where she worked and what she really did for a living.

"I haven't looked." His voice sounded bleak as he added, "I don't want to know."

"Why not? Because you disapprove of my supposed psychic abilities?"

"Yes, of course because of that. Do you imagine I'm happy about being attracted to the same type of charlatan whom I routinely expose?"

She laughed. "You are so wrong about me, Daniel."

"Come out to dinner with me, then, and prove me wrong."

"Sorry, I can't." Which was true enough. Not only did she have rehearsals, but she needed to be present each night for her company's current production of *A Doll's House*. She was the alternate for the role of Christine, which she played each Tuesday evening and Wednesday matinee so the usual actress could have some time off from a grueling schedule.

"Well, at least tell me your last name."

"Wait...you don't know my last name?"

"I'm embarrassed to confess that I didn't ask you for it when you told me you'd been married. Very annoying, the way women are always changing their names."

She began to laugh. No wonder he hadn't looked her up. "You're an investigative journalist, my friend. Figure it out."

"I could," he said gloomily. "Believe me I could. But I'm desperately hanging on to my state of denial about your blasted profession, the thought of which is driving me insane."

"Narrow minded and judgmental," she teased him. "Serves you right if you remain in ignorance." After a moment she added, "Speaking of names, what about that B?"

"In my name? That B?"

"Yes, Mr. D. B. Haggarty. Brandon? Benjamin?" She thought of Stephen's antihero from his books and added, "Bartholomew?"

"I'm not telling. You tell me yours and I'll tell you mine. Maybe."

"Maybe?"

"It's a stupid middle name."

"Hmmm. Beauregard? Basil? Bevis?"

He laughed and said, "It's actually pretty apropos, now that I think about it. It's Blaze. Daniel Blaze Haggarty."

Now it was her turn to laugh. "Blaze? As in blazing fires?"

"As in the French name, spelled B-L-A-I-S-E. I had an Irish grandfather and a French grandmother. But for some insane reason my American parents spelled it B-L-A-Z-E. Since my father's name was also Daniel, I got called Blaze a lot at home and at school. I hated it, and of course, people made fun of the name. I started calling myself Daniel as soon as anybody would pay attention, and it finally stuck."

"So now, when you go around threatening to burn women at the stake, you have the right name for it!"

"You're the first woman," he said in a low, sexy voice, "whom I have ever threatened to burn." He said it in a manner that stripped the word entirely of all its painful connotations and imbued it instead with blood-tingling sensuality. She sucked in her breath thinking, damn, I'm not going to be able to resist this guy much longer.

He called her at least once every day, usually at night before she went to bed. He texted her occasionally, too. After convincing her to give him her email, which did not include her last name, he started sending her short but engaging emails that she soon found herself looking forward to and cheerfully answering. One day he sent her a box of chocolate truffles, addressed to Kate Mystery Witch. Since he'd driven her home, he knew her address, and she was certain he could have used it–or her phone number—to discover her last name and everything else about her. But he was apparently serious about not wanting to know.

She happily devoured his truffles even as she complained to him that night on the phone that he was ruining her waistline. But she continued to refuse his requests for an in-person meeting.

He didn't let this bother him. No matter how many times she told him to forget it, he always came back with another suggestion: dinner, a movie, a basketball game, an exhibition at the Museum of Fine Arts, and so on. Sooner or later, he said, he was going to find an activity that would tempt her. In her heart, she knew he was right. Because of the calls and emails, she was getting to know Daniel Haggarty, and the better she knew him, the more she liked him.

"Hello, Daniel," she said as her cell chimed at midnight toward the end of the following week. "Doesn't it ever worry you that I might be asleep at this hour?"

"Kate?" said a puzzled female voice on the other end.

Oops! "Mom? Is everything okay?"

"Who's Daniel?" asked Iris Carter. "Is there a new man in your life, dear?"

In this respect, at least, Kate reflected wryly, her mother was as normal as anybody else's. Her patience with her daughter's widowhood had begun to wear thin.

"Nobody special. Why are you calling so late?"

"Oh, sorry, I wasn't paying attention to the hour. I just needed to hear your sweet voice. Tell me about this Daniel."

"There's nothing to tell. He's just a guy I met who keeps calling me."

"You know, dear, the time is ripe for you to fall in love. In fact, this development could well explain the slight difference in your aura that I commented on when you came over last Sunday. There was a distinct rose-colored glow."

Whoa. Another person who thought she was glowing? And unlike the guys, her mother could actually see these things. "Don't get too excited, Mom. I don't intend to see the man again, much less fall in love with him." She drew a quick breath and tried to change the subject. Once her mother got started on her love life, she was liable to go on about it all night. "Are you having trouble sleeping?"

"No, not really. I was just having a long talk with Angelique, and when she mentioned her daughter, I remembered there was something I wanted to ask you about. What was it now? Poor Angelique is having such trouble with that child of hers, you know."

"Hmm," Kate knew better than to ask for details, particularly since Angelique was an eighteenth-century French ghost. Kate vaguely remembered that she'd been guillotined in the Reign of Terror.

"Something about television. Poor Angelique didn't know what I was talking about, of course. A box where you can see people walking about and speaking as if in life. I haven't even tried to explain the internet to her. She absolutely couldn't understand when I told her that I was actually going to be on television. She was concerned that it might affect my health."

Kate snapped to attention. "What do you mean, you're going to be on television?"

"Why, darling, I had the most fascinating conversation today with such a nice man who wants to do some sort of documentary about my 'illustrious career,' as he put it. Can you imagine? And I was convinced that everybody had forgotten about me."

"You didn't agree, I hope?" Kate said on a rising note of panic.

"There, dear, you sound so concerned. I appreciate it, but you really mustn't be so protective. It sounds like such fun. He said I might even be on YouTube, and that people from all over the world would be able to see the broadcast."

"Was this 'nice man' named D. B. Haggarty by any chance?"

"Why, yes. Mr. Haggarty, I believe. But by the end of the conversation he was telling me to call him Daniel." There was an intake of breath, and Kate could feel her mother's intuitive powers flashing across the cellular network. She might be flaky, but she wasn't thick. "Your Daniel?"

"He's not my Daniel," Kate said grimly. "He's the producer responsible for a program called *Facts and Fantasies*, and he's a very dangerous man. Not to mention unscrupulous. I can't believe he called you up and pretended to be pleasant. He hates psychics and mediums."

"Really?" Iris sounded a bit disconcerted. "And I'm usually such a good judge of character."

That was a laugh and a half. Her mother could look into a person's palm and read every nuance of his or her personality, but no matter how reprehensible the faults she uncovered, she seemed to forget about them the moment she dropped the subject's hand. "I look for the good in people," she had frequently told her daughter. "Never once have I failed to find it."

As a result, Iris Carter was routinely cheated by everyone from car mechanics to financial advisers.

"What did you agree to?"

"Well, nothing yet. I explained to him that although I was flattered by the invitation to appear on this YouTube thing, I'd have to discuss it with my daughter first."

"Thank goodness, Mom. I'll talk to him and convey your regrets. He'll have to be made to understand that you're retired and don't do interviews anymore." Her voice tightened as she added, "I'll make sure he doesn't bother you again."

"But Kate—"

"No buts. Do you remember a medium called Myra Kelley?"

"Of course. A pleasant woman, and quite talented," Iris said a little uncertainly.

"She was a fake, Mom, and you know it. One of Haggarty's interviewers exposed her on his program a few months ago. They reduced her to tears and blasted what was left of her credibility. That was only the beginning as far as Daniel is concerned. He doesn't believe in supernatural phenomena, and he means to prove that all psychics are either charlatans or nutcases."

"Good heavens!" Her mother sounded shocked. "He sounded like such a charming young man on the phone."

"He's charming all right," Kate said, remembering the way he had nearly seduced her. "He'd charm the fish out of the sea and then grill them over an open fire."

It wasn't until she'd hung up that she remembered her birth sign–Pisces–and Daniel's threats, and she shivered at the aptness of her metaphor.

Kate stared at her phone for a few moments after the talk with her mother. Daniel hadn't called her today, which was a little unusual. She decided, for once, to take the initiative. She sent him a text saying:

Leave my mom alone. No way is she going on your show.

Almost instantly, she got a response. She prepared herself to be angered, but all it said was:

Heard & understood.

CHAPTER SIX

The next morning, Saturday, Kate stepped out of her swim club into the chill of biting autumn wind to find Daniel leaning against his Porsche, waiting for her. He was casually dressed in jeans and a black leather jacket, and his hair was agreeably ruffled by the stiff breeze. He looked rough and tough and sexy as hell.

Kate couldn't contain a smile as he came up to her and took her gym bag out of her hands. She was glad to see him; how could she deny it? Her body had reacted instantly with a surprisingly intense flash of lust. "What are you doing here?" She tried to sound severe and disapproving, but she suspected it wasn't working. "I don't remember telling you the name of my gym."

"Good morning to you, too," his amused voice returned. "Are you always so perky at this ungodly hour?"

She glanced at her watch. It was nine o'clock. "It's not that ungodly."

"Spare me," he groaned.

"Go away, Daniel. I am not going to let myself be ambushed by you."

He grinned and stayed put. "You've been doing your best to avoid me, but admit it—your emails have been friendly. As for how I knew it was your gym, I didn't, but this is the closest exercise club to your house, and it's the only one nearby that has a pool. You told me you were a swimmer."

"Why are you being so persistent?"

"I don't know. Personality flaw? Come on, I'll take you out to breakfast. After all that swimming you must be starving."

"Breakfast!"

"You keep turning down my invitations to assorted evening activities."

"I work in the evenings."

"Ah, yes." As always, his voice turned severe at the reminder of her work. "I keep forgetting—night is the best time for casting spells."

A puckish grin came over Kate's face. He couldn't be too heavily into stalking, or he would have Googled her by now and discovered her actual profession. He still thought of her as a professional psychic. It was remarkable, under the circumstances, that he continued to demonstrate such an interest in her. He seemed to take perverse pleasure in pursuing a woman of whom he thoroughly disapproved.

"Breakfast, huh?" Now that he mentioned it, her stomach was growling. The clever devil knew how to prey on her weaknesses. First the truffles, now this. And even yummier than the thought of breakfast was that long, strong body of his, close enough now to her to exert the full force of his sexual magnetism. She felt her resolution falter, and knew she was going to cave. Damn hormones! "Can we have pancakes?"

"I was thinking of something sophisticated and continental, like croissants and light, fluffy omelets."

"Blueberry pancakes. With maple syrup and great dollops of butter."

"With a side of bacon and a side of hash browns, and a bottomless pot of coffee." He was obviously warming to the idea.

"Sounds divine. I know a good place for that in Harvard Square, just a few minutes from here."

"Okay, but it's up to you to find me a place to park."

Thirty minutes later, after three fruitless tours of the Square, Daniel finally shelled out for a parking place in an expensive underground garage, muttering darkly about the problems of owning a car in the city, and led his captive into her favorite local pancake and waffle house. Sitting down opposite him, Kate felt the heat of his eyes. As it had before, his gaze seemed to touch her with fire. But she didn't let that stop her from digging into a huge helping of blueberry pancakes slathered with syrup.

"One of my favorite things about you is the obvious pleasure you take in appeasing your appetite," he said with a wicked grin. "Do you gratify your other desires with the same enthusiasm?"

"What other desires? Good food, in my opinion, is the only pleasure that counts."

"I could introduce you to some others."

"I knew you were going to say that." She took a slow swallow of coffee and smiled at him. He looked a trifle less dangerous by day than he had by night. His complexion was not as dark as she'd thought, and the midnight blue of his eyes seemed lighter, too. In fact, his skin was quite fair against his dark hair and thick eyebrows. His face was still scruffy, as if he used a blunt razor when he shaved and always left a disreputable shadow. There was something very sexy about that look. She wanted to stroke those rough cheeks. She folded her hands in her lap to stifle the temptation.

He'd taken off the black leather jacket, revealing a long-sleeved flannel hanging open over a grey T-shirt. Casual weekend attire, clearly. All in all, he looked somewhat less satanic than she remembered.

"And?"

"And the answer is still no."

To her surprise, he didn't pursue it. Instead, he said, "How can you eat so much and still stay so thin?"

"I'm not thin."

"Slender, then," he corrected himself, letting his eyes roam over her. She, too, was dressed casually this morning in a mauve sweater, jeans, and soft leather boots. Her brown hair, still damp from the pool, was loosely tied back with a ribbon.

"I work out, as you know. Swimming, running, lifting weights."

"You lift, too?"

"Sure. Lots of women do it, particularly in my line of work." Indeed, she didn't know a single performer who didn't work like hell to keep in shape.

But Daniel misinterpreted. "You have to be strong, I suppose, to tip tables at séances without getting caught. Everything I've researched about the history of spiritualism suggests that mediums have always been athletic. Some of them were even able to perform remarkable feats of contortionism."

Kate rolled her eyes at the ceiling in a here-we-go-again gesture.

"There was a famous nineteenth-century medium who had herself bound with cords around the neck, waist, wrists, and ankles in her cabinet before every performance. Strange figures used to materialize in her séance rooms when she went into a trance, and she had been accused of impersonating these 'spirits' herself. Her bindings were always double-checked to make sure she couldn't free herself when all the lights went out."

"But she could free herself, I take it?"

"Let me put it this way: The spirits' features were extraordinarily similar to the medium's, and spirits and medium were never seen together." He took a swallow of coffee, and his eyes glinted at her over the rim of his cup as he added, "Did your mother teach you that trick? Shall I take you home and tie you up and see if you can twist free?"

Kate nearly choked on her pancakes. His voice was so starkly sensual that it made heat wash through her. She clutched her fork tightly for a moment, and then put it down carefully on the side of her plate. This had to stop.

"Look, I don't know how to get it through to you that I'm not interested in the hot bunny sex you're offering."

"Hot bunny sex?" He was laughing at her.

"Or whatever. You don't even like or approve of me. There's no way I'm going to get mixed up with a man who regards me as an object of derision."

His hand reached out and folded over hers. She felt a rush of warmth. Why was she was so susceptible to his touch?

"Forgive me if I've given you that impression. I like you very much."

"I think you're just after me for the thrill of the chase or something." She slid her hand out from under his.

"Come on," he said a little impatiently. "If sex were all I wanted, I could get it elsewhere."

No doubt. With his looks, his charm, and his confidence, no doubt he'd been getting it regularly since puberty.

"What do you want then?"

"A chance," he said simply.

"A chance for what?"

He held up his hand, palm toward her. "A chance to channel my energy into the one deep line that comes after the ragged false starts."

She blinked at him, surprised. "I thought you didn't believe in palmistry."

"As a science I don't. As a metaphor for looking at one's life, though, it's rather intriguing." His eyes were serious for once. "I'm almost thirty-one, and I split last spring from a girlfriend who left me for some extreme sports dude who jumps out of airplanes and skis on virgin cliffs in the Himalayas. Since then I've done some random dating, but I'm disenchanted with the hook-up, hang out for a few weeks, then wave goodbye routine. I'd like to get to know someone on a deeper, less superficial level, and I sense that possibility between us. Don't you?"

Okay, so maybe he wasn't just proposing quick, wild, no-complications sex. She frowned, thinking about it. Every night that week, as she lay curled up in her lonely bed trying to sleep, she'd been fantasizing about him. She remembered the warmth of his mouth on hers, the exciting hardness of his body. She fell asleep each night imagining that he was with her in bed, pressing her down with his weight and loving her all over.

But that wasn't all she thought about. They had had some interesting conversations on the phone during the past few days, and several witty email exchanges. There was a lot more to Daniel than the erotic side of things. Most of what she had learned about him, she liked.

And yet...he was so different from Arthur—much more domineering, much more dynamic. His charisma added an extra charge to the sensual attraction between them, but there was a great deal more to a relationship than that. Life had been sunny and tranquil with Arthur; with Daniel it would be turbulent and maybe even dark.

"Well? Am I gonna get my chance?"

She stopped brooding and ate the last mouthful of her breakfast. "I don't know, Daniel. I'm a little frightened of you, if you want to know the truth."

He frowned, but she sensed he wasn't entirely displeased by her admission. He probably enjoyed frightening people.

"Are you worried I might make good on my threat to include you in my program on psychic fraud?" he inquired, his blue eyes gleaming.

"Oh, dear God, no," she laughed. "I really think we ought to clear that up before—"

"Or your mother? You're afraid for your mother? Is that it? Do you think I'm trying to get close to you in hopes of prying all sorts of anecdotes out of you about one of the best-known ghost-whisperers in the country?"

She glared at him over the rim of the coffee cup she had lifted to her lips. "That possibility has occurred to me, yes. I was pretty upset to hear that you had phoned her and tried to charm her into an interview."

"It was worth a try."

"As I told you last night, the answer is no. She doesn't do interviews."

His eyelids flickered. "In that case, maybe you could be persuaded to provide me with the intriguing details of how she rigs the room before a séance?"

"So that really *is* what you want from me?" Her coffee cup slammed down onto its saucer. "If I possessed any such knowledge—which I don't, because my mother's not a fake—there's no way I would ever divulge it to you."

"Of course she's a fake," Daniel said in a voice that was low but intense. "Even if I never get the chance to interview her, I mean to discredit her along with all the others. I want to be completely straightforward with you about that. I despise mediums, spiritualists, trance channelers, ghost whisperers, or whatever they're calling themselves these days. No matter what happens between you and me, I'll be moving ahead with my plan to show the world what frauds they all are."

"Nothing's going to happen between you and me. I've already told you, you're too narrow-minded and judgmental for me." She paused, and then added, "My mother's getting old, and she's always been a little cracked. She's living in retirement now, she's not very healthy, and she's not doing readings or séances. I hardly think she's an appropriate target for one of your muckraking attacks."

He shrugged, but his eyes were hard. He was a complex personality, she thought: hot and cold, harsh and gentle, driven in his professional pursuits and rather brutally honest. Again, she couldn't resist comparing him once again to Arthur, who had been even-tempered and genuinely kind. Kindness was a virtue she valued highly. There was too much cruelty and aggression in the world. She didn't want to get mixed up with a man whose professional goals demanded that he ruthlessly hunt down a harmless woman and expose her in the public stocks of the mass media.

"I have to go." She thrust her hand into her jeans and pulled out her wallet. Before she got it open, his hand came down over hers.

"Not this time. I suggested this, and I'm paying. As for your mother, let's put that subject aside. All I care about right now is you. I want you, and there's no way I'm letting you walk out of my life."

The steel underlying his words both chilled and excited her. Dear heavens, the man was persistent! She put her credit card away. Let him pay, dammit. "I'm sorry, but I need to leave."

He rose when she did. "Then I'm coming with you."

"You can't."

"Stop me."

She thrust her arms into her fleece jacket and turned to stalk toward the door. Daniel pulled on his own jacket, tossed some cash on the table and followed.

"Are you going to make a scene?"

"I am trying to be a gentleman. Watch, I'll demonstrate." He made a show of holding the door open for her and bowing as she stepped out into the street. "Forgive me. I've made the lady angry," he added in an exaggeratedly humble tone.

She caught the teasing look in his eyes and found herself stifling a smile. Arrogance she could resist, but his unpredictable bursts of humor left her defenseless.

"I've already told you, Kate, I won't do anything to hurt you." He paused, then added, his rueful tone testifying to the cost of his concession, "Or your mother, either, if she's really as old and feeble as you say she is."

Kate reflected guiltily that her mother wasn't as old and feeble as she'd intimated, but she kept that thought to herself.

The wind made her shiver as it whistled around the buildings in Harvard Square. The unseasonable cold they had been having this month hadn't let up. September was usually much warmer in

Boston. Daniel's arm came around her shoulders, as if to shelter her from the wind. "If it makes you feel better, I won't interview her without your permission. Or hers."

She tried to shrug free, unsure whether she could trust him. "Is that a promise?"

"Yes," he said, drawing her closer. "Relax," he added, his breath hot against her ear. "You're as slippery as a fish."

And as easily hooked, she thought sadly. "I am a fish. A Pisces."

He pulled a face. "So you're into astrology as well?"

His easy, amused tone disarmed her, and she began to feel she might have been precipitous in her desire to escape. He couldn't be as ruthless as she'd thought if he was really willing to give up his plan to harass her mother for her sake.

She allowed him to walk her back toward the underground garage. She might as well let him drive her home. It was a bit too chilly to stand outside waiting for the bus. Besides, she had left her gym bag in his car. "We psychics are all into astrology. When's your birthday, Daniel?"

"I'm not going to tell you."

"Why not?"

"You'll say we're incompatible and use it as an excuse to keep up this stubborn coyness of yours."

"Graham has you pegged as a Scorpio. Were you born in November?"

"Nope. So much for Graham's wisdom."

"Too bad. Pisces and Scorpio are among the most compatible lovers in the zodiac."

He brightened. "If I were a Scorpio, would you make love with me?"

Since he wasn't born in November, she risked a light answer. "I might consider it. Graham says the sex would be hot."

They had reached the entrance to the garage. It got dark as they descended the stairs to the lower level, and she was conscious of the increasing pressure of Daniel's arm around her. "I am a Scorpio."

"I don't believe you. When's your birthday?"

"You're going to laugh."

"Tell me."

"I was born on your favorite day of the year."

"What does that mean?"

He maintained a mock stubborn silence as they walked through the quiet garage toward the car, but he finally gave in and answered, "October thirty-first, witch."

She did laugh, delightedly. Then she stopped, because they had reached the car and he was pressing her up against it and kissing her fiercely. Their bodies melted together, and fire leaped through her. "So you are a Scorpio," she murmured against his lips.

"And the sex will be very, very hot."

His gloved hands threaded through her hair and held her motionless while his mouth played teasingly on hers. She gasped as his tongue wet the surface of her lips, and then traced tiny patterns over her cheeks and eyelids. The damp butterfly kisses were deliciously erotic, and she was passive for only a few moments before her fingers slipped into his hair and pulled his face closer to hers.

"Mmm," he groaned deep in his throat. Their tongues touched, and Kate's limbs grew heavy with desire. She pressed against him, crushing her breasts against his chest. The kiss deepened. His

tongue stroked hers with devastating expertise. Bursts of liquid
warmth exploded inside her. His hands slid down her back and
kneaded her bottom, drawing her lower body into the cradle of his
hips. He felt wonderful. He was hard, and she loved feeling it,
knowing that she had made him so. Her head tilted back as his
kisses moved ravenously down her throat. She sighed, wanting
him, needing what he offered. Her loins ached as she absorbed and
returned the pressure of his thighs against her own. He put both
hands on her hips and held her still while he rocked against her in
a manner that made her limp, hot and barely aware of who she
was or what she was doing.

"Kate," he whispered. He took up the word in a breathless lita-
ny of "Kate, Kate, Kate." He sounded as incoherent as she felt. His
body trembled; his face was flushed and damp against her own. He
slid them both sideways along the car until she was leaning
against the hood; then his strong arms lifted her so she was sitting
on it. She nuzzled his throat with her lips and teeth as he parted
her legs and stood in close between her thighs. His arms reached
around to support her back as he insinuated himself still more
tightly against her. His lovely cock was pressed right up between
her legs. She imagined it sliding into her. She moaned his name.
Her legs curled around him, and she clung to him as if the world
was coming to an end and he would be wrenched away from her.

One of his hands jerked open her jacket and sought her
breasts. His gloves made him clumsy, so he bent his head and tore
one of them off with his teeth in a gesture that was savagely exciting. She let out a gasp as his bare hand slid under her sweater,
pushed up her fragile bra, and took her flesh into his palm.

"You feel so good." His fingertips drew teasing circles around
the peak of her captured breast, making her moan and shudder in

his arms. He forced the sweater up as his head came down, and he kissed her breasts. His scruffy cheeks were harsh against her bare skin, but it felt delicious. Her nipples had turned to hard, burning points, and she thought she would die if he didn't take them in his mouth. She held his head against her while his body pressed rhythmically now, signaling his need and stoking hers to a fever pitch. She squirmed against his cock, wishing the clothing down there would simply vanish so their union could be complete. She wanted him inside her. She was spinning on waves of explosive sexuality, tossed on a storm of desire that was much more intense than anything in her experience.

She was tearing at his jacket, longing to touch his naked flesh as he was touching hers, when a sudden arc of light distracted her. The headlights of another car beamed down on their en-twined figures as somebody entered the garage. Kate buried her face on Daniel's shoulder in a sudden rush of embarrassment and slid from the car hood to her feet, her body moving deliciously along Daniel's as she regained her balance.

"Oh my god, we're in a public garage," she said, trying to catch her breath.

He had already adjusted her clothing for modesty's sake, and he sheltered her protectively against him as the car passed them. Then he reached out and flung open the car door. "Get in. We'll go to my place."

Trembling, she obeyed, sitting down and fastening her seat belt with shaking fingers. Her panties were slick and damp. Wow, she thought as her mind sluggishly began working again. This was wild. She couldn't recall ever feeling such intense, mindless lust with Arthur.

A shaft of disloyalty stabbed her, cutting right through her desire. How could she feel such yearning for Daniel when her sexual feelings for her gentle, kind husband had been tame in comparison? It didn't seem right somehow.

Maybe she just didn't remember how it had felt back then. She had been alone too long. Her natural urges had been stifled by her grief, and now that the grief had finally receded, those urges were burgeoning forth, clamoring for expression, making her eager to snatch the pleasure this very exciting man was offering. What had Jeff told her? The chemistry was a gift. It would make things easy. She should seize the gift and take joy in this aspect of living once again. It was time.

And yet... how would she feel when her physical demands were met? How would Daniel feel? He still thought she was a fake, a fraud. He still wanted to humiliate her mother.

"We're going too fast," she said as the Porsche sped out of the garage and into the light of morning. She closed her eyes against the brightness. "This just isn't right for me."

The car jerked as he shifted recklessly. "Don't say that." His voice was taut. "No second thoughts."

"Do you think it's any easier for me?" She sat upright in her seat and glared at him. "Women are as capable of gut-wrenching lust as men are, and the frustration hurts us just as much."

"I know that. But neither of us is committed to another partner, so there's no reason for you to condemn us both to frustration."

"There's one very good reason. I'm not ready yet."

"Yet?" he repeated, zeroing in on the operative word. "Do you want me to wine you and dine you for a couple of weeks first? You

can't accept the explosive chemistry between us until some deco-
rous courting period has elapsed? Is that it?"

"No, that's not it."

"You won't even accept a normal sort of date with me."

"I know. I'm sorry. Just take me home, please. To my house, I
mean."

Instead, he slammed on the brakes and pulled the car over to
the side of the road. By some miracle, a parking place had opened
up, and he slid the car into it and shut off the motor. Her entire
body tensed as he turned to her, a grim look etched on his face. He
noted her stiffness, and his eyes turned sardonic. "Relax. I can
take no for an answer. I just hate to, dammit."

She smiled faintly and relaxed against the seat. He has a beautiful mouth, she thought involuntarily, staring at it. Desire twisted in her again.

Daniel took a deep breath and closed his eyes. Kate stared at
his thick eyelashes, which were even denser than her own. His face
was drawn with emotion, and she felt an unexpected tenderness
for him.

"You said yourself that I was a man of unruly passions," he reminded her, raising his lashes again. "You were right. You also
said sex was important to me. You were right about that, too."
The look in his blue eyes intensified. "I've been tortured since I
met you. I lie in bed at night, unable to sleep, tormented by fantasies of you. If I weren't so positive that witchcraft and voodoo and
all the black arts were a crock of bull, I'd be certain you'd put a
spell on me."

"Daniel, I—"

"I'm going to ask you one question, and I need an honest answer. What does it mean, you're not ready yet? Are you ever going

to be ready? Just how serious were you when you told me last week that you don't sleep with men? Are you afraid of sex? What the hell is the matter with you?"

She felt herself smile. "That's five questions."

One hand cupped her chin, forcing her to face him. "Answer me."

"Okay." She urged herself to be as honest as he was. "You're not the only one who lies awake at night and fantasizes. I was attracted to you the instant I saw you, leaning up against the wall at that party and glowering at me."

There was a glint of satisfaction in his eyes. "Go on."

"I'm not afraid of sex. Sex is awesome. The trouble is, I was very much in love with Arthur."

"Your husband?"

"Yes. He was the only lover I've ever had. We started dating in high school, when I was fifteen years old. We were both virgins, and we learned about sex together, taking it slowly and amazed at everything we discovered. It was always a very intimate act for us."

She could see Arthur then, in her mind's eye, on their last night together—the night before the accident. They had made love so sweetly, and he had smiled at her, his fingers framing her face as he'd gazed into her eyes and whispered, "Forever and ever, Katie. I adore you, and we'll always be together." Never had it entered their minds that this would be the last time they made love.

Did you ever know it was the last time? Couples broke up, separated, divorced, and if you were young and very unlucky, sometimes your partner died. If you had known you were making love for the final time, would it be different? Would you try to make it even more special, or would the sadness of the coming separation make it horribly sad?

She shook her head, trying to push the vivid memory away, but it was gnawing at her insides, making her feel as though she might start to sob. She fought the feeling. She hadn't cried for months, and this wasn't the time. "I'm sure it sounds really lame and old-fashioned," she plunged on, "but I just can't leap into bed with a man I hardly know. I wish I could. My life has been so empty since he died." Another wave of sorrow engulfed her, and she was mortified to feel her eyes begin to water. She coughed, trying to hide it. Arthur was gone, and she had grieved deeply for him. Why wouldn't the pain fade, lessen, go away?

She was about to lose it, dammit. She didn't want that to happen, not while she was with Daniel. Her grief was too private. This was exactly what she had been avoiding dating. She had never learned how to do the casual, get off in bed but don't feel any deeper emotions thing.

Showing more tact that she would have given him credit for, Daniel said, "Let's go for a walk along the river. It's a bit windy, but we should be all right. Come on."

The tasks of removing her seatbelt and tightening her jacket against the wind gave her the moment she needed to recover, and she was grateful to him for providing her with that escape. By the time they had crossed Memorial Drive and strolled down to the riverbank, she had succeeded in swallowing her tears and gaining control of her uncharacteristically wayward emotions.

* * *

A half hour later, after a brisk walk along the Charles River with Daniel companionably holding her hand, Kate sat beside him once again as he drove her home. The walk had been pleasant.

The crisp air had brought on the colorful glory of autumn a bit earlier than usual, and the tree-lined streets of the city were ablaze in bright reds, oranges, and yellows. It was beautiful. She loved the fall. Even so, she was glad to be back in his car. The morning had clouded over, and it looked as though the hurricane that was churning off the coast might bring some in some nasty weather.

They hadn't talked a lot, but the silence felt comfortable. His expressive eyes had offered her sympathy and understanding, along with a calm acceptance of her grief. He didn't seem to consider it strange that she was still mourning her loss. If he thought it lame that she hadn't had sex for three years, he gave no hint of it.

As a result, she felt more at ease with him than she had felt since they'd met. Her respect for him had increased, as had her affection. Daniel Haggarty was turning out to be a good deal kinder than she had originally thought.

Maybe she should just go ahead and get naked with him. He hadn't said it, but the bitter truth was undeniable: Her idyllic relationship with Arthur was over forever. She had avoided sexual intimacy for three years, and her body was rising up now in rebellion against the persistent self-denial. It wasn't realistic to keep reining in her natural desires because she didn't feel the same emotional bond with Daniel that she'd felt with Arthur. She was just getting to know Daniel, and the bond might grow between them.

On the other hand, it might not. She shivered, hugging herself. She was such a mess!

"Cold?" asked Daniel, turning up the heat.

"Uh, no, not really."

"What are you thinking?"

"Nothing much."

He pursed his lips, looking strained again. A couple of moments passed before he said, "I want to see you tonight. I'll make dinner for you. How about that? I'm not a bad cook, you know."

"I'd like to, but I can't; not tonight."

"Kate, I respect your feelings, and I understand your reservations. I can't promise you anything at this point; I'd be a liar if I said I could. I want you desperately, but I'll do my best not to coerce you into bed before you're ready. I'll do anything you want, in fact, except go away. So stop arguing. We're going to get to know each other better, and we're going to start by being together tonight."

"I really can't," she said with genuine regret. "I'm working tonight." *A Doll's House* was being presented this evening at a local university theater, freeing up the company's own theater. The *Macbeth* cast would be running a full rehearsal there after the matinee performance of the Ibsen play.

He took his eyes off the road to stare at her, and then had to swerve to avoid a bus. He cursed. "What is it tonight—another charitable party? Gull a few superstitious idiots while collecting their money for a worthy cause?"

She shook her head. It was time to tell him. This had gone on long enough. "No, it's far more sinister than that. Tonight I'm going to be dressed in black, leaning over a cauldron, prophesying and murmuring incantations of doom." She wagged her fingers at him like a spook. "'Double double, toil and trouble, fire burn and cauldron bubble—'" she intoned, then stopped abruptly. It was unlucky to quote from The Scottish Play, as just about all Shakespearean actors called it. Productions of *Macbeth* had a reputation in the theater for being fraught with disaster. Citing a line from the play was every bit as hazardous as mentioning it by name.

"Very funny," said Daniel.

She tossed her hair back over her shoulder and grinned. "I'm serious. An important personage is coming to consult me and my colleagues. We're going to predict great glories for him. We're going to tempt him by appealing to his overweening ambition."

She expected him to understand the reference, but Daniel glared at her. "You're actually sitting there plotting what to say to some poor sucker?"

A ripple of pure merriment went through her, and she had to look away to contain her laughter. "I swear to you that every prediction I make for this man will come true. Even the manner of his death."

"You're going to predict somebody's death?!"

"Take it easy," she said as he careened around a corner.

"That's despicable. I can't believe you'd do such a thing." He shook his head, looking grim. "Dammit. Every time I begin to think maybe I can deal with this, you toss me another curveball."

"Come watch me," she challenged.

"What do you mean?"

"Exactly what I said." Her eyes were twinkling. Let him see for himself what kind of witch she was. "Come watch me perform, act, practice my witchcraft, do my job. You said you wanted to get to know me better. Something about relating to me on a deeper, less superficial level?"

"I've seen you perform," he growled. "Once was enough. I don't like it. I don't even want to think about it."

"If you can't accept my professional life, I really don't see how you can expect to have any sort of relationship with me. Suppose we got serious. Before long you'd be insisting I quit work."

"Damn right. You can't go around predicting people's deaths. Some folks are susceptible to the power of suggestion. You could be condemning some poor sod to die from sheer terror."

"Don't worry, Haggarty. This particular client deserves it. He's terrorized quite a few people himself, and besides, he's a ruthless, power-seeking murderer."

Daniel pulled the car to a jolting stop in front of her house. "Where are you performing tonight, in the state prison?"

When she just grinned at him, he relaxed and leaned back in his seat. "Okay, witch. You're having a little joke, aren't you?"

"Sort of," she confessed.

"Sort of?"

She swung open the Porsche's door. "Come tonight and find out. One thirty-seven Liberty Square," she added, giving him the address of the theater. "It'll be early—6 p.m. Tell the guy at the door you're a friend of Kate Kingsley."

His eyes lit up. "Kate Kingsley?"

"And don't Google me first. You've waited this long. I want you to be surprised."

"I don't like surprises," he groused.

"You'll like this one," she predicted. "See you later." She laughed and jumped out of the car.

CHAPTER SEVEN

"Is he out there?" an uncharacteristically nervous Kate demanded of her fellow actor, Graham.

"If he is, he's sitting in the back. I couldn't see the guy," Graham answered. He was adjusting his doublet and hose for his role of Malcolm, the dispossessed heir to the throne of Scotland who prevails in the end of the play, after the death of the tyrant Macbeth. "These blasted tights are baggy," he complained. "How am I supposed to look dashing and heroic in this getup?"

"I think it's rather sexy."

"Yeah?" Looking pleased, he preened in front of the greenroom mirror, and then glanced over at Kate. "You look pretty hot yourself. I thought the three Weird Sisters were ugly old hags. How come you look young and beautiful and delicious enough to eat?"

"Paul agreed with me that the ugly old crone interpretation is a cliché. A witch should be lovely and feminine and powerful in her sexuality. That's what makes you men afraid of us, after all."

"Rot. I think you're just trying to knock the socks off D. B. Haggarty, luv. And you will, too, if he sees you dressed like that."

She smoothed the front of her black Renaissance gown. It had a square, low-cut neckline, and scarlet laces held the bodice together. The silken skirt of the gown was slashed down the front to reveal a scarlet underskirt, the flowing sleeves similarly slashed to reveal a scarlet lining. Her dark brown hair was loose about her shoulders and threaded with narrow black and scarlet ribbons. The overall effect was dramatic and sensual.

"He probably didn't come. He said he wouldn't. Anyway, there's that hurricane threatening, so the roads are probably a mess."

"Don't worry; the hurricane's supposed to miss us, and I doubt if a little gale would faze that crusader. He probably doesn't give credence to weather reports. Don't you know that all weather prognosticators are frauds?"

She smiled a little, and then chuckled. "I can't wait to see his face when he realizes I'm an actress and that it's the Scot's death I'm predicting. You should have heard him this morning, Graham. He was appalled."

"I hope for your sake he can take a joke. Otherwise he's not going to be too pleased when he finds out you've been scamming him."

"Serves him right," she laughed. "I told him at the start that I was an actress, but he paid no attention. He might be annoyed at first, but I can handle that." She reflected a moment, remembering both the sense of danger in Daniel and his underlying tenderness. "I hope."

Graham made a show of buckling his sword belt. "You've got it bad for this guy, don't you?"

Kate tightened the laces of her bodice. "I'm trying not to get involved with him."

"Yeah? Tell me another."

"I mean it." She had been stressing about the matter all day. Ever since Daniel had kissed her in the garage, dissolving them both into a state of intense sexual urgency, she'd been able to think of little else. "I'm a quiet-living widow. He's way out of my league. I'd be crazy to let anything happen between us."

"I'm glad you realize that. I was afraid you might be getting in too deep. He's not your type."

Kate flashed him an annoyed look. It was all right for her to tell herself that, but she didn't appreciate hearing it from Graham.

"I heard from a friend of a friend that Haggarty is quite the player." Graham went on. "He's apparently left several broken-hearted women in his wake."

"Are you jealous?"

Graham moved a step closer to her, his eyes running over her figure in the provocative manner he usually reserved for other women. "Maybe," he admitted. "You know how I feel about you, luv."

"I know you're my friend." She was unwilling to think of him in any other way. He occasionally teased her with sexual innuendos, but he had never made any concerted attempt to alter the status of their friendship. Which was good, because she had never been physically attracted to Graham.

Like her college buddies, Graham had been good to her in the aftermath of Arthur's death, coaxing and cajoling her into taking an interest in life again. She would always be grateful to him for that, and she enjoyed their camaraderie at work, but that was as far as it went. "Stop rolling your eyes at me and let me finish getting ready," she said lightly. "We've got more important things to do than worry about my love life or lack of one. I have to open this play, you know."

As if on cue, a man's voice bellowed, "Kingsley! Where the hell are you, dammit?"

"Oh, jeez," she muttered as Paul Tiele, their director, stormed into the dressing room, smoking a forbidden cigarette and looking more than usually agitated.

"What is this, *Antony and Cleopatra*?" he mocked when he found Kate and Graham together. "We got a play to do, remember? The hundreds of dollars' worth of cloth you're draped in is supposed to be exhibited onstage, not back here for our resident Lothario to admire. Admirable though you may be."

"Thanks a lot."

Tiele, a thin, prematurely gray man in his early forties whose nervous energy and peremptory manner annoyed his actors just a little less than his brilliance and originality dazzled them, considered her for a moment in silence, then stalked over to her, blew smoke in her face, took the bodice of her dress in his two strong hands, and jerked it up an inch. "You're too sexy. You're supposed to be seducing Mac—" he stopped just short of speaking the name "—the Scot with visions of power, but one look at you and he'll send his dreams of kingship straight to hell."

"I thought that was the way you wanted me to play it, Paul."

"It is. But I usually see you in jeans and a T-shirt. You look different in that dress." He glanced at Graham. "What are you smirking at, Hamilton?" He gave Graham's costume a critical examination, too. "Nice legs. But your hose is baggy."

Kate coughed from the cigarette smoke and laughed at Graham as he cursed and once again attacked his costume.

Five minutes later, they were ready to begin the rehearsal. Then Kate remembered. "Paul, wait. I almost forgot. I inadvertently quoted a couple of lines from the play today. I'd better do the exorcism first," she said, referring to a ritual known by Shakespearean actors the world over.

Tiele choked on his own smoke and groaned. "Shit, Kingsley. You never quote from The Scottish Play, particularly on dress rehearsal night. Are you deliberately courting disaster? Just because you're one of the Weird Sisters doesn't mean you can take liberties of that kind. If anything goes wrong, I'll hold you personally responsible."

"Take it easy, Paul. Nothing's going to go wrong."

Tiele was known for being the most superstitious member of the company, and Kate was well aware that he was none too comfortable about doing the play at all. It was considered the unluckiest play in the entire theatrical canon.

Like all the actors in her theater company, Kate knew the details of every disaster that had ever occurred during a production of *Macbeth*. There were a lot of them. Supposedly, Shakespeare himself had had to take the role of Lady Macbeth in the first performance of the play when the young man playing the role had suddenly taken ill and died. In 1849, a riot had broken out during a performance in New York that had killed 31 people. Sir Lawrence Olivier had almost been killed by a freak accident in 1937 when he played Macbeth at the Old Vic, and in one of Sir John Gielgud's productions, three of the actors had died during the run. Charlton Heston had been severely burned onstage during one of his productions of the play. The stories went on and on—accidents, murders, and other mysterious deaths plagued both the actors and the people connected in other ways with the play. Kate had heard these tales told over and over. Tiele had never directed *Macbeth* before, and, quite simply, he was petrified.

The time-honored method of dealing with the fatal slip of either naming the play or quoting lines from it was to perform a simple, though somewhat odd, ceremony. Kate knew the routine.

She went out of the room, knocked, reentered, turned around from left to right three times in a circle, then burst into the most vigorously obscene swear words she knew. Graham, who was watching, raised his eyebrows. "Is that the raunchiest you can get? Quiet-living widow, indeed!"

Kate was glad Daniel wasn't backstage to witness the ritual. It was exactly this sort of superstition that he loathed.

Shortly thereafter, the rehearsal began. As First Witch, Kate had the opening line of the play. Everything was set up onstage as it would be for an actual performance, and after some initial problems with the technical crew, she got her cue and began. "'When shall we three meet again? In thunder, lightning, or in rain?'"

She was too absorbed in her role to notice whether Daniel was in the theater or not. As always when she acted, she was lost to thoughts of anything else. During her performance, she felt as though she actually was one of the witches tempting Macbeth with the possibility of kingship.

Wrung out after her two brief scenes in Act I, she walked blindly offstage, fingering the bodice of her gown, which was a little tight. She gave a cry of surprise when she collided with a tall man whose arms went around her, trapping her hands against the soft material of a blue and green plaid flannel shirt.

"Double, double, you're in trouble, witch," he whispered crushing her so hard against him that her breasts were flattened by his pectoral muscles.

"Daniel!"

"You're an actress."

"Yes. I am." Her voice was muffled by the warm line of his throat. Held close to him, she felt the same sensual vertigo she'd experienced that morning in the garage. "I told you that the night we met."

"This is what you meant this morning by prophecies of doom? This is what you meant when you told me to come and watch you 'perform'?"

"Well, of course. What else?" she said innocently.

"And this is where you come when you go to work? All the evenings I've called you and you haven't taken the call, this is where you've been?"

"Rehearsing a play is time-consuming. Particularly so close to opening night. Besides, I'm an alternate in the play that's running now. I perform Tuesday evenings and Wednesday afternoons, and I'm on call in case the main actress for my role can't play the part on any other night."

"In *A Doll's House*? What part do you play in that?"

"Nora's friend Christine."

"So you're not a psychic or a medium or a Wicca or a Gypsy fortune-teller?"

She shook her head. "Nope. Graham does astrology part-time, and he sometimes works with a psychic. When she got sick right before that party, he asked me to fill in for her. It's the first time I've ever done such a thing, and, considering the grief you gave me over it, it'll be the last." She leaned back in his arms and grinned up at him.

"You're laughing at me."

"You deserve it, Mr. Daniel Blaze Haggarty."

His dark eyebrows arched wickedly as one of his hands moved threateningly down to the curve of her bottom. His eyes were twinkling. "I'll get you for this. Nobody makes a fool out of me."

"I'm trembling."

"You should be. Why didn't you tell me before?"

"I tried to, several times, but you absolutely refused to listen. Anyway, I didn't want to spoil your fun. You seemed to take such pleasure in trying to intimidate me. 'I'm going to lead you to a very public stake... and then I'm going to burn you!'" she quoted, mimicking his intonation perfectly.

"You're in big trouble, Kate," he repeated with a grin. "For almost two weeks you've played havoc with my peace of mind with this little act of yours. I was tempted to look you up before coming tonight, but I didn't...which means I suffered through several extra hours of suspense. I promise you, I am going to have my revenge."

His roughly sensual voice sent shivers through her, and she had to bite her tongue to stop herself from inviting him to go right ahead and avenge himself.

His eyes sparked as if he'd read the invitation in her expression. He leaned his head down but didn't kiss her. "What's this gook all over your face?"

"Stage makeup, obviously. Don't mess it up; I've got another big scene later."

His gaze wandered to her bodice. "I like your costume," he said warmly. "Are you allowed to wear it home?"

"Of course not. It goes back to the costumers to be cleaned and pressed for opening night."

"It's very provocative. I'd like to have the pleasure of unlacing it for you."

His heated words aroused her to an alarming degree. Once again, things seemed to be escalating out of control. The chemistry between them was incendiary.

"Did you like my acting, Daniel?" she asked in a desperate attempt to change the subject.

"You're good," he said, sounding serious for once. "You'd certainly tempt me."

"Stop that," she insisted, slapping his hands away from her bodice laces. "Do you have any idea what a costume like this costs?"

"Nope." His hands went instead to span her waist, and he smiled at her with eyes that were both teasing and lecherous. "What have you got on under it? Your waist is slim but your skirts are all puffy."

"If you must know, I'm wearing an old-fashioned petticoat. No matter how much women's underwear you've seen—and I imagine you've seen a lot—I doubt you've ever encountered a whalebone petticoat before."

"No, but I'd like to. Are you wearing one of those old-style corsets, too? I love those. How about garters?"

"Maybe I should drop you off in the costume department?" she laughed, pulling away from him. At this rate, they'd be ripping off each other's clothes before the evening was over. When he held her close, all her doubts and fears went flying out the window.

"You're a very beautiful and desirable witch, Kate Kingsley. And a terrific actress, too." He smiled. "I'm proud of you."

She flushed with his praise. The sexual electricity abated slightly as they met each other's eyes with a different kind of warmth. Yet again he had surprised her, reacting with good humor to the deception she'd foisted upon him for so long. *I like him,* she thought in a sudden blaze of insight. *I like him a lot.*

"Thanks." Impulsively she squeezed his hand, and then reached for a smock from a hook in the greenroom, donning it carefully to protect her costume. "Let's go out front and watch the play. I have to listen to what my director thinks of my performance. Unfortunately he's not likely to be so complimentary."

"He'd better be," Daniel growled. "Okay. I'm pretty fond of *Macbeth*, as a matter of fact."

"Ssh. Don't let the other actors hear you naming the play. It's bad luck. We call it 'The Scottish Play.' We're not permitted to quote from it, either, except on stage when we're saying our lines."

"Why not?"

"This play is haunted, of course. Terrible things happen to actors who perform it unless we're very careful."

Daniel gave her one of those looks. She recognized it from the night of the party. "You may not be a psychic, but you're clearly eccentric," he said with a long-suffering sigh. "I must be out of my head, falling for you. I should have turned and run the other way the moment I saw you."

"On the contrary." She grinned at him. "Maybe I'm exactly what a stick-in-the-mud rationalist like you needs. Everybody should have some mystery, some magic, some witchcraft, in their lives."

His eyes caressed her with something more than passion. There was affection there, she was certain. He opened his mouth as if to speak, then shook his head faintly and smiled instead. "Come on. Let's watch the haunted play, my love."

The possessive way he'd said "my love" warmed her for the rest of the evening.

* * *

"You really shouldn't do anything adventuresome tonight, luv," Graham said to her as she was hanging up her costume after the rehearsal. Daniel was waiting for her outside. "Baleful planetary influences, you know. According to the charts, a Pisces like you should lock all the doors and windows and crawl safely into bed alone. It's definitely not the time to take any risks."

"Oh, great. That makes me feel terrific, Graham."

"And whatever you do, don't travel. Not that you need an astrologer to tell you that. Just look out the window."

It was pouring. In fact, during the hours they'd been in the theater, the outer bands of that offshore hurricane had struck the city, dumping several inches of rain and shaking the trees with high winds. "I have to travel to get home," she pointed out. "So do you, for heaven's sake."

"Go home, by all means. Just don't go anywhere else."

She caught her lower lip in her teeth in a brief nervous gesture. "You don't like him, do you?"

"Not really, no."

"You were the one who abandoned me to him at that party. You blithely told him I was a witch and took off."

"I was an idiot. He'll walk all over you."

"He's a Scorpio. You said we were compatible."

"Scorpios are ruled by the planet Pluto, who was the god of the underworld, if you remember. They're hard, dark, and fierce. And they're hell on women. Remember what happened to Persephone when Pluto decided he wanted her? He thundered up out of the ground in his chariot and dragged her screaming down to the Underworld."

"He released her when her mother went crazy with grief and brought winter to the world."

"Only because the other gods insisted. And he demanded that she spend half of every year with him." He looked dramatically out the window at the raging storm. "She's with him now, languishing in heavy darkness, held in thrall by that overpowering sensuality all Pluto people possess."

"Chill, Graham."

"Why don't you find yourself a nice Cancer? That's the other sun sign you're compatible with, and they're much safer and easier to get along with."

"I like Daniel."

"You're going to do it with him, aren't you?"

The little throbs of excitement that had shivered in her all evening erupted again. Her heart was beating twice as fast as usual, and her skin felt so sensitive that she was aware of every inch of her clothes. She fussed with her costume and didn't answer.

She heard the crack of Graham's knuckles and heard him moving close behind her. "Just be careful, okay?". He touched her shoulder. "I'd hate to see you get hurt."

She turned spontaneously and hugged him. "I'll be fine. Don't worry about me."

Graham kissed her forehead, and then pushed her away. "Go on. He's waiting."

* * *

A half hour later she and Daniel were standing on her front porch, shaking themselves like bedraggled animals after being pelted with wind-whipped rain.

"You'd better invite me in this time, lady, or I'm liable to blow away."

She laughed as she struggled with her keys. "Not even I could be so cruel as to send you home on a night like this without a nightcap or a hot cup of coffee."

When she finally managed the lock, Daniel pushed the door open, and they stepped together into the house. "Yes!" he said as he moved into the warmth of her front hall. He pushed back his hood and tore off those sexy driving gloves, and before she could blink, his jacket was unzipped.

"The night creature is in." He backed her against the nearest wall. He tipped up her chin with his fingers and thumb and stared at her parted lips for an instant. "You're doomed," he added before covering her mouth with his.

CHAPTER EIGHT

Kate melted into the kiss as the rain from their jackets dripped into tiny puddles on the floor. Daniel's lips were hotly possessive, his body strong and all-encompassing. I want you so, she said silently as she slid her hands up his arms to tangle her fingers in the damp, dark waves of his hair. He was delicious—a warm, vital force, a dynamic whirlwind of masculinity.

"Mmm," he murmured against her mouth. His tongue completed a lazy tour of her lips that made her entire body glow. "I've been dreaming about this all evening. All day. I've been walking around in a daze of desire since this morning." He stripped himself and then her of their jackets in a few economical moves. One hand skated down her throat, opening the top three buttons of the lavender top she wore over her jeans, and he lightly massaged the hollow between her breasts. "I've been aching to do this," he whispered. His thumb splayed out and rasped over a nipple. She shivered and curled closer to him. "And this." He coaxed the nipple to hardness with rough yet tender fingers. "There are so many things I want to do with you tonight."

"Me, too." Leaning her head against his throat she said, "But let's take it slowly."

"I'll try." He moved her head slightly so he could nibble on her earlobe and run his tongue along the hairline where her thick tresses sprang.

"Rumor has it that you hook up with a lot of women." As soon as the words were out, she wished them unsaid. It sounded too much like a demand that he offer her something more than he usually offered his bedmates.

"Don't listen to rumors." His hands moved down her back and curved over the soft flesh of her bottom, cupping her tightly against his thighs. "Trust me. I'm quite an honest man, you know."

"I remember. One of your good points." She leaned back and grinned at him. He unhooked one of her hands from around his neck and held the palm up for examination.

"What of your heart line? Are our palms as compatible as our horoscopes?" He brought her hand to his lips and ran his tongue over her palm. The sensual muscles inside her convulsed, and she felt as if her legs were going to give way. A soft sound of pleasure rose in her throat as his clever tongue slid in between each of her fingers, circled the base of her thumb, then devilishly probed the sensitive hollow in the center of her palm.

"Daniel," she whispered.

He dropped her hand and kissed her mouth again with a passion that she matched blindly, fiercely, and without thought— until Chester meowed and shoved his body between their legs.

"What the hell?"

"It's okay. It's only Chester. He must be jealous." She stooped down to ruffle the tawny creature behind the ears. "Hi, baby. I want you to meet Daniel."

Chester rubbed his head against his human's fingers and pointedly ignored Daniel, who stared down at him, saying, "That's the biggest cat I've ever seen. Is he domesticated?"

"Just barely," she laughed.

Daniel gamely attempted to pet Chester, but the huge orange cat lurched out of his way, swatting the leg of a small table with his tail. The table tottered, and Kate reached out to steady it as Chester slunk away into the kitchen. "Unlike most cats, he's clumsy. He's forever knocking something over."

"I don't think he likes me," Daniel said as Chester gave him a haughty amber-eyed stare from the kitchen doorway.

"He's suspicious of males. He rarely sees one."

One of Daniel's hands lightly clamped her wrist. "I still find that a little hard to believe, Kate."

"Well, it's true." She tried to withdraw her arm, but it was held fast by his strong fingers.

"I'm glad, though. The less competition, the better."

She leaned her head back and opened her eyes wide. "Getting possessive already, Blaze?"

"Did you miss that when you were studying my palm? I've been possessive of you from the moment we met."

His gruffly assertive tone thrilled her at the same time that it made her a trifle wary. She had no experience dealing with a willful, passionate man like Daniel. Arthur had been so even-tempered and serene.

"And don't call me Blaze," he added.

"Why not? It's a romantic name—sounds like something from one of those old bodice rippers. Those heroes were always very sexy, if a trifle overbearing."

"Well, sexy sounds good, but I'll try my best not to be overbearing."

Would he? she wondered. He'll try to dominate you, Graham had warned that first night. Kate knew that, good-natured though she was, she lacked a submissive spirit. If Daniel did indeed try to dominate her, they would end up fighting.

She and Arthur had rarely fought. In retrospect, it seemed a bit odd. Certainly there had been occasions when she had felt angry with him, and he must have been angry in return, but she could probably count the times they had seriously quarreled on the fingers of one hand. Arthur had been a peacemaker. He had been good at defusing tension, and he would set his own needs and feelings aside if doing so could prevent a fight.

She wondered, maybe for the first time ever, how many of her husband's own needs had never been met? He had always put her first. Had their harmony been, in some ways, bad for Arthur? A memory of the accident flashed: had she imagined it, or had Arthur, realizing their car was out of control, somehow managed to turn the wheel just enough so that he, not she, took the brunt of the impact? Had the final act of his life been an attempt to save her?

"What are you brooding about?" Daniel asked, watching her face.

She snapped back to the present. "I was just thinking about Arthur."

Damn. She knew as soon as she spoke the words that she shouldn't have said them.

There was an edge to his voice as he said, "Do you often brood about Arthur?"

"I'm sorry. That was tactless of me."

There was a moment of taut silence before the tension in him dissolved. He ran a hand through his black hair, unconsciously mussing it. "No. My bad." His blue velvet eyes glinted with self-deprecation. "I like it that you're honest with me. It's just that I guess I'm what you might call a territorial male."

"Hmm. You and Chester probably have a lot in common." At the sound of his name, Chester meowed plaintively. "He's hungry. Let me get him settled." She moved down the hall to the kitchen, where Chester was expectantly circling his supper dish. "He's actually my mother's cat, but I've been taking care of him lately."

Daniel followed, bumping his head on the low archway to the kitchen and cursing. Chester gave him a haughty glare.

"Be careful," she warned too late. "It's an old house."

Daniel looked around the modern kitchen. "Looks pretty contemporary in here."

"We renovated the kitchen and the bathrooms. In fact, we had to renovate the entire house before we could live comfortably here—new floors, new windows, insulation, a new heating system, new plumbing and wiring." She opened a cupboard and took down a can of cat food. Chester was head butting her ankles. "It was quite a project."

"We refers to you and Arthur? You lived here with him?"

"Yes. We actually inherited the place when a rich aunt of his died; we couldn't have afforded it otherwise." The aunt had also left them some cash, which had come in handy. Kate didn't make a lot of money as an actress, although recently she had landed a few commercials that supplemented her income.

There was a short silence. Daniel leaned back against one of the countertops and folded his arms across his chest, considering her as she dumped the cat food into Chester's dish and placed it on the floor. Chester pounced.

"You said Arthur died in a car accident?"

"Yes. I was in the car, too. He swerved to avoid a child who had run into the road, and we crashed into a tree."

Daniel crossed to her, cursing softly as he took her in his arms. He cradled her face in gentle hands. "I'm so sorry."

"Arthur was killed instantly. I was trapped in the mangled car, going in and out of consciousness. I have nightmares about it sometimes." She shuddered, not wanting to relive it. "Afterward, when they admitted to me that he was dead, I didn't want to go on living. But I wasn't hurt badly enough to die."

"Thank God for that."

"I was hospitalized for a while, though, with broken bones and lacerations. I caught a hospital infection, and was very sick for a couple weeks. My mom took great care of me, and my friends were wonderful, too. If it hadn't been for the people who love me, I don't think I would be here now."

Daniel held her close for several minutes while she regained her composure. She could feel his compassion washing over her. His hands massaged her shoulders and fiddled with her hair.

"But I'm okay," she said, pulling away from him. Was she? Her memories of Arthur were immediate and strong tonight. What would he have thought of Daniel? Would he have liked him? Maybe they wouldn't have gotten along.

She carefully covered the cat-food can with aluminum foil and put it away, feeling uncomfortable under Daniel's steady gaze. "Do you want a drink?" She pulled open the cupboard over the refrigerator to reveal her small cache of alcoholic beverages. "I think I have some wine, and maybe even some whiskey."

"No, thanks." When she turned and inadvertently bumped her head against the cabinet door, he added, "Am I making you nervous?"

"Nervous?" She smiled, determined not to appear edgy, but she found herself taking a step backward as he advanced toward her.

She felt the edge of the sink against the small of her back as his hands settled on the counter on either side of her, trapping her. He was so close. His warm breath on her face, the coiled power of his hard-muscled body only centimeters away. She felt caged, cornered.

"How long has it been, Kate?" His voice was low, sensual.

She turned her head away from his tantalizing eyes and mouth and stared out the small kitchen window at the darkly falling rain. "I told you."

"There's really been no one since Arthur died? No sex for three whole years?"

"I'm sure it's hard to believe."

His fingers trailed over her cheek, caressed the curve of her mouth. "You loved your husband. I can understand that. But it does seem an enormous waste." He lowered his head until his lips whispered over hers. "A beautiful, vibrant woman like you shouldn't lock herself away from the males of the world. It only makes us more determined to seek you out and make you feel alive again."

He kissed her deeply then, but she resisted, not knowing why. He could bring her body to a riot of wild sensations, but again she sensed he would demand much more from her than he would be willing to give in return. All Graham's warnings came back to haunt her. She was Persephone, tempted to the feast by the dark lord of the underworld. If she gave in, and ate, she would be forever subject to his will.

"Relax," he murmured. His kiss became gentler, more seductive. When her mouth refused to open to him, the tip of his tongue flicked her, coaxed her, entreated rather than demanded. "Nothing's going to happen unless you want it to. I can't seem to stop trying to make you want it, though. It's my nature, I think."

"Sex is important to you." She felt her resolve weakening as fine wires of sensation curled through her.

He moved his hips against her. "Yes."

"I guess I am a little nervous," she admitted. Her fingers moved lightly over his shoulders, feeling the strong contours of hard muscle and sinew beneath the flannel of his shirt. "But I'll be fine."

"Let's sit down." With one arm cradling her to his side, he steered her into the living room and dropped them both down on the plump-cushioned ivory-colored couch. He gathered her close, practically into his lap, but his beguiling caresses ceased. She felt his chin rest on the top of her head as he said, "There's no rush. I want you to feel comfortable with me. Can you tell me what you're worried about?"

"It's just jitters. Stage fright. It's common among actors, you know."

"No acting, Kate. Not when we're together like this."

She laughed softly. "Do I look as if I'm acting? You wouldn't think so if you knew me better."

"We know each other better than you think. We looked into each other's eyes on the night we met and learned all the important stuff right then and there."

"I don't believe it! D. B Haggarty, professional rationalist, proclaiming the virtues of intuitive communication?"

She could feel him smile. "Not exactly. It's all due to the sense of smell, you know. Perfectly rational and scientific. Intuition has nothing to do with it."

"Smell?" She sniffed dubiously. He did have a pleasant natural scent about him. A faint glimmering of woodsy maleness.

"Sure. Haven't you heard that explanation of instant attraction? It's no longer termed love at first sight, but a bonding of the olfactory senses. My nose and yours are soul mates."

Kate giggled. He lifted her chin and rubbed his nose back and forth against hers. "You see? They're crazy about each other."

The conjunction of noses brought their mouths within a whisper of one another. Kate's chest tightened as he said against her moistened lips, "It sounds crazy, even to me, but I honestly feel that there's a lot more at stake with you than there's been with any other woman in my life."

"At stake? As in burning at the?"

He lowered his lips to her throat, letting her feel his teeth. The tiny threat made her breathless. "Why do I have the feeling you're not taking me seriously?"

I'm afraid I'm taking you all too seriously. You're too passionately emotional, too dynamic, and much too sexy for me *not* to take you seriously. You're tearing my quiet existence to shreds. "You promised you wouldn't rush me."

He smiled wistfully. "Did I? Stupid me." He pulled her closer, nestling her head against his shoulder. "Do you want me to go?"

She felt the warm, solid length of him beside her, his hands gently caressing her, his comfortable shoulder, his strong thighs just beside hers on the sofa—all the things that testified to his incredible hotness. If he stayed, they would make love, which was what they both wanted. They had both wanted it since the night they'd met. "No. Don't go."

He shifted, pressing her back against the arm of the sofa, fitting one long leg between hers so she could feel his hard muscles against her inner thighs. At the same time one of his hands settled lightly over one of her breasts, reminding her of how wonderful it could be between them.

"Not that you were seriously thinking of going," she added, smiling.

"I'd be crushed if that's what you really wanted." His lips moved deliciously on her throat. She groaned and circled his neck with her arms. There was no real doubt about it, of course. She was about to suggest that they move to the bedroom when Chester pounced, landing squarely on Daniel's back and digging in his claws.

"Dammit, not again!" Daniel rolled defensively off the couch, and Chester neatly took his place on Kate's chest, flopping down against the warmth of her body and beginning to purr loudly. On his knees on the Oriental rug beside the couch, Daniel glared at the two of them—Kate, who was laughing, and Chester, who was giving Kate an indignant look as if to demand why her comfy breasts were shaking up and down.

"Ornery cat," he snarled, grabbing the orange tomcat and putting him down firmly, but not roughly, on the floor. Chester yowled in protest. "He's territorial all right. I think he's planning to fight me for you." He reached awkwardly over his shoulder to rub the spot where Chester had landed. "You never warned me he was trained to attack. He's fierce as a lion."

Kate's laughter escalated. "Daniel in the lion's den."

"Very funny."

She controlled herself sufficiently to ask if Chester's claws had done any real damage. "Let me see," she said, pulling Daniel down beside her again and working the buttons on the front of his shirt.

She bit her lip as she watched the smooth sculpted muscles of shoulders and chest emerge. 'Take it off," she said, dry-mouthed.

"Are you kidding? With him running around loose? That thick shirt's the only thing that saved me just now." But his hot eyes were flaring with barely contained passion.

"Let me see your back."

He turned, slipping the shirt off his shoulders. Beneath his smooth skin, muscle could be faintly seen to ripple, but there were no deep scratches, only a few red marks. "I think you'll live, Haggarty," Kate said, her voice husky from the longing she had to run her hands over the naked flesh before her.

He turned back and met her eyes. Sparks sizzled between them, and the wires tightened within Kate's body. It was going to happen. She couldn't stop it.

Chester prowled around the sofa, eyeing Kate's cozy body and Daniel's bare back. Daniel shot the cat a cautious look. "He's planning his move. He's going to pounce when I least expect it— and I can just imagine the moment he'll choose. I'm beginning to think you've lured me in here so your familiar could finish me off, witch." He sidled up against her and ran the tip of one finger from her collarbone down along the open buttons of her top, between her breasts and across her stomach to the snap that closed her jeans. "Can you put him out?"

"No, sorry, but he's an indoor cat."

"Then come with me to my place. I'd prefer it that way. If I'm going to be the first man to make love to you since Arthur's death, I want it to be special for you." He glanced around the room of her old Victorian house. "I don't want to do it in the house where you lived with him. Come home with me tonight."

She could feel her heartbeat kick and scamper in her throat. "But the driving's terrible."

"I live in Winchester—it's not far away." When she hesitated he added, "Humor me. I feel strongly about this."

"What if the storm keeps up and I get stranded? I have rehearsals tomorrow."

"Tomorrow's Sunday. Don't they ever give you people a break?"

"Usually I have Sunday and Monday off, but that changes depending on our schedule. The theater is always closed on Monday, but we have performances every other day, plus matinees on Saturday, Sunday, and Wednesday."

"So you'll have Monday off?"

"Not this week. We have extra rehearsals right before a new production opens."

"Well, I'll get you back, I promise. Besides—" He was drawing breath to continue, but he ended up turning his face away and sneezing explosively. "Dammit," he swore, unsuccessfully searching his pockets for some tissues as he sneezed again.

She caressed his hair. "It's cold and wet out there, Daniel. Let's stay here and build a fire. Your hair is damp, and your cold'll get worse if we go out again."

"I don't have a cold." Bending over, he sneezed again, six times in rapid succession. "There's only one thing that could cause this." He turned his glare accusingly on the huge mound of tawny fluff who was hostilely contemplating him from the other side of the coffee table.

"Oh, no," Kate said. "Chester."

"Chester," Daniel repeated with a scowl before sneezing again.

She disentangled herself and got up from the sofa to coax the unsuspecting Chester into her arms. She rubbed his head vigorously as she carried him toward the rear of the house. "I'll put him down in the basement. His box is down there, and he's made himself one or two cozy beds there, too."

But when she opened the basement door, Chester, sensing he was being banished, leapt out of her arms. Crash. He knocked over a broom and mop that were propped in the back hall near the basement door as he tore off in a blur of orange. But he didn't anticipate Daniel, who brought him down on the hall carpet with an impressive tackle.

"No more claws, big fella, or... " Daniel's voice trailed off as he hefted the creature and carried him gingerly back to the basement door. "It's hard to think of a threat that'll impress a cat." He was having quite a time holding on to the squirming animal.

"What's the matter?" Kate asked a moment later when Daniel closed the door with Chester still on their side.

He sneezed and looked a little sheepish. "It's dark down there. I can't just heave him somewhere he doesn't want to go."

"You can't?"

"You monster," he said, rubbing a suspicious-looking Chester behind the ears. "Don't fret, buddy; it's your house, after all."

As she stared dumbfounded at the handsome, sneezing devil cuddling the cat he was allergic to, Kate once again knew that she liked Daniel Haggarty very much indeed. Their eyes met, and warmth drifted through her. It was a different kind of warmth from the sensual heat he inspired, although that was there, too. It was a quiet, intimate communion between two sympathetic hearts and minds—a golden, timeless moment she wished would never end. And she knew that Daniel was right: On some profound level, they did know all the important things about each other.

Daniel set the cat down as his vigorous sneezing started up again. Once again, he patted his pocket. "Wouldn't you know it? I forgot to bring my medication. Do you suppose there's a pharmacy open around here?"

"You needn't suffer." She reached for his hand. "I'll come with you to your place. Give me a couple of minutes to get ready."

The banked fires in Daniel's eyes leaped to flame again. "What about Chester?"

"He's got his cat box and lots of food." She opened the door to the basement so he could go down when it suited him. "He'll be all fine for the night."

Daniel smiled wickedly. "So the damn allergy is good for something at last."

* * *

Chester was lying on the rug in front of the fireplace when Kate came downstairs with her backpack, but there was no sign of Daniel until she heard a muffled sneeze from the small study that opened off the living room. Arthur's study. Most of his things—books, papers, personal effects—were still in there. Although she had meant to do it many times, she had never had the heart to sort through them and decide what to keep and what to throw away.

"What are you doing in here?" she asked when she found Daniel examining a photo of herself and Arthur on vacation in Montreal.

"Trying to escape from your cat." His voice was faintly sarcastic as he added, "Is the shrine off limits?"

"It's not a shrine."

"Arthur Kingsley, M.S.W.," he read from one of the degrees mounted on the beige-papered wall. "What was he, a social worker?"

"Yes. He worked with disadvantaged kids."

"A noble profession," Daniel said in a neutral tone. He picked up a wedding photograph in a silver, heart-shaped frame and examined it. "He was a good-looking guy," he said, staring at Arthur's tall, lanky form. "Very attractive."

Kate took the picture away from him and placed it back on the desk. She treasured that photograph. When she was seated here at the desk, she could always see it. She and Arthur had had the heart-shaped frame made for an earlier photograph of them together in high school. Even though the frame seemed kitsch now, she still loved it. She felt almost protective of it, and she didn't want Daniel to touch it.

Undeterred, he picked up the other picture that she always kept on her desk, the one of her and Arthur surrounded by their college friends. It was the same photo she used as a computer screen saver. "You look so young," he noted. "Who are these other guys?"

"They're the same friends I play Hunt the Night City with, that computer game I told you about. It's a good way for us to stay in touch."

"So you still hang out with your husband's old friends?"

"They're my old friends, too. We met them in college. Arthur and I went to the same school. When Arthur died, they took care of me. They were awesome, and I loved them dearly."

He said nothing. He studied the photograph for a few more seconds, and then put it down. She watched a little uneasily as he continued his exploration of the room, running his fingers over the volumes in the bookcase. His mood had changed again. Dear heavens, what a volatile man he was.

"Do you spend a lot of time in this room?" he finally asked.

"I use it as a study. All my computer stuff's in here. This is the desk I sit at when I play the game with my friends. Do you want to check out my gaming rig? It's pretty sweet."

But he continued prowling around, not showing any interest in her computer equipment at the moment. He picked up a journal. "The Proceedings of the American Society of Spiritualists?" He shot her a dark look. "What's this doing here, Kate?"

"My mother gave me a subscription for Christmas last year."

"Ah, yes. Your fascinating mother." His tone had hardened. He picked up a deck of tarot cards and shuffled them idly. "It's clear where your talents as an actress come from. That's all you share with her, I hope?"

"What are you getting at? I thought we were leaving."

He waved his hand at the wedding picture and Arthur's effects. "We are. There's one thing I want to settle first, though, Kate. You know now that I'm possessive. This mausoleum annoys me. He's been dead for ages, but all his stuff is still here, as if he just stepped out for a trip to the grocery store."

Kate flushed with irritation. "You seem to have knack for spoiling things."

"Look, I'm just trying to understand you. I know you haven't completely gotten over your husband's death. I get that. But I don't want to make love to a married woman."

"Married!"

"I know the sort of people who subscribe to these journals; I've researched the subject, remember. A faithful widow for three years. It reminds me of many cases I've investigated. The surviving spouse who can't accept the fact of her partner's death." His face had turned rigid with his "Scorpio brooder" expression. "How often do you go to séances, Kate? How often do you have cozy little conversations through a medium with your dear deceased Arthur?"

Kate's breath left her in a gasp. Her eyes closed automatically. "I don't go to séances. You can be very cruel sometimes."

When he spoke again it was from right beside her. "Maybe. But it's cruel of you to ask me to compete for your attention with a ghost."

"I'm not asking any such thing. I'm not a spiritualist, for godsake."

"I once heard you talking out loud to Arthur," he persisted. His hands had fallen heavily upon her shoulders, holding her still for his questioning. She had a sudden image of herself sitting before a video camera, being interrogated by this sometimes-ruthless man.

"Talking to Arthur?"

"On the stairs, after the party, on the night we met. You were saying you missed him."

She remembered his sardonic remark about communicating with the spirit world.

"In my experience, people who talk to the dead are either crazy or duped."

"How about lonely?" She tore herself away from him. "Or have you never known what that feels like?"

He stared at her in ominous silence for several seconds before saying, "Swear to me you're not involved in spirit circles, Kate. It's the one thing I don't think I could take."

"Why not? What have you got against mediums, anyway? You're fanatical on the subject."

He just scowled.

"I resent being hounded by you about this, Daniel. A few minutes ago you wanted to make love to me."

His eyes seemed to darken as he stared into hers, the blue irises retreating as the pupils dilated. "I still want to make love to you. There's nothing I want more. But I won't share you with anybody, least of all a ghost."

She drew a deep breath. She didn't understand this side of him. It had disturbed her from the start, and she knew with every ounce of intuition she possessed that there was going to be trouble between them because of her mother, her crazy upbringing, and even her personal beliefs in the extraordinary powers of the human mind. She wondered what Daniel would think if she told him about her childhood, growing up in a haunted house.

How could she ever explain to him about those years? He would think she was inventing the whole thing.

She sighed. "I'm not a spiritualist, Daniel. I still miss my husband, but he's dead and I'm alive. I've accepted that. I'm sorry if I seem to you to be carrying around an excess of emotional baggage from my marriage. I'm trying to shed it. It may still take a while; I may have to ask you to be patient. If that's too much to ask"—she paused, not wanting to say it, but feeling it necessary to make the point—"there are plenty of other women you could be pursuing instead of me."

His hands were on her once more, and she could feel his tension. "I don't want anyone else. I want you."

"You have me." She pointed to her backpack. "I've got everything I need, and I'm going home with you tonight."

His fingers tightened slightly, and she felt dizzy with awareness of his sheer physical power. She wondered why she felt no fear of him. Emotionally he frightened her, but not physically. He was much taller and stronger than she, but in that realm, at least, she trusted him. It must have been so from the moment they met, or she never would have accepted a ride from a dark stranger on an even darker night.

"Don't ask for patience from me. When I get you into my house, into my bed, I won't be capable of much restraint. If you come with me tonight, please be sure you want my loving, because I don't think I could bear if it you changed your mind."

She raised her hands to his face and touched the feathering of hair above his ears. "Patience with my emotions, not with my person. I give the latter to you willingly."

He sighed and pulled her almost savagely close. She could feel his accelerated heartbeat against her breasts. One of his hands slid into the hair at her nape and forced her head back. He kissed her hard, his tongue invading her with a furious passion, which she met with the surge of her own body. She felt alive, very much alive. She could feel Daniel's warmth flowing into her body, making every cell cry out with the joy of living.

Breathing unsteadily, Daniel disengaged himself enough to see her passion-flushed face. "You turn my bones to water, you know that?"

She smiled at him and slid her fingers through his dark, silky hair.

"Let's go," he agreed, taking her arm and leading her out of the study. She caught one last glimpse of her wedding picture as she shut the study door behind them. She spoke again to Arthur, silently this time: "Wish me luck, love."

CHAPTER NINE

The driving sucked. Kate sat huddled in the seat next to Daniel, staring through the fogged up windshield and trying by sheer force of will to keep the car safe from the tangled branches that were being torn off by the high winds. Massachusetts Avenue in Cambridge was a mess, with a couple of power lines down from the wind. Conditions got even worse as they drove through Arlington Center toward Winchester, the wealthy suburb where Daniel had his home.

Once, when the car skidded on the rain-slick road before straightening out, Daniel reached to cover her hand with his. "Scared?"

"A little." She had never felt completely safe in cars after the terrible accident that had killed Arthur and injured her.

"Nothing bad's gonna happen—I promise. It's blowing much harder than it was an hour ago, but we'll be fine. I'm being very careful. Do you trust me?"

His tone inspired confidence. He seemed so competent, so capable. "Yes."

His mouth turned up in a lecherous grin. "Big mistake, lady. You'll be marooned in the storm with me—completely at my mercy."

She grinned back, waves of excitement churning within her despite her nervousness about the storm. "I just might enjoy that."

Half an hour after leaving Cambridge, they finally pulled into the long driveway that led to Daniel's house. There their luck ran out. A small tree was down, blocking their way. "Everybody out," said Daniel cheerfully. He grabbed her overnight pack from the back seat and slung it over his shoulder. "We hike the rest of the way."

The rain seemed to be pelting down even harder in Winchester than it had been in Cambridge, but the worst hazard was the ferocious wind. She didn't even want to think about what would happen if they were struck by a falling tree limb. It was also cold, much chillier than usual for this time of year. Before they had gone more than a hundred yards, Kate was shivering.

"How much farther?" she gasped, clinging to Daniel's arm.

"What?" he yelled back.

"Where's the damn house?"

"Sorry, it's a long driveway. More of a private road, really. But we're almost there," he promised while pulling her along, forcing her to keep walking what felt like miles.

"And it's uphill," she complained, wishing they'd stayed at her place. She jumped as a dead branch hit the roadway just ahead of them, but Daniel had already leapt protectively in front of her. He cursed softly, then bent and pressed his warm mouth against hers. "We're fine. Don't fade on me now."

"I'm not fading," she insisted even as she burrowed closer against him.

He pushed her away gently, keeping one arm around her waist. "Let's move faster. We'll be safe inside."

"Graham warned me not to travel tonight. I should have listened to him." She couldn't see a thing, but she kept walking, clinging to him as the wind buffeted her. She was seriously relieved when they rounded a curve and she saw the house before them—a huge silhouette with one light gleaming like a beacon.

"Thank God the power's still on," said Daniel, and with a renewed burst of energy, he hoisted her up into his arms and carried her the rest of the way. "I was a little worried about that."

She put her face against his neck and murmured, "So heroic! I'm perfectly capable of walking, Blaze."

He laughed. "Think of it as a romantic abduction: He lifts her high in his arms and strides forcefully down the hall to the master bedroom."

"I always wonder why the guy doesn't get a hernia. Put me down. You'll hurt yourself. I may look thin, but that's on a five-foot eight-inch frame. Do you know how much I weigh?"

"I know I'll never send you chocolates again. There. Whew." He dumped her unceremoniously to her feet on the bottom step of his front porch and bounded up to unlock the door.

She was about to follow when a flash of lighting skewered the sky above the treetops. For no reason she could fathom, her mood changed, and she smiled. She liked storms. Now that warmth was guaranteed, the rain didn't feel so chilly. She spread her arms out wide and twirled, tilting her face back so the rain hit it full on. It felt sharp and fresh and curiously sweet.

"What are you doing?" Daniel growled.

"Dancing in the rain," she laughed. "Come join me."

"I thought you were freezing and desperate to get inside."

"I was. But the sky, the trees, your house, the storm—what a magical night."

"Has anyone ever told you," he said, bounding back down the steps and sweeping her into his arms for several more twirls on the soggy lawn, "that you're completely and delightfully unpre-dictable?"

She laughed and hugged him. "Nope. It's the way you affect me, Blaze. You make me a little dizzy. A little crazy."

"What I want," he whispered, his lips against her cheek, "is to make you happy."

He did make her happy, she realized. For the first time in ages, she felt brim-full of happiness.

"But don't call me Blaze."

She danced away from him and ran up the stairs to the porch. "Blaze, Blaze, Blazity-Blaze," she teased, shaking rain off herself like a puppy. Daniel joined her, grinning and looking pretty damn happy himself.

Inside the house, she couldn't help a few expressions of delight as he led her through a large, airy front hall lit by a crystal chandelier to the curved staircase, which rose elegantly to the second floor. "Wow, the place is a mansion," she said, noting the quality of the art on the wall. "Are you rich?" She abruptly remembered the hundred-dollar bill he'd so casually donated to the National Foundation for the Blind. "TV must pay an awful lot better than theater."

"You don't care much about money, do you?"

She could honestly say she didn't. "I wouldn't turn my nose up at it, but, no, it's not something I waste much time thinking about."

"My father cared about little else," he said as they mounted the stairs after shedding their coats at the bottom. "He literally worked himself into the ground making it, lots of it. He died a long time ago. My mother, too. I was their only child. All the fruits of his labors came to me, including this house."

"You sound kinda bitter."

"The house is beautiful, as are many of the things in it. But I'd rather have had my parents."

She squeezed his hand. He moved her heart in ways she wouldn't allow herself to put a name to. How could she care so much, so soon?

He led her down a cherry-wood-paneled hallway to the bedroom at the far end. It was cozily masculine, papered in autumn tones, a large, old-fashioned room with an antique bureau, a rolltop desk, and a couple of easy chairs in front of a mammoth fireplace. But it was the huge four-poster bed that really caught Kate's attention. It was covered with a flame-colored spread, which seemed so appropriate to Daniel's nature that she laughed out loud.

"The sizzling setting for your seduction," he whispered just behind her, his breath hot against her ear. His hands rested lightly on her shoulders, then moved down slowly, deliberately, to cup her breasts. "Still chilly?"

"A little."

"We should have stayed at your place, cat or no cat. I'm sorry, babe. I had no idea the driving would be so bad." His fingers slipped lower to the waistband of her jeans. "These'll have to come off. They're wet."

Her pants were soaked from her thighs down. Daniel's hands hovered at her waist, awaiting her signal. She smiled at him and nodded. She could feel his tension as he somewhat awkwardly unfastened them. He hesitated a moment before he pushed them over her hips and off, leaving the lower half of her body bare except for a pair of bikini panties. The touch of his hands electrified her. Her skin felt sensitized, alive.

"Come on," he said, taking her hand. He walked her across the room to a door on the left and into the bathroom, which was as large as a bedroom in any normal house and as thoroughly modern as the house itself was antique. It was equipped with a large stall shower and a separate sunken bathtub that was unquestionably the biggest she had ever seen.

"You could keep a whale in there."

Daniel skirted the tub and led her to a door on the other side of the double marble sinks. "A sauna," he said, fiddling with a dial on the door. "This should take the chill off."

"A sauna? Good grief, you live like a king."

'Take off the rest of your clothes."

She slowly unbuttoned her top, and he followed suit by unfastening his own shirt. She paused to watch, transfixed at the rapidly emerging sight of his well-defined chest muscles lightly dusted with wiry black hairs. She remembered thinking on the night they'd met that he must hit the gym regularly. His firm, sculpted muscles proved it. His body was taut, strong and beautiful. The flannel shirt came off, and then he unbuckled the leather belt at his waist.

"Don't stop." His tone had roughened.

"I'm just taking it slowly while enjoying the view."

He whipped off the belt and leaned closer to kiss her firmly on the mouth. "Nothing will happen too fast. Are you going to strip the rest of those clothes off, or do I have to do it for you?"

She hesitated for a moment. No one had seen her naked since the accident. She had several scars on her torso from her injuries. They weren't horribly disfiguring, but neither were they pretty to look upon. She had had one scar on her back covered with a tattoo, but the tattoo artist had told her that the skin was too damaged in the other spots for tattooing to make much of a difference. When she swam, she always wore a one-piece bathing suit now. No more bikinis for her. What if Daniel was put off by her scars?

Coward, she told herself impatiently. It's a little late to fret about that now.

She slipped off her top and added it to the pile. She was left in a matching bra and panties of sheer material, and she knew without even meeting his eyes that Daniel was watching her, his gaze licking over her, kindling sparks everywhere it touched.

She heard him suck in his breath and take a step closer. He had seen the scars—one curving down her ribcage towards her navel, and the other on her right hip. He was near now; she could feel the heat he was radiating. Her heartbeat slammed into high gear.

Daniel touched one hand to her ribs, his thumb sliding slowly along the scar there. "Are you embarrassed about these marks? To me they are beautiful. They testify to an ordeal you endured and survived." He stroked the other scar on her hip. "Your entire body is beautiful. And I am very glad you survived."

She melted. It was all good; everything was going to be fine.

One of his hands slid up to the curve of her breast. In response, her nipples peaked against the silken cups of her bra. "Ah," he breathed. "So lovely. I can hardly believe you're here, finally, in my keeping."

As he drew her against his naked chest, she thought what an odd, old-fashioned word that was: his keeping. It made her feel special, cherished. Their coming together in the parking garage had been raw sexual passion, unalloyed with gentler emotions, but it felt as if there was something more between them now.

His hands moved around behind her back, seeking the clasp of her bra. In a whisper of sound, the flimsy garment slipped down her arms and off. He cupped her breasts in the palms of his hands and rubbed them up and down against his chest.

The feel of his hard muscles against her delicate skin sent spasms through her. She sighed and leaned into the caress. Daniel's thumbs skated deliciously over her nipples, urging them to even greater arousal. They ached and peaked against him. Liquid pulses throbbed between her legs at every touch.

He pushed her back a little, his eyes drinking her in. "Your breasts are beautiful. I knew they would be."

"Somehow I don't think this is very therapeutic," she murmured, gazing up at him through half-closed eyelids.

"Oh, I don't know. We're doing a nice job of staving off hypothermia." His hands eased down her backbone to the base of her spine and pulled her lower body into the cradle of his hips. She had just a hint of his arousal before she wriggled away, exclaiming, "Your jeans are sopping wet and cold!"

He stepped back and began to tug them off. "Last one in is condemned to be the other's slave for the night."

Moments later Kate sprawled nude on a wooden bench inside the sauna, laughing through the door at Daniel's attempts to peel the stiff, waterlogged jeans from his legs. "Oh good. I've always wanted a sexy male slave."

But when he joined her, his body magnificently toned and blatantly aroused, she felt a thrill of apprehension. The intense chill of the trek through the rain was rapidly fading into unreality as that drugged, dizzy feeling she'd experienced in the parking garage took hold of her again. If anybody were going to be enslaved, it would probably be she.

As promised, Daniel didn't allow anything to happen too fast. With tantalizing slowness, he lowered his body to the bench beside her, stretching his legs lazily. He didn't touch her. "This is great, isn't it? Are you warming up?"

"Um-hmm." If he tried to measure her sexual temperature, she thought wryly, the thermometer would explode.

He turned slightly toward her and shifted her until her back was nestled against his chest. Just the light touch of his hands on her arms, moving her, ordering her position, made her tremble with anticipation.

She leaned her head back against his shoulder. Her long hair brushed his chest, and he fondled it, running the wet strands of it through his fingers. Catlike, she arched her back.

One of his hands dropped to her breasts, slowly molding one, then the other. Her skin was beginning to dampen from the heat, and his fingers slipped over it easily, exploring and teasing and probing. "You have the sweetest breasts. They fit my hands so perfectly."

She couldn't speak.

He moved in closer behind her. "Bend forward a little," he instructed her.

She brought her legs up on the bench in front of her and bent from the waist, resting her head on her raised knees. Daniel brushed her long hair forward over one shoulder and kissed the back of her neck. He paused for a moment, and his fingers traced the lines of the tattoo on her back. It was an abstract design with swirls and curves shaped vaguely like a rose. "This is beautiful. I didn't know you had a tattoo."

"I got it to cover one of my scars."

"Well, the artist did a great job, because I can't even see the scar."

"When I had it done, my friends from the game–my friends from college–went with me and got tattoos too, in solidarity."

"Seriously?"

"Yes. It may have been the nicest thing anyone's ever done for me. It was Stephen's idea, I think–he'll do just about anything, but Jeff and Nick decided to do it too. We all went to the tattoo parlor together. Later, I think Max got one too, although I haven't seen his. Can a vampire even get a tattoo?"

"Uh....what?" Daniel was briefly distracted from his ardent caressing of her back and shoulders. "Please don't try to tell me you've got a friend who's a vampire. Ghosts are bad enough."

She laughed. "He likes to tease us. I'd love you to meet my friends, even if they're all a little crazy."

He growled. "Can we talk about your friends later? I've got other priorities at the moment." He pressed her forward a little more, which made her breasts slip fully into his hands. He took merciless advantage of this. After kneading, caressing, and pressing them together, he began to work on the erect nipples, rolling them between his fingers and gently tugging on them until she thought she would die. Every touch reverberated in her sex, flooding her with unbearable heat. Before more than a couple of minutes had passed, she was squirming on the bench, longing for relief.

"I'm hot, Daniel. I need to cool off."

"Mmm." He was kneeling behind her now, and his lips were nudging the nape of her neck. She could feel the slight coarseness of his scruffy whiskers against her tender skin. "That can be arranged."

She was conscious of tiny sparks of excitement mixing with the heat of the sauna to make her liquid all over. She could hear the sound of his accelerated breathing, could feel the beating of his heart beneath her shoulder blade.

His fingers slid over her belly to crinkle the down at the apex of her thighs. Then he touched in between her legs, lightly, delicately. "You're beautiful here, too," he told her. She felt him shudder, and he withdrew his hand. His naked body was taut and silky against her. She heard him curse softly. "I'm trying to go slowly, but..."

She twisted in his arms, turning to face him and kneeling up on the sauna bench to brush a lock of damp hair out of his eyes. "It's okay," she reassured him. "I'm not nervous anymore."

He folded her against him, whispering, "I am. I want to make it good for you. I want your first time after three years to be special." He nuzzled her throat, his teeth teasing an earlobe. "Come on, let's get out of here before we faint."

Under the shower, they washed the sweat off each other... ever so carefully. Kate reveled in running her hands all over his firm, aroused body, and his barely restrained passion excited her further. He was as taut as an arched bow and as devastating in his potential power. It awed and amazed her that all this pure masculine energy should be focused on her.

When they stepped out of the shower and she tried to dry him with one of the huge bath towels, he pushed her away and did it himself, motioning her to do the same. He was staring at her with such naked lust that she felt another tiny frisson of apprehension. He was so intense!

When she was dry, he caught her wrist and fairly dragged her out of the bathroom toward the huge bed that loomed on the other side of the bedroom. He jerked the bedclothes out of the way and sat down, pulling her close. "Let's both take a couple of deep breaths."

"Deep breathing? Is that your secret formula for sexual success?"

"Right now it's a last resort against sexual humiliation."

"You don't have to impress me." Having expected smooth sophistication, she was touched by his anxiety. She leaned over and kissed the top of his head. "Anything that happens is okay."

He smiled and kissed the soft flesh of her breasts. "You're too good to be true, you know that? Hush now. Don't talk anymore. Lie down."

He pulled her into bed and caressed her slowly from shoulder to thigh. She could feel his hands tremble as they explored her, and she knew she was trembling, too. Her palms trailed over his skin, tingling. His muscles rippled beneath her touch, and when she pressed her face to his chest, she heard the driving tempo of his heart.

He rolled her onto her back and threw a heavy thigh across her legs. "You like this?" He kissed her roughly, then tenderly, then roughly again. His hands moved on her pliant flesh, touching, smoothing, stroking, loving her everywhere.

"Mmm, yes." She shifted slightly, enjoying the feel of his weight upon her, his hard sinews against her softer, more yielding flesh. "So much."

"Kate." He kissed her throat and then her breasts, one after the other, sucking the rosy tips into his mouth and sighing with pleasure. "You taste of honey and flowers and wine."

Arching beneath him, she slid her hands down his naked back, kneading the hard muscles that shifted under her fingers. His teeth nipped her breasts, gently at first, harder as her excitement spiraled. First one, then the other, his tongue and teeth worshiped her breasts until she was crying out for his possession. But he paused for a moment to kiss her scars tenderly.

At last his fingers slipped lower, homing in, finding the spot. She tossed her head back and forth on the pillow. He knew how to tease, how to touch, how to tune her to a fever pitch. Even though he was flushed with his own desire, even though his hands were shaking with restraint, he took his time about exciting her and giving her pleasure.

"My turn," she gasped, doing her best to stave off the end for a few more moments. She pushed at his shoulders until he rolled over onto his side. She wanted to please him as much as he was pleasing her. "Hold still."

"I don't think I can."

"You have to. I'm ordering you to, Blaze."

He laughed softly. "Stop calling me Blaze."

"I like it. It's perfect for you, witch-hunter." Reaching out, she found a nipple and rolled it between her finger and thumb. His growl of satisfaction pleased her. It made her feel powerful, and at the same time, very feminine.

"I love you touching me," he admitted as her explorations continued. "Makes me feel wanted."

"Oh, you're wanted all right."

Her fingers walked over his tautened stomach, probed the hollow of his navel, and then sought the magnificent thrust of his cock. He groaned as her light fingertips ventured along the shaft. He was throbbing, and she felt an answering series of spasms deep inside her.

"Nice," she told him, meeting his eyes with a mischievous smile as she stroked him harder. "When am I going to get it?"

"Witch." He delved into a drawer in the bedside table and came out with a handful of condoms. She giggled at the number, but for once Daniel didn't join in her laughter; he moved swiftly to break open a packet and get one on. Then she found herself beneath him again, held immobile by his powerful body, his cock pressing insistently against her moist folds. "Never tempt a starving man."

But he waited one more second, his hooded eyes asking for her permission. "Yes, for godsake, take me, take me, take me..." The words formed an urgent rhythm as their bodies slowly merged. Kate glowed with happiness because it felt so perfect, so right.

For a golden instant, they were still, their eyes open and looking directly into each other's, and Kate felt all her defenses crumble. Smiling, she opened herself to him, body and soul. His hips plunged, and she met his thrust with her own. Both cried out with the sheer pleasure of it. They drew apart, then joined again, and she felt herself spinning as the tension in her core wound ever tighter. Closing her eyes, she saw colors, just as she had on the night they met—passionate blues, steamy yellows, hot pinks, and crimsons.

Her hands slipped down over his tense body, exploring him, reveling in his virile strength as he forced her into a wild, haphazard rhythm. Holding him tightly, she let herself go, trusting him to take her higher and higher until her breathing grew shallow and her limbs started to dissolve. There was one more moment of almost agonizing pleasure before she slipped over the edge. She was only vaguely aware of Daniel's hoarse cry as his body went rigid a few seconds later with his own climax, but in the aftermath, they clung to each other, making small sounds of wonder and awe at the extraordinary mutuality of their pleasure.

Afterward Kate's head rested on Daniel's shoulder, his arms holding her body loosely, their legs tangled. She was falling into a light slumber when she vaguely heard him say, "Sleep, my magical witchy woman." His lips touched her eyelids tenderly. "Sleep."

* * *

Kate woke up gasping, her heart sprinting. She'd seen Arthur in her dreams, his limp body lying on the ground beside the car, not moving while she strained to free herself from the wreckage and smelled the ominous scent of gasoline. Then he was beside the bed, lightly caressing her hair and telling her he still loved her. "I'm still here," he said to her. "Believe. *Believe.*"

But when she opened her arms to him, he glared at her with Daniel's sardonic blue eyes.

Then Daniel's voice was comforting her, saying, "Ssh, love. You were dreaming." His strong arms enfolded her, and he lifted her atop him, his thighs parting to imprison her between them. She felt his crinkly chest hair brushing against her breasts. "It was only a dream."

"It was Arthur," she said shakily. "He told me to believe."

A fierce light sparked in Daniel's eyes. "Believe what?"

Realizing where she was, and with whom, Kate rapidly pulled herself together. "Uh, nothing." Daniel was the last person she could ever tell that she and Arthur had once lightheartedly agreed that whichever one of them died first would try to send the other a message from the Other Side, assuming the Other Side really existed. The message was to be the simple word "believe." It would mean that somehow, somewhere, Arthur's spirit still survived. "I'm sorry. I must still be half asleep."

Daniel's voice was kind. "It's natural, Kate. Don't worry about it. It's the first time, and you feel a little guilty. It'll pass."

She pressed her face against his shoulder. Although she tried to stifle them, the dream images still flitted across her mind. "Sometimes I still dream about the accident."

He held her tightly, and after a time he said, "Tell me about Arthur, Kate. You've been unusually loyal to him. He must have been really something."

She was surprised and touched. Usually he didn't want to hear about Arthur. "We grew up together," she answered slowly. "He lived down the street from me, and we were friends long before we started having sexual feelings for one another. We started dating in high school, and everybody kept telling us that high school relationships don't last, and that we'd never end up together, but they were wrong."

"So, you never even dated anybody else?" He sounded awed at the thought.

"Not seriously. There was some teenage flirting and crushing in high school before Arthur and I got together, and later, in college, we broke up for a couple of months. I guess we were both curious about what it would be like to see other people. I fooled around a bit with one or two guys I knew (including Stephen, she was thinking, amused at the memory). But I never actually had intercourse with anybody except Arthur. Our wedding was on the Saturday after our college graduation." Her voice dropped as she remembered the carefree pleasures of those happy days. "We both thought we'd be together forever. I couldn't believe it when he died. It didn't seem possible. It was as if I'd been severed from an essential part of myself."

Daniel muttered something under his breath.

"What did you say?"

"I was cursing. It's even worse than I thought. I suppose the guy was perfect, too? Handsome, great personality, terrific in bed?"

Actually, Daniel was a more exciting lover than Arthur had been. Or maybe it just seemed that way because her body had gone so long without sex. Once again, she felt a faint disloyalty to Arthur. She had thought their relationship so perfect, yet the first experience she'd had with another man had been more intense and ecstatic than anything she remembered experiencing with her husband. It shook her a little. "He was a sweet, kind, gentle man. He wasn't perfect, but who is? I loved him."

"How long were you married?"

"Nearly five years."

"Were you planning to have kids? From what you say, Arthur would have been an awesome dad."

Kate's hands touched her empty belly in an instinctively protective gesture. She rolled off Daniel and curled up beside him. "We did want kids." She was not going to cry, dammit.

Daniel propped himself up on one elbow and frowned into her eyes. "And?"

"We had just started trying when he died." To her horror, she felt her eyes fill. Not again! She turned her face into the pillow and fought to fend off crying jag. Nearly losing it in his car this morning had been bad enough. He was going to think she was some kind of basket case.

But once again, Daniel showed more sensitivity that she'd been giving him credit for. He lowered his body over hers and silently comforted her. "I'm sorry if my questions upset you," he murmured against her ear. "I want to know you, to understand you,

but the last thing I want is to hurt you. Any time I ask you something that disturbs you, you're free to tell me to shut the hell up."

As it had earlier, his tenderness moved her. Because he seemed
to be such a forceful, aggressive man who would think nothing of
riding roughshod over everybody else's feelings, Kate still felt
surprised when he offered her kindness and consideration. "I
will," she said, grinning at him, "but so far you've been very nice."

He turned her over and gently stroked her cheeks, letting the
ball of his thumb caress her bottom lip. "Nice?" His mouth curled
up in a dangerous smile. "Is that the best you can manage?" His
hand slipped down to smooth over her throat and breasts. His legs
captured hers, and she felt his body stir and harden with renewed
desire. "Let's see if we can find a better adjective than nice."

The husky promise in his voice incited a yearning deep inside
her. When he kissed her, she rocked her pelvis against his until he
groaned and slid between her thighs.

"I want you again," he said.

"Me, too."

"This time I'll do better. The first time was too fast."

"I loved the first time."

"Second time's the charm." His voice was determined, almost
harsh. "I'm going to give you something new to dream about,
babe."

He kept his promise. The Daniel who made love to her now was
a different Daniel from the man who had exploded in her arms
two hours before. No longer trembling with his need for release,
he courted her in a more leisurely manner, showering her with his
devastating sensual skills. She was dazzled. He knew exactly
where to touch her to give her the most exquisite pleasure. He
knew how fast, how hard. He knew when to tease, and when to

satisfy. He even seemed to know what made her shy, and how to overcome her inhibitions.

The first time he used only his hands and his mouth to lead her to the edge of bliss, to hold her there for endless golden seconds, and finally to hurl her over. Thinking herself replete, she curled up and tried to rest against him, only to discover that he had no intention of letting her stop. Once again he aroused her, patiently seeking out every pleasure point on her body, finding many in the process that she'd never been acquainted with before. She felt like a virgin again, being introduced to pleasures that were beyond her experience and almost beyond her imagination.

"Lie still," he ordered at one point.

"Why?" she gasped, barely able to obey.

"Just feel me loving you." He moved inside her with tantalizing slowness, withdrawing and coming back to her after a breath-stealing delay. "I want you to feel me staking my claim on you, witch."

"Staking?" she said, giggling. "As in burning at the..."

He cut her off with a kiss, adding, in a pause after thoroughly plundering her mouth, "I want it to be clear to you exactly how alive we both are."

When he began to retreat again, she clasped her arms tightly around his back and tried to prevent him, but he was inexorable. "Lie still," he repeated as her hips strained upward in protest. His hand slipped between their bodies, seeking out the place where they were joined. As he moved out of her, he stroked her sex with a light, maddening touch. "I'm going to heighten your pleasure, but I want you to stay perfectly still for me."

On some deep level, his domination of their lovemaking thrilled her. It was new to her, this wild desire to surrender. Panting, she obeyed him, fighting the almost irresistible urge to move and feeling his slightest touch in every cell. "Some slave," she murmured as he continued the delicious torment. "You've got our roles reversed."

He chuckled, but his voice maintained its gently aggressive edge. "Speaking of roles, my darling witch"—he moved deeply within her while she gritted her teeth in her effort to prevent her body from undulating wildly beneath him—"I haven't forgotten the way you deceived me. You're no more qualified to tell fortunes than I am."

"Well, maybe a little more. I have powers that I've, uh, never really bothered to develop. They run in the female line of my family."

He muttered a skeptical expletive and thrust into her with such force that she thought he must surely hurt her, but she felt no pain, only pleasure. "Dear God, Daniel!" She let out an involuntary moan. "You're driving me crazy! May I move now?"

"No."

But she could tell from his breathing that his own control was slipping, so she defied him. His carnal lips moved in a brief, dark smile as he grabbed both of her wrists and held them down on the pillow. She struggled, but of course he was stronger, and a wave of delicious helplessness washed over her. This kind of edginess was new to her, but she liked it. She struggled some more, not because she really wanted him to release her, but because it felt incredibly hot to feel him holding her down. He was careful not to hurt her, and he whispered her name tenderly against her lips as he plunged deeply into her, his hips guiding her wildly into his rhythm. At some point, his hands fell away from her wrists. She wrapped her arms around his muscular back, unconsciously digging her nails into his flesh as they rode the final surge to completion, neither controlling the other now, both of them equal in the face of a storm of passion whose powers were greater than anything either of them possessed alone.

Afterward, lying flung out on her back in pleasant exhaustion, she murmured, "Wow. That was awesome."

He grinned and kissed her affectionately. "You're quite a woman."

"I've never been able to come twice in a row like that."

He chuckled. "You see what you've been missing? These are your golden years; you're approaching your sexual peak."

"And you're past yours," she teased him. "Don't men peak at nineteen or thereabouts? I should find myself a college student."

"No way, darling. You're mine now." His voice was fiercely possessive. "Deprive me for a few days, and you get hot-blooded lust; satisfy me, and you get slow, sensual seduction. What more could you want, you lucky girl?"

"Humility?"

He rolled on top of her, laughing, and she hugged him, feeling deliriously happy. He was tough, tender, and playful, all in one. She nestled closer, reveling in the feel of his hard, sweat-slick body. What more could she want? His love, of course. How easy it would be to fall in love with him.

Kate stiffened as she realized the unruly direction of her thoughts. Fall in love with him, indeed! This was exactly what she'd feared, dammit. Spend the night with a man, and—bingo!—she was imagining herself in love.

Careful, girl. She warned herself not to get carried away just because she was enjoying the pleasures of sex after three years of abstinence. It would be crazy to fall for D. B. Haggarty, no matter how much he prattled about the more he supposedly wanted from her. He was a whirlwind—pure passion, pure energy. No doubt he would blow out of her life as wildly and swiftly as he had blown in.

"What're you thinking?"

"Scorpio lovers," she said, closing her eyes.

"I looked us up on some astrology website this morning," he confided. "You're right: We're a perfect match."

"Ah-ha, the skeptic's walls are beginning to crumble!" she whooped. "Next I'll have you going to table-tappings and reading your horoscope each day."

"Don't be absurd," he said fiercely before kissing her into silence.

CHAPTER TEN

It was still raining hard when they woke up on Sunday morning. Kate called Paul Tiele from Daniel's bed and was told that rehearsals had been canceled because of the storm. The entire city was paralyzed. There were trees and branches down all over the place, blocking many roads.

"Be in here tomorrow morning at ten," Paul said grouchily. "I don't care if you have to swim to work, Kingsley. This is probably all you fault, you know. Quoting from the play."

Daniel scowled when she switched off her phone and repeated her director's words. "Superstitious jerk." Then he grinned. "You got the day off, huh?"

She laughed, noting the lecherous gleam in his eyes. "I can't imagine what I'm going to do with my time."

Daniel promptly pounced. They rolled over once, wrestling playfully, before he trapped her against the headboard. The now-familiar melting heat washed through her with an intensity that made her groan and press herself against him. "I don't believe this. I feel depraved."

"From deprived to depraved in one night's time," he laughed, kissing her.

Later in the day, the rain finally stopped and they went for a walk to inspect the local damage. Daniel's home in Winchester was just across the road from a golf course, so there was a huge area where they could walk. The damage from the hurricane had assured that there would be no one golfing today. The ground was wet and there were broken branches tossed all over the fairways that they had to step over, but the exercise felt good.

When they returned from their walk, Daniel used a chainsaw to remove the tree limbs blocking his driveway. Watching, Kate thought he looked outrageously sexy, assaulting the poor dead wood. When the driveway was clear, he drove his car up to the house, and he looked outrageously sexy doing that, too. There was something about the way he moved the gear stick that really turned her on, particularly with those black driving gloves...

"Why are you staring at me?" he asked.

"I can't stop thinking about how much I want to get you naked again."

"That can be arranged."

"Daniel....when you take off everything else, could you maybe leave on the driving gloves?"

He grinned. "You like leather, huh? That gives me some truly wicked ideas."

* * *

Later that afternoon, Kate made tea while Daniel built a fire in the living room hearth, and they snuggled down on a thick carpet in front of the fireplace to talk. Kate tried to explain to him what it was like growing up with a mother who saw dead people on a frequent basis. "Living with my mom was, well, unusual. I know you don't believe in this stuff, so it's difficult to explain. You had to be there, in our house, I mean. And even then..." She stopped, helpless to describe what her childhood had been like to D. B Haggarty, professional skeptic and witch-hunter.

"What was it—haunted?" he asked with a disparaging laugh.

"I know you don't believe me, but yeah, it kinda was. Listen to me, and try to understand. When I was growing up, there was never a question of 'do you believe in ghosts' because some of my mother's best friends were ghosts. She'd go around talking to them half the time."

"She sounds psychotic to me."

"No, she's not psychotic." Kate looked earnestly into his face, trying her best to explain. "She's a little flaky, but she was never incapable of taking care of herself, or of me, or of running the house and coordinating all her nutty activities. Besides—and I know you're going to mock me for this—the ghosts used to answer back."

"I suppose you talked to them, too?"

"In a way. Some of them rapped. Once for no, twice for yes. Codes for letters of the alphabet. You could carry on a conversation with them if you wanted to."

"Knee joints."

"What?"

"Don't you know that the two sisters who started the spiritualist movement in this country admitted before they died that they had made their mysterious rapping sounds by cracking their knee joints? Or maybe it was their toe joints."

"You're referring to the Fox sisters?" Kate knew about the Fox sisters, famous psychics who had lived in the middle of the 19th century. "There has always been controversy about Margaret Fox's supposed confession."

"Really." He sounded skeptical.

"Yes. According to many sources, she was coerced into it, and she later recanted. Kate Fox, her sister, was by all accounts a powerful medium. She was examined and tested in every way that was possible during that era, but no one ever proved her to be a fraud. In fact, some scholars have asserted that the Fox sisters were attacked because they were successful women. Their psychic abilities brought them the sort of income and independence that was traditionally reserved for males."

Daniel made a dismissive gesture. "Hey, I believe in the equality of the sexes. Women are just as capable of being deceptive scam artists as men are."

She smiled. "Well, I don't know about the Fox sisters, since they died long before I was born, but in my mom's case I do know. She uses no tricks. As for the rappings I used to hear as a child, they were very loud noises. Sometimes the sounds emerged from the wall, or from the ceiling, or right out of thin air. And that's not all. You know about telekinesis—things moving around by themselves, defying the law of gravity? Mom has some telekinetic abilities, too. And of course clairvoyance. She can predict all sorts of events."

"How's her luck with the state lottery?"

Kate shook her head, laughing a little. "You don't believe me, do you?"

"Nope."

"Jerk," she teased him. "We can laugh about it now, but it was scary sometimes when I was little, living in that spooky house of hers."

"Now that I can imagine. I believed in monsters under the bed, too, when I was a child." Daniel stroked her hair with soothing fingers. "Poor kid. You must have been frightened a lot of the time."

She considered. "Occasionally, yes, but it also seemed ordinary to me. I thought everybody's mother practiced some sort of magic and consorted with spirits."

"I wish I were recording this. Why won't you let me interview your mother? I'll probably do it anyway, you know. This material is too good to pass up."

"What do you mean, you'll do it anyway? You promised you wouldn't interview her without my permission."

"Your permission or hers was what I promised."

"Well, you won't get hers without mine," Kate said uneasily. The subject made her uneasy. Her mother on YouTube? That would be a disaster. Iris didn't possess an ounce of caution or common sense. She would answer all the interviewer's questions with complete honesty and directness, admitting that she communed with spirits long dead as freely as any normal person would admit to switching on her phone and chatting with a friend in another city. She would come across sounding certifiable.

"You'd better forget the idea. She might be a little odd, but she's my mother. I've heard about the kind of thing you do on your show. You and your crusading minions would eat her alive."

Daniel's eyes were dancing wickedly. "You mean you're not going to introduce me to your mother? But mothers usually adore me. I'm considered such a good catch."

She punched him gently on the shoulder and suggested a few choicer terms for what he was.

"So you know about my crazy upbringing now," she said a few minutes later. "How about you? Tell me more about yourself. How did you get into the work you do now? Were you a more conventional journalist first, or did you move straight into internet media?"

"Conventional. Like all starry-eyed young journalists, I envisioned working for one of the top newspapers. Despite growing up with the internet, I still labored under the illusion that print journalism was here to stay. I even had a paper route as a boy. I wonder what kids do now to earn extra spending money?" He grinned at her. "How do they pay for their monthly gaming subscriptions?"

"They probably charge their parents to repair the household computer network when it goes down. Did you work as a reporter for a newspaper?"

"I started out freelancing, but after a couple of years I got a job for a news magazine. I worked my way up and spent a few months as a war correspondent in the Middle East. Was in Afghanistan for a time, too, embedded with a medical unit. It wasn't supposed to be a combat situation, but we came under attack more often than I care to remember."

Kate shivered and reached for his hand to squeeze it. "I can't even imagine what a nightmare that must have been."

"Yeah. They were good men. And women—no sexism there. Amazingly brave bunch of people, putting themselves into danger to save their comrades. And the stuff they could do in the field to preserve life was amazing. Did you know that civilian emergency medicine has improved considerably because of techniques that were developed in the war zone?"

"I've heard that. In fact, one of the surgeons who handled my case after the accident had done some training in combat medicine." They hadn't been able to save Arthur, though. He had died instantly from the impact.

"Were you close to death at any point?"

"I don't know. I don't think so. My memory of exactly what happened in the hospital is a little fuzzy, and, honestly, it's something I can't bear thinking about." What she remembered most clearly was the crushing grief she had experienced upon learning of Arthur's death. "I hate hospitals."

He gathered her closer. "That's understandable. I'm not fond of them myself, after some of the things I saw in Afghanistan."

Kate didn't know anybody who'd been there who actually liked to talk about it, so she changed the subject. Asking him about his family didn't prove to be a safer topic, though. He elaborated on what he had told her about his parents the night before, explaining that his mother had been devoted to his dad. "He was a commodities broker, as lucky as he was skillful at predicting trends. But he was obsessed with it. He was only 42 when he had a heart attack on the trading floor. He never even made it to the hospital."

"How old were you?" she asked gently.

"Twelve." He said the word offhandedly, as if it didn't matter, but she guessed that he was trying to contain some painful memories.

"I'm so sorry. That's awfully young to lose your dad."

"Yeah." He cleared his throat, and then went on, "I was broken-hearted, of course, but it was even worse for my mother. She was devastated. Diminished, in a way, if that makes any sense. She lost a lot of weight and got smaller, it seemed, but of course, at that age I was getting taller. She had loved him deeply, and she couldn't handle the shock of his death."

He sipped the last of his tea and leaned back with his head against the sofa cushions. "She died too, less than four years later. Cancer. She didn't have the will to fight it. She just wasted away. She was never the same, after—" he stopped abruptly, shaking his head as if regretting that he had told her any of this. After what? She wondered. But she could sense his abrupt withdrawal.

Four years later. He had been left an orphan at sixteen, she realized, aching for him. She touched his arm gently, but he drew away from her. His muscles had gone tense.

"Who took care of you?" she asked, wondering if he would even answer. After a short pause, he did:

"My uncle. My mother's brother lived here in town. He and his partner—they're gay. He's a lawyer, a litigator. They were great. I lived with them, and we rented this house out for several years. I finished high school and went away to college, but for some reason I didn't want to sell the house. Eventually, after I'd been out of the country for a while, I came back to Boston and moved in here.

"Uncle Jon and Cameron are married now and living down on the Cape. I see them whenever I can—they saved my life, you could say. I was messed up for a while after my parents died. Did some wild stuff, drinking, riding a motorcycle at crazy speeds, skipping school, not studying, not caring what happened to me. They settled me down and helped me get back on track."

"They sound awesome."

"They are."

"Well, even if, for obvious reasons, you never meet my mom, I'd love to meet your uncle and his husband." She said this unthinkingly, but wished the words back as soon as they were out. They had spent exactly one night together, and she was asking to meet his family? She felt her face and neck go red with embarrassment.

But Daniel didn't seem fazed at all. He smiled and said, "You'll like them, and I'm sure they'll like you."

Relieved, she nestled against him, her hands in his, her face near his shoulder.

"Kate..." He stopped.

She leaned her head back until her eyes locked with his. "What?"

"I don't form attachments easily, but—"

She quickly withdrew one of her hands and stopped him by placing her fingers on his mouth. "Ssh. Don't say any more." She didn't want him to say anything he might later regret.

He smiled and kissed her fingers. His eyes searched hers; then his hand slipped around to the back of her head and tilted her face to his. They kissed sweetly, without lust or urgency, and settled closer into each other's arms.

CHAPTER ELEVEN

If Kate had expected Daniel's take-charge domination of her life to end when he returned her to her house on Sunday evening, she was soon proven to be wrong. He called her from his home Sunday night, texted her from his office several times during the day, and on Monday in the late afternoon he showed up at the theater to watch her rehearse. It was the beginning of a pattern that continued steadily over the next couple of weeks. D. B. Haggarty didn't do anything halfheartedly. "I'm your lover now. I intend to share your life."

They spent every night together. He would drop her off at home on his way to work so she could feed Chester and play with him for a while before she reported to the theater. Evenings Daniel spent backstage with her, usually bringing his laptop so he could work while she was busy. He was putting together a new broadcast on government surveillance of the internet, which had grown exponentially in recent years. Wrapped up in that issue, he had temporarily set aside his vendetta against spiritualists, for which she was grateful.

He worked energetically, giving his full attention to whatever it was that absorbed him. He had the ability to narrow his concentration, never noticing a thing around him except what he was doing at the time. He made love the same way—totally absorbed, in her, in the experience, in the magic they wove between them.

At night, late, when Paul Tiele finally released the exhausted company, Daniel drove Kate home once more to check on Chester, and then on to his house in Winchester. One night they stayed in Cambridge because Kate was feeling guilty about the cat. "He's lonely," she explained as she cuddled the huge purring feline. "I've never left him alone so much before. Maybe I should take him back to live with my mother again."

"How'd you end up with him, anyway, if he's hers?"

"She was hospitalized for a couple of weeks last year with pneumonia, and I took charge of him then. I got attached to him, and he seemed happy with me. Mom has two other cats, and she thought I could use a little company."

Daniel took Chester from her and patted him warily. The cat was surprisingly tolerant of this large, male stranger. "I like cats," Daniel told her. "Always have. I really wish I weren't allergic."

"Have you taken your allergy medication?"

"Yup. I probably shouldn't push my luck though." Reluctantly, he set Chester down, but the cat continued to cheek-rub against his legs, which eventually resulted in Daniel having to pop another antihistamine pill.

When Kate went into her office–Arthur's office–that night to check her email, both Daniel and Chester trailed after her. Something about the room always made Daniel prickly. Tonight he refrained, with obvious effort, from making any snarky comments about its being a shrine to Arthur, but that didn't stop him from glaring at the picture of her and her husband that still held the place of honor on her desk. Trying to distract him, she said, "I should teach you how to play Hunt the Night City so you can meet my gaming friends. It's actually a lot of fun."

"Crank it up, then, and show me."

She did, with Daniel hovering over her shoulder, watching as the bright colors of the game came up on the big screen. Daniel quickly established his familiarity with games of this genre, although not with this particular one. He asked some intelligent questions about the game environment, the story, the typical group make-up, and the in-game economy. When she asked if he wanted to take her place and play her character for a bit, he agreed. It only took him a couple of minutes to get used to the controls.

"That looks like a pretty cool sword," he noted, examining its skin and its stats.

"Legendary drop from an end-game raid boss."

"Woo-hoo. You're some kind of hard-core raider? My dearest girl, you have all sorts of hidden talents. Hey, I think someone's sending me a private message. Who's Nekrotic?"

Oh jeez. Her character's name would have popped up when she came online, and Nekrotic, of course, was awake and playing the game. "That's my friend Max. He plays a vampire character."

"'Hey, babe,' Daniel read out loud, 'Why U logging in? How come you're not banging the BF?'"

"Oops," Kate said, laughing.

Daniel started typing a response. He typed very fast. "R U implying I can't bang the BF & kick undead ass at the same time?"

"Babe, if U could do that, we'd know it by now. But lately Uv been like, gone girl. He must be blazin," Max typed back.

Daniel shot Kate a nasty look, mouthing, "Did you tell your friends my middle name?"

She shook her head, laughing. She hadn't. "It's just his slang."

Daniel looked skeptical, but he returned to the keyboard, typing, "He's blazin all right, dude. U can count on that."

There was a slight pause, and then Max responded, "Now if I really believed U could do the dirty & game at the same time, I'd of moved my gaming rig down to ur place & bounced U on my dick during raids."

Oh dear. Max wasn't usually so graphic. Stephen was the one who casually employed crude language. Max had probably figured out he wasn't typing to Kate, who rarely used texting shortcuts. Max had good instincts about that sort of thing.

"Where's your voice program?" Daniel asked in a deceptively mild tone. "Start it up for me." As she leaned over his shoulder to do so, he wrestled her into his lap, in front of the screen's camera so they would both be visible when the program came up. Daniel, who had obviously used gaming voice software before, snapped on her microphone and pulled it toward his lips. He left the sound to emerge from the main speakers. He had no trouble locating Nekrotic's group and joining their video channel. The familiar faces of Jeff and Stephen popped up on screen, grinning. Max's face, as usual, was hidden.

"Hello, gentlemen," he said calmly. "Which one of you charmers is Nekrotic?"

"That would be me," came Max's low, sexy voice. "Sorry, no vid feed. Those other two idiots are Jeff and Stephen. You, presumably, are the Unbanged Boyfriend?"

"I'd try the lap thing," Daniel retorted, "except that I don't really like to multitask. So much nicer for the lady, don't you agree, if she receives her lover's complete, undivided attention."

There was a considerable amount of chortling from her friends. Grinning, Kate put her mouth near the mike and said, "Hey guys! How's it going?" To Daniel she said, "Stephen's the one with the Harry Potter glasses. He's a writer. And that's Jeff with the light hair. He's a history professor. I guess Nick's not on. As for Max, he's kind of a phantom."

"Hey, Kate," said Stephen. "So that's him? Very rugged. You'd better treat her right, New Guy. She's our girl."

"She's my girl now," Daniel said, doing the male territorial thing. Kate could almost feel the waves of testosterone coming off him. "But I'm more than glad to meet her gaming friends, even if one of them is missing a face. Hiya, Jeff, Stephen. Hey, Phantom Max. Why the mystery?"

"He's a night creature," Stephen said cheerfully. "You know the type—can't be photographed? Doesn't show up in mirrors?"

Max chuckled and answered, "I keep a low internet profile for professional reasons, running my connection through a variety of proxy servers and anonymizers."

"Not for gaming, surely? Wouldn't your connection be too slow?" said Daniel.

There was a longer than usual pause before Max responded. "I know a few ways around that problem."

"Why the secrecy?" Daniel asked. It struck Kate that she had never asked Max this simple, direct question.

"You're media, right?" Max said. "I don't make a practice of explaining myself to the media. No offense."

"None taken. You got something to hide from the media? Or maybe from the law? You a hacker?"

Max laughed. "Why does everybody think that?"

"You're not putting Kate into any danger by association, I trust? Internet activity and contacts can be tracked."

Jeff, who hadn't yet spoken, presumably because he'd been staring into the camera and evaluating what he could see of Daniel, responded to this. "None of us would ever put Kate into danger. On the contrary, we look out for her. As for Max, he's an old buddy of mine and a standup guy. I can vouch for him."

Daniel studied Jeff's face for a long moment before asking, "You're Jeff, right? Who vouches for you?"

"I do," said Kate. She was feeling a little dismayed by the direction the conversation had taken. "These are my friends, Daniel, my very old and dear friends. They're not just online personas; most of us went to college together."

"Except for Max, of course," Stephen put in, joking around as usual. "Last time he was in a university was in the 16th century, right, Nekrotic? Or am I mixing you up with one of Kate's ghosts? I get my supernatural creatures confused."

"Kate's ghosts lack fangs," Max snarked. "And their inability to move a mouse or a keyboard makes them lousy gamers, so I've got no use for them. Sorry, Kate. I hope I'm not riling things up in the spirit world with my dark, demonic energy."

Her friends laughed. Daniel didn't. Kate decided this was quite enough for an introductory meeting. "G'night, guys," she said. "I just signed on to show Daniel the game, and to say hi. I'll see you all later."

"Later," they agreed, and she waved to their collective video feeds and logged out.

She twisted on Daniel's lap to see his face, half-expecting him to make some sort of snide comment. But all he did was quirk his eyebrows a bit. "Gotta love gaming geeks," he said. "Colorful bunch."

"I think they may have literally saved my life after Arthur's death. I was pretty depressed and felt as if I had nothing to live for."

"In that case, I owe them big-time," he said, snuggling her close.

It turned out to be the only night they didn't make love. Daniel was so doped up on anti-allergy medication that he fell asleep almost as soon as they fell into bed.

In the morning, though, he woke her from a deep sleep and took her in the fiercely exciting manner to which she was becoming accustomed. When she cried out in ecstasy, Chester meowed worriedly at the door.

"It's all right, Chester," she called, wiping a swathe of sweat-damp dark hair out of Daniel's eyes. "He thinks you're hurting me."

There was a crash in the hall, which Kate recognized as a vase shattering under the influence of Chester's swatting tail. Fortunately, she didn't own any expensive vases.

Daniel swore. "That damn cat."

"You should be grateful to him," she laughed. "We both got some sleep for a change."

His laughter was a low growl. "You mean I work you too hard, woman? These dissolute nights getting to be too much for you? Maybe you're just out of shape. I notice you haven't been leaping out of bed at dawn to go swimming lately."

"I stop for a swim on my way to work," she informed him. "You're the one who could use some exercise. I bet you haven't been hitting the gym lately."

"I run four or five miles every day at lunchtime, and I've got some free weights at the office."

"I didn't know that." She was surprised because she already felt as though she knew everything about him.

"Thought you had an indolent layabout in bed with you, huh?" He bent his dark head and dabbed a rosy nipple with the tip of his tongue. "Maybe I'll just resign myself to being late to work this morning in order to prove my stamina."

"I thought you'd just proved it." Incredibly, his ministrations were causing that familiar tightening in her supposedly satiated body.

"I'll just have to prove it again. We wouldn't want there to be any doubt in your mind, would we?"

She shook her head. With Daniel she'd discovered that intense multiple orgasms weren't mythical.

CHAPTER TWELVE

"I'd really like to interview your mother," Daniel said on a Sunday evening, the night of the final rehearsal before the official opening of the play. *A Doll's House* had closed, and *Macbeth* would open on Friday.

They were in his car on the way to the theater, but Daniel's mind was obviously still on his work. His program on surveillance had wrapped the day before. She knew he had various other projects in the works, too, so she had hoped he'd put the idea of interviewing her mother aside. "I'm still planning to do an entire hour's program on so-called psychics, and I've lined up three séance-goers, the president of some international spiritualist society, and a photographer who shoots pictures of what he claims are ghosts. All I need now is a medium. Your mother's probably the most famous."

"I said no, Daniel."

"Come on, Kate. What are you afraid of? She seemed willing enough the one time I talked with her about it."

"There are plenty of other mediums you can use."

"I want Iris Carter. Long before I knew you, I intended to have her on the show. She's the best. Exposing her as a fraud would present the greatest challenge."

Kate's felt her face darken with anger. "Is that the way you regard attacking somebody in front of thousands of people—as a challenge? You're talking about my mother."

He shrugged. "Maybe I'd fail. If she really has as much power as you claim she has, why do you fear for her? Maybe she'll turn my interviewer into a bat."

"Very funny. Why are you so down on mediums and psychics, anyway? I can understand that you're a skeptic on this subject, but why do you care if other people believe in things like telepathy and the Other Side? What harm does it do?"

"It does incalculable harm." His voice had gone cold, his blue eyes glacial.

"You claim to be the most rational of men, but you're obsessed with this subject."

"With good reason," he said darkly.

"What's your reason? You've yet to explain it to me."

But he didn't. Instead he repeated, "I want her, Kate."

"Then choose between us. Because I promise you, the day you go after my mother will be the day I break off our relationship."

Daniel pulled into a tiny parking lot behind the theater and shot her an ominous look. "You really think you can walk away? No, Kate." His voice was soft, deceptively mild. "It's too late for that."

She could feel the aura of masculine power he projected. Every now and then, he still reminded her of the Scorpio brooder he'd been on the night they first met. Hot, dark, and a little bit dangerous. "What does that mean?"

"Think about it," he suggested as they stepped out of the car. He flashed her a disarming grin. "If by any chance you're still in doubt, I'll be happy to demonstrate when we get home tonight."

She did think about it several times during the course of the evening. *You really think you can walk away? It's too late for that.* What did he mean? He wasn't in love with her. As passionate as his lovemaking was, he'd made no further attempt to say anything that would confirm a growing emotional bond. He'd told her at the start that he could make her no promises, and she'd accepted that.

But her own feelings for him deepened with every night that she spent at his side. The more she learned about him, the more he seemed to typify everything a man should be: strong, yet gentle; aggressive, yet kind; serious in all his purposes, yet blessed with the gift of laughter. She'd stopped comparing him to Arthur. She hadn't thought much about Arthur in days. This realization made her feel guilty. She certainly didn't want to forget Arthur.

She daydreamed about Daniel when he wasn't with her, and she chattered about him to her friends in the cast until they all began to tease her about the new love in her life. All of them except Graham.

"Scorpio," he'd been muttering all week long. "Wait till you feel the slash of the scorpion's tail. Don't cross him, Kate, or he'll turn on you for sure."

She'd scoffed at Graham's predictions, but they made her uneasy.

Graham stirred her anxieties a little more that night after the rehearsal. Daniel had disappeared for a few minutes to make a phone call, and Graham snatched the opportunity to say, "Of all the men to pick, Kate—why him? I watched *Facts and Fantasies* the other day. They were doing a thing on child abuse. I never thought I'd feel sorry for a child abuser, but by the time D. B. Haggarty's vultures had finished with her, I actually wanted to comfort the poor woman. The people they interview on that show take more punishment than the bad guys at the end of a cop show."

"I've never actually seen the program," Kate confessed.

"You really ought to check it out. Is he still hunting witches, by the way? I hope you haven't given him any dazzling demonstrations of your psychic talents lately, luv."

"My psychic talents, if I have any, are not the stuff exposes are made of."

"I don't trust him. Sorry if I'm clucking over you like some bloody mother hen, but I have feeling he's going to hurt you. I still don't understand why you fell for him. You loved Arthur, and he was so easy-going and safe."

"I don't really want safe anymore. I mean, the world isn't safe, is it? You can't always count on things, or even on people. Anyway, it's not as if everything was always one hundred percent with Arthur. That is—" She stopped, flustered, not sure what she was saying.

Graham was staring even more intently. "Were there problems with your marriage?"

"No, no, there weren't any problems. Arthur and I were happy together." She struggled as she tried to verbalize feelings she didn't entirely understand. "It's just that, we never fought over anything. Don't you think that's a little strange? He was so, I don't know, so perfect."

"I can see why he might seem perfect in comparison with Haggarty," Graham said. Then, looking over Kate's shoulder, he broke off.

"Who might seem perfect in comparison with me?" said a low, dangerous voice from the doorway.

Kate bit her lip as she turned to face Daniel. That had been a quick phone call.

He came in, his hands thrust into the pockets of his jeans making fists that bulged the already tight material. He looked from her to Graham and back. "Who's this paragon of perfection you're comparing to me?"

"Nobody."

"Arthur."

Kate and Graham both spoke at the same moment. Kate immediately turned to glare at Graham. She had learned that Daniel didn't care to hear references to her dead husband.

"Oh, Arthur," said Daniel, scowling at Kate. "We all know that no man could ever hope to measure up to Arthur."

Kate quietly put on her coat. It had been more and more evident that Daniel and Graham could barely tolerate each other, and she didn't want to see the situation degenerate into total war. "I'm ready. Let's go."

"Show a little caution for the rest of the night, Kate," Graham advised. "Venus is moving into opposition with Mars, and as for your planet, Neptune—"

"We're not interested in that drivel," Daniel snapped.

"Excuse me. The voice of reason speaks. When are you going to have a priest on your program, Haggarty, so you can mock his silly belief in the existence of God?"

"I might decide to go after an astrologer or two first," Daniel shot back. "How would you like some TV exposure, Hamilton? Or are you afraid some big Hollywood casting director might see you making a fool of yourself?"

"If astrology is such drivel, I wonder why it describes your personality so accurately. I also wonder why you're pursuing Kate. You know her background; she's her mother's daughter. What are you going to do if she goes into a trance on you someday? YouTube it for your viewers' amusement?"

Daniel stared at him without answering, but Kate said, "I don't go into trances. I might indulge in a temper tantrum, though. It's not gonna take much more from either of you to set me off."

But Graham wasn't finished. "You're not her type, Haggarty," he plunged on. "And I don't get how a woman who was happy with a warm, gentle man like Arthur Kingsley could long put up with a witch-hunting devil like you."

Kate stiffened when Daniel reached out and seized her hand in one of his. Although he seemed cool enough, his palm was damp with tension. He really didn't like Graham, and the growing hostility between them worried her sometimes.

"She knew what I was from the start," Daniel said, as much to her as to Graham. "I've always been honest. She knew, and she took me anyway. Now she's stuck with me."

Kate tried to free her hand, which he was holding rather tightly. "Will you let go of me, please?"

"Never," he said darkly, releasing her hand, but putting an arm around her shoulders and steering her toward the door.

"You're all wrong for her, you know," Graham called after them. "You'll lose her, coming on like a bloody warlord."

Daniel thanked him ironically for the advice.

They drove home in silence. Kate was annoyed, and Daniel operated the car in a jerky fashion, his hands hard on the wheel, his foot pounding the clutch. When they got to her house Kate hurried inside and cuddled Chester, pressing her face into his thick orange fur and thinking that maybe her life would have been less complicated if she'd run away from Daniel Blaze Haggarty the moment she met him.

He followed her in and stood watching her, his eyes gleaming beneath his thick dark lashes. Chester was kneading her forearm. "Poor baby," she soothed the neglected cat. "Did you miss me?"

Looking up at Daniel, she said, "I should really stay here with my cat tonight. It's cruel to leave him alone so much."

Daniel reached out and scratched Chester's head. The cat paid him the unusual compliment of purring. "You ought to start giving that problem some thought. I'm fond of the beast, but I don't think I can live with him. Chester's probably going to need a new home. Will your mother take him back, do you think?"

Kate gathered Chester even more tightly against her. "You're not going to separate me from everyone I love—my colleagues, my friends, my gaming buddies, my mom, even my cat." She hadn't played Hunt the Night City for multiple nights in a row. Ever since she'd introduced him to her friends, Jeff, Stephen and Max had been texting and emailing her, demanding to know more about Daniel. "Good looking guy," Jeff had emailed, "so I'll forgive you for being so out-of-touch. He's not entirely lacking a sense of humor, though, is he?" This was so Jeff. He fretted about her.

Max had written, "Sorry about the dick remark, that was crude. But I knew it wasn't you at the keyboard. You type about half as fast as that guy. Does he write code? Ten to one he's done his own share of hacking in his youth."

Stephen's contribution has also been typical: "You'd better be having a wild and crazy time, 'cause that's what I'm imagining for you, babe. Is he kinky? He's got that vibe. If so, and you're feeling adventurous, call me, and I'll hook you up with the Boston clubs." Stephen's own kinkiness had long been a source of much teasing among his friends. It amused her to think that he might have read a similar tendency in Daniel. So far, at least, he hadn't tried to tie her to the bed or anything (that might be interesting, she thought, getting hot at the idea), but his character could certainly be described as alpha male.

"I'm not trying to separate you from anyone," Daniel declared now, his gorgeous eyelashes flicking up and down over his burning eyes. "I just want to spend as much time with you as possible. Don't you also want to be with me?"

"Yes, of course. I love being with you. I'm just trying to find my footing in this brave new world that my life has become."

"Brave new world—isn't that Shakespeare? I thought you weren't supposed to quote from the play."

"That's from *The Tempest*. It's perfectly okay to quote from Shakespeare's other plays."

"Well, that's a relief. Anyway, get your things together. We're going to my place."

Her eyes narrowed, and her nostrils flared. "What if I don't want to go? You'll get primitive and club me over the head, Caliban?"

He looked annoyed, too. "I have read *The Tempest*, you know. Caliban was a monster and a would-be rapist. I really don't appreciate the comparison."

She was instantly contrite. "I'm sorry. It's just that... I'm a bit off-balance with you, Daniel. You're very intense sometimes. And you have a tendency to be controlling."

He reached out and negligently stroked the side of her neck, much the same way as she was stroking Chester. An involuntary shiver took her, and her lips parted slightly. As always, his touch unleashed floods of erotic signals. Her body made up its mind that it wanted him, and her brain went all fuzzy.

"This thing between us is intense. I don't think either one of us can resist it, no matter how angry we get with each other." After a brief silence he added, "As for controlling, I don't mean to be. It probably comes of living alone and fending for myself for so many years."

She put the cat down and opened the basement door for him. "Can I ask you why you flip out every time Arthur's name is mentioned?"

"Nobody likes being compared with a saint."

"I wasn't comparing you. Graham was."

"He doesn't like me. He's trying to make trouble between us."

"Don't blame Graham for that," she said, recalling their earlier argument about her mother. "We seem to be able to fight pretty well without any outside interference."

He ran a hand through his hair and seemed, briefly, to be fumbling for words. "Look, Kate, you're a strong independent woman, and I love that about you, even if we butt heads sometimes." He moved closer, drawing her against the warm sinews of his body. "There's something powerful between us. I know you feel it, too. I don't want to control you, but at the same time, I don't want anyone—not Arthur, not Graham, not your college friends, not even your mother —to come between us. Not now, not ever."

Kate's head ached slightly. He tossed around words like "ever" and "never" rather easily, but it wasn't as if they had been dating long enough to make any sort of commitment to one another. She could sense his masculine arousal, his desire to possess her in the most ancient, basic way. But was there anything more to it than that? If so, he hadn't made his feelings clear.

"What do you want from me, Daniel?" She deliberately rocked her hips against his. "Just this? You have my body. Does it satisfy you?"

"I love your body," he said with a sudden devastating smile, "but now I want your soul."

"You're beginning to sound like the devil you resemble."

He shot a glance at himself in the hallway mirror. "I resemble the devil?"

"Not all the time." Remarkably, the mood had lightened. "Let's just say you have your moments of deviltry."

He grinned and hooked his hands on her shoulders, drawing her closer. One of his hands stroked down her spine, cupped her bottom, and pressed her against him. His head lowered, his tongue washed over her lips, preparing them for his kiss. "As you have your moments of witchcraft. It's appropriate, you know. One of the attributes of witches is that they consort with the prince of darkness. Wanna consort, sorceress?"

She laughed and rubbed herself sensuously against his hips. She couldn't help herself; he was irresistible. "Do we really need to go all the way to your place?"

"Maybe not," he conceded. But a few seconds later, he was seized with a sneezing fit, and she took pity on him. To his place they went.

When they entered his house a little while later, Daniel took her straight up to the bedroom. She recognized the glow in his eyes, and it sent her body leaping into glorious arousal.

"Get undressed," he ordered, his voice harsh and gravelly.

She felt a primordial feminine desire to tease him. She removed her clothes with maddening slowness, her eyes never leaving his. Her top had a prim line of tiny buttons down the front, and she painstakingly undid every single one while he stood stiffly facing her, a flush of barely contained excitement evident over the hard bones of his face. When she slid sensuously out of her skirt, she noticed that he was breathing rapidly through parted lips. Knowing she had the power to arouse him so much thrilled her. It also made her flirt, a little, with danger.

She approached him wearing only a delicate black bra and matching bikini briefs. "What about you?" She tunneled a hand under his sweater, finding the hard muscles on his abdomen and curling her fingers into them. Her bare legs brushed against his trousers while her fingers fumbled with his belt. Her green eyes met his. "I want to see your body, too." The hand that was under his sweater found his nipple and sensuously toyed with it. The other hand slipped inside his loosened trousers and captured the hard thrust of his cock, making him groan.

The next thing she knew the room was arcing around her as Daniel swooped her up in his arms and carried her to the bed. He fell on her, clothes and all, and after a few rapid fumblings with her panties and his trousers, they were naked from the waist down. She could feel his body tremble as he lowered his full weight upon her and parted her thighs. The wool sweater he still wore was faintly rough against her lace-covered breasts. They made no move to finish undressing; there was something fiercely exciting in their mutual urgency to complete the union. His rapid donning of a condom was his only concession to good sense and rationality.

"You really shouldn't taunt me," he growled, closing his mouth over hers. His hips drove against her, and she arched to accommodate him, sighing with pleasure as he sank into the slippery folds of her body, filling her exquisitely.

"I wasn't taunting you." She had wrapped her arms around his back, under the sweater. She could feel the driving tension of the muscles that bunched and relaxed as he began to move within her.

"You're mine, Kate. I want to hear you say it." One of his hands slid between their bodies to tantalize her breast through the fabric of her bra. Simultaneously he slowed the rhythm of their loving until he was barely moving. He ignored the way her body strained for a quick, violent conclusion.

"Daniel," she protested as he withdrew. A quick look at his taut expression told her he had somehow marshaled the strength to control his body. Supporting his weight on his strong arms, he slid himself back and forth between her thighs and watched her in narrow-eyed satisfaction as she pleaded for him to forge their union anew.

"Say it." There was a sheen of perspiration on his brow, and Kate knew he couldn't keep this up much longer. "Admit that you belong to me." His head dipped to tongue an aching, lace-clad nipple. The exquisite friction made her moan.

"I'm yours, dammit," she cried, pulling furiously at his shoulders.

He made a noise that might have been an exultant laugh if he hadn't been so close to the limits of his willpower. But he still didn't take her until, incensed, she reached down and fondled him fiercely. He surrendered to her then, driving raggedly into her yielding body, taking her higher and higher until she felt shards of pleasure piercing her and the explosive burst of glory that briefly made their spirits one. Dimly, in the aftermath, she heard herself saying, "Yes, yes, I love you, I love you, Daniel. I'm yours for as long as you want me."

His mouth met hers, and she felt him smile in satisfaction, but he made no reply.

CHAPTER THIRTEEN

When Kate opened her eyes the following morning she found Daniel already awake, propped up on one elbow, watching her. Memories of the night flooded her, making the color rise in her cheeks. He smiled slightly and brushed a lock of untidy hair out of her eyes.

"Morning, sweetheart." His voice was husky with unmistakable male satisfaction.

"What are you smirking about?"

He was all little-boy innocence. "Smirking? Me?"

"You look the way I'd imagine Chester would look if he ever actually caught one of the birds he's always watching through the windows."

"Poor Chester. He's too fat and clumsy ever to catch anything." He ran a finger down the side of her throat. "I'm a better hunter than he is."

Kate was astonished at the resentment that flashed through her. He looked so pleased with himself—oh, didn't he just! She rolled away from him, threw back the covers, and got up.

"Where are you going? It's Monday. Your theater is dark, and I'm planning to work at home today. We can stay in bed."

"I don't want to stay in bed." She jerked open the curtains and let the sunshine into the room. "I feel like getting up and being active."

"If it's exercise you want—" he began, but he broke off when he saw the way she was glaring at him. His expression changed, becoming wary, even a little concerned. "Hon? What's the matter?"

What's the matter? I told you I loved you last night, that's what the matter is. And you didn't even acknowledge my words. "Nothing."

"Then come back to bed."

"Not right now." She grabbed her clothes, walked into his bathroom, and shut the door.

She half expected him to come storming in after her, but, as usual, Daniel surprised her. When she returned, washed and dressed for the day, Daniel was sprawled out across the bed, sound asleep. "You're pretty damn sure of yourself, aren't you, Haggarty?" she said aloud.

He didn't respond.

* * *

A couple of hours later, Kate was curled up on the sofa in Daniel's living room reading Stephen's latest mystery novel on her Kindle when Daniel came downstairs and said a bit sheepishly, "I fell back asleep."

"There's fresh coffee in the pot on the kitchen counter."

"You're an angel." He returned from the kitchen a couple of minutes later with a mug of coffee and a bowl of cereal. "Did you get the newspaper in?"

She'd forgotten that Daniel still had the *New York Times* delivered to his front door. "No, sorry, I read the news on that." She nodded to her IPad sitting on the coffee table.

He strolled over to the front door to get his paper. "I'm a Luddite, I know, but there's something solid and reassuring about dirtying my fingers on real, old-fashioned newsprint."

She didn't respond, but kept her eyes on her book. Daniel ate his cereal, sipped his coffee, and read his newspaper in silence. Every now and then, Kate could feel him looking at her. She refused to meet his eyes, but her concentration on the book waned as she remembered the night before. She loved the way he made love to her, and she continued to find the physical domination he exhibited in bed wildly exciting. Obviously, she liked that sort of thing more than she'd realized. But he was also a generous lover, who reveled in giving her pleasure. He could be sweet and tender.

Even so, she felt as though she had taken a huge risk last night in voicing her feelings, particularly since she wasn't completely certain about what she'd said. Was she really in love with him? Could you be in love with someone you had only known for a few weeks? She and Arthur had known each other for years before falling in love.

Anyway, love or no love, Daniel hadn't responded. He had just smiled with a kind of satisfaction that might have been masculine pride or territorial possessiveness. Dammit, she didn't know what that smile had meant, if anything.

"How's your book?" he asked, speaking for the first time in several minutes.

She glanced up at him, then back down at her screen. "It's very good. A page-turner."

"Is it, like, a romance or something?"

"It's a mystery. An historical mystery, actually, by Stephen Silkwood."

"Really?" He sounded surprised. "You like his books? They're pretty violent, with that torturer hero of his. The guy's kickass, though. Is that the new one? I haven't read it yet."

It was her turn to be surprised. She knew Stephen's last couple of books had been bestsellers, but it had never occurred to her that Daniel might have read them. "The author is a friend of mine. Have you really read his books? You read mysteries?"

"Yeah, sure. I love mysteries and thrillers. You know the author? Seriously?"

"It's Stephen. You met him. Or at least, you talked to him via the game video voice program."

"Whoa. Stephen Silkwood is one of your gamer friends?"

"Yes. We went to college together. He's one of my best friends in the world. He's like a brother to me."

"Is he one of the guys who got a tattoo for you?"

She was half-laughing now because he seemed so nonplussed at this revelation. "Yes. It's on his butt."

Daniel's eyes widened for a moment, and then narrowed. She laughed out loud. "Of course he'd get it there. Jeff got his tattoo on his shoulder, but Stephen loves to be outrageous. I think it's his artistic personality."

Daniel digested this is silence. At last he said, "I've met a few writers, just never one whose books I actually liked. Why's he playing computer games when he could be writing?"

"Recreation? Camaraderie? It's a fun way for us to stay in touch. When he's on deadline he gets a lot more scarce."

"I can't believe I didn't know that about you," he said after another pause. "That one of your best friends is an author."

"There's probably a lot we still don't know about each other."

"Well, it seems we like the same books." He laughed. "Who'd have thought? I guess it's yet another thing we have in common."

She made a non-committal sound and went back to her reading.

Several minutes went by before he asked somewhat hesitantly, "Are you mad at me?"

This time she set her e-reader down on the coffee table. "Maybe a little," she admitted.

"I wondered, because you're being unusually quiet today. I'm not always good at telling when women are pissed off. Unless they're yelling. That's a dead giveaway, even for thickheaded males like me."

She smiled in spite of herself. He was usually so confident. She found it endearing that he felt bemused when confronted with feminine anger.

"So, what are you mad about? I fell asleep on you this morning, I know, but I wouldn't have thought..." his voice trailed off.

Did he seriously not know? Maybe he hadn't heard her last night when she'd said "I love you." Twice. He had been deep in an erotic cloud at the moment she'd said it. Had it flown right over his head and under his radar? If so, she certainly wasn't going to repeat it now.

"I think I've told you before that I feel a little overwhelmed by you at times."

Daniel pushed aside his newspaper and rose to pace about the room. "What exactly do you mean by overwhelmed?"

"Just...you're judgmental. And possessive. You've swept into my life like the hurricane that struck on our first night in bed. Hurricane Daniel," she added in a lighter tone.

"Don't you trust me?"

"I trust you. I just...I don't know. I feel as though I'm getting in very deep here, and I'm not sure whether you feel the same way."

He hesitated, then said, "You're all I want, Kate. Ever since I met you, you've been the only woman I think about. It's disconcerting for me, I guess. I don't usually feel this way."

This wasn't exactly "I love you," but it felt good to her nevertheless. She was all he wanted? Since she wasn't entirely sure about the love thing herself, this was good enough for now. In fact, it was terrific! She was giving him a big grin when he added,

"There's one thing I'm still struggling with, though. Well, maybe two things."

Uh oh. There was a "but?"

"Which two things?"

"Well, Arthur, obviously, and the fact that you still love him." He put up a hand as she started to speak. "Which is totally all right. I mean, I get that—he was your first love and your husband, and you lost him suddenly and in a horrible way, so of course you still love him; no doubt you always will. I understand that. I know what it's like to lose someone. It took me years to get over my parents' deaths. I was messed up for a long time."

He had told her that, she recalled. He'd credited his uncle Jon and his partner Cameron with finally helping him sort things out.

"I did the opposite of what you've done, I think," he went on. "It sounds as though you've been self-contained, going on with your life in an orderly way, and letting people like your close friends support you. Me, I was defiant. Mad at the world." He paused for a moment, and then began again almost reluctantly, as if he had to force the words out. "I didn't want help. I didn't even want to think about it. So I screwed around, did some drugs, lived recklessly and made a bunch of new friends who were just as wild and out of control as I was. Grief does strange things to you, especially when you refuse to acknowledge the monumental sadness that won't stop clawing at you."

"Yes," she whispered. She was both touched and ashamed. This was difficult for him. She remembered the deep sorrow in his eyes on the day he had told her about his parents. Sadness was not an emotion that Daniel was comfortable expressing, but that didn't mean he didn't feel it. She had thought he didn't understand her grief, but of course he must know what she'd been through. How terrible it must have been for a young boy to lose first his dad, and then, only four years later, his mom. He'd been a teenager when he'd been left alone in the world.

"In earlier centuries," he said, "it wasn't unusual for a parent, a friend, a sibling, or a spouse to die young. But today that rarely happens."

She nodded agreement. "Medical advances and healthier lifestyles have pushed death back. The Grim Reaper's no longer staring us in the face all the time."

"Exactly. Other people our age may have been separated from a parent or a partner through divorce, but not usually by death."

"So if we're unlucky enough to lose someone, it seems harder, because we don't have the community support and understanding that earlier generations would have had."

He nodded and she smiled at him. It was almost as though they were finishing each other's sentences.

"So I get it, Kate. I really do. But it's still tough for me to know he's always in your mind."

"But he's not. Lately he's hardly been in my mind at all. That's what I was trying to tell you—"

He put up a hand again, interrupting her. "And that's not all," he said in a determined tone, as if intent upon airing all his grievances.

"Right. You said there were two things bothering you. I can guess the other. My mother?"

He sat down beside her on the sofa. "Yes. Well. Not your mother, precisely, since I haven't even met her, but people like her. Mediums. Ghost whisperers. Trance channelers. Psychics." He paused briefly, and then added, "You see, there's something I haven't told you."

She waited, worried. He looked so grim. This was turning into the most serious and honest talk they had ever had. "I'm listening."

"You asked me again last night why I hate those frauds. Why I can't accept the notion that it's all just a lot of harmless fun. I guess it's time explained about my own experience with a so-called trance channeler."

It hadn't occurred to her that he might have had a personal experience. Why would he ever have consulted a medium? Knowing what she knew about Daniel the Skeptic, it seemed impossible.

"I told you about my father's sudden death," he went on. "How my mother couldn't handle it. She used to talk out loud to him, the way I heard you speak to Arthur that first night. Only she did it constantly. She couldn't accept what had happened; she couldn't let him go."

Fine shivers threaded over Kate's skin as she realized where this was leading.

"She became obsessed with death, and the possibilities of an afterlife. She started going to church a lot more often, but she didn't find the comfort she was seeking there." He stopped, saying nothing more for several seconds.

"Daniel, listen to me. You needn't tell me if this if it's too painful to talk about."

He flashed her an appreciative look, but there was pain gleaming in his eyes. It made him look younger and more vulnerable than she had ever seen him. Usually he was so direct and so self-assured, but he was clearly having a tough time handling his emotions.

"Thanks, but you should know. I mean, it's relevant, isn't it? You have to hear it sometime."

She swallowed, pretty sure that she knew what he was going to say.

He cleared his throat and seemed to harden his resolution. "One day my mother was visited by a friend who was into spiritualism. The 'friend' did a reading on my mother, aided, no doubt, by whatever information she had picked up about her and my dad in advance. It's so easy to get personal info off the web these days, but even back then, the data was starting to become available. The medium convinced my mother that my father was still there, watching over her and taking an interest in her life. She suggested that there might even be a message waiting for her from the so-called Other Side."

There it was, thought Kate. This was why he had such a loathing of spiritualists.

"She began attending readings. Soon she was 'communicating' on a weekly basis with my father. Miraculously, she seemed happier, more alive, as if her newfound belief in life after death had given her the strength to enjoy her own life again.

"Then one day she decided to take me along to the channeling session. I'd been in a couple of fights at school, and apparently my ghostly 'father' thought I needed a good scolding." He paused a moment, his voice bitter. "All sorts of weird things happened, and I was scared out of my wits. When a face vaguely resembling my father's materialized out of the darkness over the medium's shoulder, I was so shocked that I tipped my chair over backward. Purely by accident, I tripped the lever that opened the wall panel where the projector was concealed. My 'father' disappeared, and the medium was so rattled that she fell out of her fake trance and started screaming obscenities at me."

Kate silently soothed him, surprised at the amount of resentment she felt toward the fake medium. It was people like that who gave her mother's profession a bad name. Iris would have been angry, too.

"We went back there the next day with my uncle Jon, the attorney. He forced the woman to admit she had been conning my mother for months. There had been no 'messages' from my dad. It was all a hoax."

"That must have been terrible, for both you and your mother. I'm so sorry."

He nodded. He was speaking in a matter-of-fact tone now, his emotions well leashed. But his blue eyes still burned with remembered grief. "Mom went into a deep depression that lasted for months. She was never really the same afterward. It was as if everything vivid and alive had been sucked out of her. She was diagnosed with stage four cancer about a year later." One of his hands was tightly clasping hers; the other clutched the arm of the sofa. "That's why I've always hated spiritualists."

"No one could blame you," she said softly.

A minute went by, then two. Daniel's hand moved, his fingers interlacing with hers. "When I met you I thought you were one of them, and it tore me apart because I knew I wanted you. I knew I had to have you."

"And I taunted you by letting you believe it." She hated the thought that what she'd regarded as her harmless teasing during those early days had caused him pain. "I shouldn't have done that. I'm sorry, Daniel. Please forgive me."

He looked into her eyes, and the world narrowed to just the two of them. He moved his thumb, gently wiping away some dampness at the corner of her eyes. "Look at you. You're tender-hearted as hell, you know that? I'll bet you cry buckets over sad books and movies."

She smiled.

His expression softened, and his own tenderheartedness showed clearly in his eyes. "I felt so vulnerable then. I was just a kid, and I've grown a thicker skin over the years. But I don't like remembering how it felt to be so confused and helpless and alone. Does that make sense?'

She nodded. "Totally." Every time he confronted the fact that her mother was a medium, he was forced to confront a particular-ly tragic and devastating time in his childhood. No wonder he got so hostile when the subject came up.

He had leaned back against the sofa cushions and shut his eyes. She really ought to leave it at that, she knew, but there was some-thing else she had to know.

"The medium, Daniel," she said hesitantly.

"What about her?"

"It wasn't my mother, right? I mean, it couldn't have been. My mother never used tricks or projectors. She never willfully deceived anyone or abused her gift."

He frowned. "Your mother's a fake like all the rest. But, no, she wasn't the one. Her name was Myra Kelley."

She remembered the name, of course. Myra Kelley had been the fake medium he had viciously exposed on one of his earlier programs.

Let my enemies beware...

"I dealt with her," he said with the harshness that was just as much a part of Daniel Haggarty as the tenderness was. "She didn't know when she agreed to come on the show that I was the same kid who had tipped over her projector years before. But I won't really feel satisfied until I roast all the false witches of spiritualism."

Including your mother. He didn't say it, but Kate was sure that's what he was thinking.

CHAPTER FOURTEEN

"I keep feeling as if something awful's going to happen," Kate told Graham backstage on the night of the official opening of *Macbeth*.

"Stop whining, girl. It's Opening Night Fright."

"It doesn't feel like that. It feels like something else. It feels as though there's a shadow gathering around me."

"Yeah, yeah, tell me about it." Graham was unsympathetic, no doubt because he had the Opening Night jitters himself.

Kate always got nervous before a performance, but it usually waned as soon as the play started. Tonight, though, the feeling persisted even after she had successfully completed her first scene.

She suspected that this was because things had been a little strange with Daniel. After their heart-to-heart talk a few days before, she had expected them to grow closer. But it felt instead as if he had backed off. They still spent a lot of time together and made passionate love, but he was acting distant. He avoided speaking about anything personal or intimate. He fell asleep right after sex. A new project had come up at work, and once again, he was deeply involved with planning and researching his programs. He bristled every time he encountered Graham, and Graham, in turn, bitched about him far too much in front of her.

Was he freaked out by the degree of closeness they had briefly attained? That could happen with guys, she knew; her girlfriends talked about such things all the time. She was tempted to challenge him on his subtle withdrawal, but she didn't want to push him. Anyway, there was no hurry. Men like Daniel could probably only cope with so much intimacy at a time.

He'd promised to be at the play that night, and she presumed he was in the audience, even though she couldn't see him over the glare of the stage lights.

Everyone in the cast seemed nervous, and the actor who was playing Macbeth had spilled hot coffee on one of his costumes and given himself a slight burn, which had freaked out the more superstitious members of the company. Paul Tiele kept muttering that he must have been out of his mind when he had agreed to direct the unlucky Scottish Play. But the play went off more smoothly than ever, and the audience was warmly enthusiastic. By the time the final curtain fell, Kate's gloom had vanished and she, along with everyone else in the cast, began to share the heady feeling of having successfully accomplished exactly what they'd set out to do.

The cast and their friends, including Daniel, were milling about toasting each other backstage after the performance when Graham called Kate from the backstage door.

"Kate, luv, there's somebody from the audience who wants to congratulate you," he told her. Kate turned, and saw her mother.

"Mom!" she cried, staring at the small, white-haired woman decorously clinging to Graham's arm. Oh, no! Daniel had gone stiff and silent at her side. The confrontation she'd been trying to avoid was upon them.

Blinking in dismay, Kate ran to throw her arms around her mother. "What are you doing here?"

"I came to watch your performance, of course. I didn't want to tell you beforehand, in case it made you nervous."

"But how did you get here?"

"I took a taxi," Iris said proudly, as if taking a taxi were a marvelous feat. For her mother, Kate reflected wryly, it probably was. She lived close by, but she rarely went out alone these days. "You were wonderful, as always, but Kate, really, the spell doesn't go quite like that. You got several of the exhortations wrong."

Kate was conscious of Daniel hovering over them, listening to every word. She laughed nervously. "I said it the way Shakespeare wrote it, Mom; that's what they pay me for. Good heavens, this is such a surprise!" *I wish you'd warned me.* "Come in and say hello to everybody."

Daniel, naturally, was the first to demand an introduction. He bowed in a courtly fashion and took Iris's hand as if he meant to kiss it. "I've been looking forward to meeting you for a long time, Mrs. Carter."

"Really, young man?" Iris looked him over. "You're not a member of the acting company, are you?"

"This is Daniel, Mother. A friend of mine."

Iris smiled a little vacantly as her spooky blue eyes wandered again over Daniel. "Ah, yes, Daniel. Something to do with television, wasn't it?"

"We spoke on the phone," he confirmed. "About doing an interview."

"Oh, yes. Kate told me some rather uncomplimentary things about you, Daniel," Iris said with her usual unblinking honesty. "I must say I'm surprised you and she are still friends."

"We're very close friends as a matter of fact."

Iris's smile grew warmer. "Really? Then perhaps you're the one I've been expecting. You took your time about it, didn't you? My daughter has been alone far too long."

Daniel raised his eyebrows at Kate as he answered, "I intend to see that she's alone no longer."

Iris was beaming now. "Such an authoritative tone." She sighed. "These are the times when I do so wish Kate had a strong father who would stand beside her and demand to know whether or not your intentions are honorable." She paused. "But, of course, you and I know the answer to that, don't we, Daniel?" She peered directly into his eyes as, for a few instants, a battle of wills seemed to flare between them. Then Daniel broke eye contact, darting a glance at Kate. He looked disconcerted.

"Willful and stubborn," Iris chided him. "You guard your mind well, but you are curious, aren't you? The drive to know the truth is stronger than your prejudice. Can you feel yourself changing? Loosening up? Becoming a little more open-minded?"

"Mother..." Kate interrupted. Daniel's face was flushed, and for the first time since she'd known him, Kate saw him at a loss for words. She didn't know whether to laugh or slink away in embarrassment. A few years before, embarrassment would have won out, but recently Kate had stopped feeling so defensive about her mother. Once she had longed for the ordinary sort of mother everybody else had, but now she was proud to be the daughter of such an original.

Still, given Daniel's feelings about psychics, she could see nothing but trouble ahead. Certainly he was the last person she wanted her mother to exercise her powers on. It wouldn't take much to incite him. Poor Iris had no idea what she was up against.

"Don't narrow your devilish eyes at me, young man. I'm far too old to be intimidated in that manner," Iris went on blithely. Smiling, she turned back to Kate. "Good for you, my dear. It's about time you chose the alpha of the pack. You need a man with spirit."

"Don't say anything," Kate whispered to Daniel a few minutes later as they stood together watching Iris chat animatedly with Paul Tiele.

"Who's saying anything?"

"I told you she was, um, different."

"She's different all right." He was still flushed and tense. "She tried some kind of weird mind trick on me."

"Mind trick? How would you even know that? According to you, telepathy of any kind is impossible."

He frowned, but didn't answer directly, saying instead, "She's lucky she wasn't born in an earlier century."

"It's lucky we all weren't. You'd have been the first to demand the witches' execution if you'd lived back then."

"You're probably right. I suppose a TV program like mine is about the closest this society comes to public shaming and execution." His gaze flicked thoughtfully over her mother as he added, "Damn. I wish I had a videographer here tonight. Maybe if I called the studio—"

"No way, Daniel." She touched his arm lightly and said, "We should go."

He ignored this sensible suggestion. "You led me to believe she was foggy-brained and tottering on the brink of the grave."

"What I said was that she was retired and that she didn't do interviews."

"I don't know why you're so protective. It's evident she can fend for herself."

"Look, I'm totally cool with why you feel the way you do, but she's my mom. If you ever so much as point a cell phone camera in her direction, I'll be very angry and upset."

Daniel glared at her for a second before his features slowly relaxed into a smile. "Fine. But don't expect everything to go exactly the way you want it to go. You're with the alpha of the pack now, remember?"

Yeah, that part of her mother's nonsense he'd obviously liked! She had a flashback to the last time he'd gotten really alpha in his lovemaking, and how it had excited her. She remembered the words he'd wrung out of her—words of love, words of commitment. And from him? Nothing.

Maybe she should consider breaking things off with him. (*No!* something inside her cried). Maybe she should turn her back and run before she sank without a trace into the heartless pit he was digging for her soul. The dark lord of the underworld...

"Kate?" His fingers traced over her cheeks. "I'm just teasing you. Are you okay?"

She shook herself. "I'm fine," she said brightly. "Did somebody mention a party?"

Somebody had. Graham was inviting everyone in the cast over to his place for an impromptu celebration. To her dismay, his summons had already been accepted by Iris, who announced happily that she hadn't been to a party in years. Kate hadn't expected this; her mother usually retired early. "Aren't you tired, Mom? Why don't I just take you home?"

"No, no. Dear Graham has a psychic friend he's going to introduce me to. He's already offered me a ride, and I've accepted." She looked at Daniel, who was frowning. "But if you and your young man are tired, my dear, why don't you go along home? Don't think about me. I'm sure I can spend the night at Graham's apartment if it gets too late."

"Of course," Graham said smoothly. He and Kate's mother were old friends, and Kate knew he was fond of Iris. "My guest room is at your disposal." And without allowing Kate to say anything more on the matter, he bundled Iris off to his car.

"I think we should go home," she told Daniel as they got into his Porsche in back of the theater.

"We're going to Graham's party."

His peremptory tone annoyed her. "I thought you couldn't stand Graham."

"Surely you're not going to abandon your mother at this hour of the night."

"My mother understands that I want to be alone with you."

He flashed her a look. "We'll have plenty of time to be alone later."

"Look," she said, exasperated. "I'm sure you don't really want to spend any more time around my psychic mother. Can't we just leave it at that?"

"No. We can't."

"You're hot on her trail, aren't you, witch-hunter? Can't bear to let the quarry out of your sight. Have you ordered a video crew to meet us at Graham's apartment?"

He glowered at her, not answering, following the car in front of them toward Graham's apartment. Kate fumed in silence. He would do whatever the hell he wanted, of course. He always did.

At the party, Kate was so irritated with Daniel that she spent the next half hour chatting with other friends and avoiding him. He didn't seem to notice; he was too busy hanging around her mother.

Kate didn't tune into the general discussion until she heard somebody mention the infamous curse on *Macbeth*. "Maybe Iris can help us get to the bottom of that superstition," Graham suggested. "She knows all about spirits and witches and things."

Uh-oh, thought Kate, noting the way her mother snapped to attention and demanded an explanation. She also noted the devious look Graham directed at Daniel. Graham had made it clear that he resented and distrusted her boyfriend. She wouldn't put it past him to turn his party into a forum on superstition and psychic phenomena just to anger the skeptic among them. She liked Graham, but his delight in causing mischief could be excessive. He didn't always consider the consequences of his actions.

"I've heard that there's an actual witches' spell in Act Four," said Paul Tiele. "One theory has it that the evil spirits called up by the spell must wreak some havoc before they're allowed to return to wherever it is they came from."

"There is a witch's spell in the play," Iris confirmed. "But it's worded incorrectly, so I doubt it would call up any spirits. On the other hand," she went on after pausing for thought, "some of the darker spirits are notorious rascals. Perhaps one of them has an aversion to the incantation used in the play. He may even have been offended by the playwright, either here or in the Other World."

"Offended by the playwright?" Daniel repeated in a low, sarcastic tone. He had edged around the guests and was now standing just behind Kate, his fingers lazily massaging the nape of her neck.

"Shut up."

"My kingdom for a camera crew."

"It would be nice to know exactly what it is that brings down the ill fortune," Paul mused. "This play's got several weeks to run. I'd very much like to avoid disasters."

"Why don't we summon the spirits and ask?" Graham suggested. "We've got a famous medium here, after all. We could hold a séance. How about it, Iris, are you up to it?" he added with a malicious glance at Daniel.

"I could attempt it, of course. One never knows what might happen, though. The spirits do not always come at the beck and call of those of us who are still in the fleshly realm."

"Oh, dear God," said Kate. She glared at Graham, who blithely ignored her. "Really, Mom, don't you think it's much too late at night for that sort of thing? I'm exhausted. Daniel and I were just about to leave."

"Run along, then, dear. I've decided to stay with Graham tonight anyway. I'll talk to you tomorrow."

"Mom!"

Kate felt the light touch of Daniel's fingers on her arm. "Leave her alone. If she wants to do it, let her."

She turned to look at his face, but Daniel's attention was on Iris. She recognized his expression. It was the same one he had worn on the night they first met, when he looked into her eyes and threatened to burn her. "Let's get out of here."

Daniel's eyes were gleaming beneath his thick lashes. "Soon. Not yet."

"Please, Daniel. I want to leave."

"Take my car, then. I'll catch a cab home."

The bad feeling that had been bothering Kate on and off all day returned in full force. The last thing she wanted was a confrontation between her mother and Daniel on this explosive issue.

"You hate this sort of thing. You don't want to witness my mother doing a séance."

"On the contrary." He smiled grimly. "I can think of few things I'd rather witness." And he refused to budge.

While chairs were being arranged in a circle in the living room, Kate tried again. "Please, Daniel, let's go. Graham should never have suggested this. I think he's trying to taunt you. Don't play his game."

"It's your mother's game I'm interested in," he said tightly.

"If you insist on staying, I'm going to wait outside."

But he had apparently changed his mind about her leaving. She felt his fingers closed around her wrist. "Stop pretending this has no connection to you. I want you to stay and see how it plays out."

For a moment, Kate felt a surge of fury toward witch-hunter D. B. Haggarty. But the feeling swiftly changed as she realized that he might want her beside him for some sort of emotional support....the sort that he, big tough alpha male that he was, couldn't admit. Besides, his thumb was rubbing sensuously over the pulse point on her wrist, while his entire attention was on Iris. She doubted he was even conscious of the tiny massage he was giving her or of the shivers of desire it sparked within her.

She was worried and upset, but even so, he could arouse her. She was really hooked. She shared at the fingers that enclosed her wrist like a manacle. Just as she'd feared, she was out of her depth in this relationship. It had been true from the start.

The dark cloud settled over her. Being with him was such an emotional roller coaster—wildly exciting but scary as hell. Arthur had never jerked her around, or tied her insides in knots.

When the séance began, Kate sat as far away from her mother as possible. Daniel took the seat beside her, with Paul Tiele on her other side. Paul was chattering nervously, but Daniel stayed silent, watching the medium's preparations. These were simple enough, Kate was glad to see. Iris Carter did not require a special table, a particular position with respect to doors and windows, or even a completely darkened room.

She sat in a comfortable chair within the circle of guests, closing her eyes and relaxing her thin, birdlike body. She gently requested that they join hands to form a circle, then, without giving further instructions, she retreated into silence.

"What's she doing?" Daniel asked after several minutes had passed uneventfully. "Meditating?"

"Something like that. She's emptying her mind and body so she'll be able to receive whatever messages the spirits wish to send through her."

"Has she got a spirit control who guides the 'dear departed' to her?"

"Yes. His name is Sir Godfrey Vernon. He's an eighteenth-century British squire. A friend of Samuel Johnson's, I believe. He reported once that Sam was delighted to find out there was a life beyond. Apparently his faith wavered greatly during his sojourn on earth."

Daniel muttered something under his breath.

"You insisted on staying, so spare me your scoffing."

Almost immediately thereafter, a convulsion shook Iris's body, and the muscles in her face altered in an eerie fashion, changing her appearance dramatically. One of the women in the circle let out a small cry of alarm, and somebody else shushed her. "Good day to you," said a hollow-sounding male voice from Iris's throat. "For what purpose am I summoned?"

Daniel made another disapproving sound, which Kate endeavored to ignore. She was, as always, more than a little awed at her mother's strange transformation. Far better than Daniel, she was aware that "Sir Godfrey Vernon" knew things that Iris had no way of knowing. He spoke with a polished British accent, using words and idioms that had been current in the 1700s, and he was almost completely ignorant of the conventions of modern life.

Kate had heard theories suggesting that Vernon and other spirit controls like him were actually submerged aspects of the medium's own personality. It was possible, she supposed. She had never known exactly what to make of him.

"Who's going to talk to him?" Paul Tiele hissed. His face was white, and he was holding Kate's other hand nearly hard enough to cut off her circulation. "She's your mother, Kingsley. Say something."

Kate shook her head. There was no way she was going to involve herself in this. She glared at Graham. This had been his clever idea; let him do it.

Graham was looking a little peaked himself. He ran his tongue nervously over his lips and said, "Who are you?"

In a dry voice Vernon identified himself, adding, "And who, might I ask, are you?"

"I'm, uh, Graham Hamilton, an astrologer," declared Graham in an obvious attempt to jump on the psychic bandwagon.

Through Iris, Vernon snorted loudly. "Fiddlesticks! All astrologers are charlatans, the buggers! I' faith, I've no wish to speak with one."

Graham was momentarily speechless, but Kate could feel Daniel chuckling. "Your mother has quite a sense of humor."

"Be quiet." She glared at him.

Instead, Daniel raised his voice. "Will you speak to a man who hates charlatans as much as you do?" he asked the medium. "A rationalist who doesn't accept the existence of ghosts?"

Iris looked in Daniel's direction, and Kate shivered slightly. She would have been willing to swear on the Bible that the intelligence staring out of her mother's eyes bore not the faintest resemblance to sweet, flaky Iris Carter.

"I' faith, why not?" responded Vernon. "Verily enough I was a rationalist myself, in life. What would you ask of me?"

"Ask him about the play," Paul Tiele prompted.

"I myself would ask you for details about the so-called Other Side, but—"

"I' truth, I am not at liberty to divulge them," interrupted Vernon.

"I suspected as much," said Daniel. "The other people present are curious about a supposed curse on the play *Macbeth* and wish to contact someone who can set their minds at ease."

"You're not supposed to name the play," Tiele complained. "It calls down the curse."

"Did you hear that, Sir Godfrey? You address a group of actors who are shaken with superstitious fear."

Iris's head turned as Vernon examined the faces of those present. "Scurvy lot," he said dismissively. "Never cared for actors myself. Although Davy Garrick, now, there's as fine a tragedian as ever walked the boards. Shall I see if I can locate Davy and ask him if he ever feared such a curse?"

"I thought we might ask old Will Shakespeare himself if he ever willfully offended any demons," Daniel suggested so sarcastically that Paul Tiele was moved to object.

"If you're not going to take this seriously, Haggarty, why don't you leave the circle?"

"Now, Shakespeare, there's a rollicking fine fellow," said Sir Godfrey Vernon. "Never read 'im myself, o' course, but Johnson says he's a remarkable dramatist, with some flaws, of course. I hear he wrote some right bloody tragedies and some foot-pounding comic romances. As to demons, though—" He stopped abruptly, and Iris's head fell forward. Kate tensed—these sessions were a strain on her mother, who was no longer young and strong. But almost immediately, Iris raised her head again, and Vernon said in a different tone, "Wait. There's someone here. There's... i' faith, I cannot tell exactly. Aye. A most determined young man. 'Ey? What's that you say?" Vernon looked inward, speaking not to the group, it seemed, but to someone—or something—they could not see. "Wait. I will inquire. A young man is here," he said, addressing Daniel again. "Seeking his wife. He has something to tell her. Fretting about it, too. Is there a young woman present? A widow?"

Kate cleared her throat, telling herself that her mother must be in a genuine trance, or how could she ask such a question? Daniel's fingers were crushing the bones in her hand. She couldn't tell if he was trying to be reassuring or if he was about to erupt.

"D'you mean me, Sir Godfrey?" she asked. "Have you forgotten me? There was a time when you and I were pretty good friends."

But the spirit was apparently immune to sarcasm. "Are you the widow? Good. I have a message for you from"—there was a pause; then the medium continued with slight questioning intonation—"from King Arthur."

Somebody giggled. Daniel distinctly muttered a curse, and somebody said, "Ssh!" Kate felt her lover's body shift as if he were going to jump up and put an end to this, so she resolutely kicked him in the shin. "It's dangerous to the medium to interrupt in the middle of a sitting," she whispered. "You asked for this; now accept the consequences."

He was tense as a board, but he didn't interrupt. Kate turned back to Sir Godfrey. "King Arthur?" Was her mother entering another of her periodic Merlin the Druidic priest phases? "Are you sure that's his name?"

There was another long pause. "King Arthur, aye. Or Arthur King. Are you acquainted with such a man?"

"I might be," Kate ordered herself to stay calm. It's not really Arthur, she told herself. It's just my mother, doing something she's done a thousand times before.

"It's your husband," the control rasped. "He cannot stay. He must go back. He only wants to say... what? I cannot hear you, lad. What? Danger?" There was a short silence, and Kate tried to ignore the way her heart was throbbing. "He says someone's in danger of... what? The fall? Falling?"

"Am I in danger of falling?" Kate asked, bewildered. On stage, she wondered? Or was the warning metaphorical?

Sir Godfrey's voice grew louder, clearer: "Beware the fall. Nothing will be the same after the life-changing fall." He stopped for a moment, before adding, "Beware the fire."

"This is positively Biblical," Daniel snarked.

"Both a fall and a fire?" Kate's mouth was dry.

"The fire will burn you," the hollow voice continued, more loudly now. "Do not try to salvage your heart from the ashes. Let it go."

Kate shivered and withdrew her hand from Daniel's. Since the night she had met him, the image of fire had symbolized Daniel and the passion between them. "Is that all?" she asked. Daniel seized her hand again, holding it fiercely in a grip she could not break. His palm was hot and moist—a telltale signal of his agitation.

"Goodbye, he says. He's slipping away. He says goodbye, and he's repeating the word believe."

"Dear God," Kate said, her voice a mere wisp of sound. Her body began quivering slightly. She wrenched her hand from Daniel's and broke the circle. Then she rose from her chair and ran from the room as if she had indeed seen a ghost.

CHAPTER FIFTEEN

"I'm all right."

It was five minutes later, and Kate stood shivering in the circle of Daniel's arm as he zipped her into her jacket. She had successfully fought back tears, but more than anything else in the world she longed for the privacy of her own home, where she could bury her face in her pillow and try to make sense out of what had just happened.

"Are you sure, babe?" Daniel's hands were firm but gentle as he drew her into a warm, comforting embrace. He was quivering even more than she was, though, and she knew that for all his solicitude he was beside himself with rage. So far, thank goodness, he'd left her mother alone, taking out his anger on a subdued-looking Graham. Snarling obscenities, he had flung the other guests' coats all over the bedroom floor until he found Kate's, then ushered her toward the door. On the way out, he had said to Graham, "I hope you're happy now, you spiteful little worm. It was me you wanted to get with this masquerade, but it's her you've hurt."

Having followed them to the foyer, Graham now protested, "It never occurred to me that anything like this would happen. How did I know that Iris would—that she could—that—" He paused, shaking his head. "I don't believe in spirits," he said, not sounding very convincing.

"Spirits, my ass! Call up the grieving widow's husband? It's the oldest trick known to these charlatans. But it works, and you know why? Because the widow wants to believe it." Kate felt Daniel's arm tighten around her shoulders. "She insists on believing it even when her own common sense tells her she's been the victim of a sadistic trick. Get out of my way. And keep Iris Carter away from me. It never crossed my mind that a mother would do something like this to her own daughter."

Kate was barely listening. "Where's my mother now?" she asked, craning her neck to look back into the apartment. "Is she all right?"

"She's resting," said Graham. "She doesn't seem to remember anything that happened."

"I'll bet," Daniel said nastily. "You can damn well keep the freak here, Hamilton. If I get my hands on her, I might be tempted to send her to join her spirit friends."

"Oh, for godsake, Daniel." If Kate was certain of anything, it was that her mother hadn't been responsible for what had just happened. "Chill. I'm not leaving without seeing for myself that she's okay."

Daniel's arm tightened around her. "We're leaving. Right now." He was guiding her toward the elevator.

"Don't worry," Graham assured Kate as she sought his eyes in concern for her mother. "Iris is fine; she'll be with me."

Kate had to be satisfied with this, because Daniel was relentless about getting her out of the building without further argument.

In the car, she huddled in her seat, unable to get warm despite the blasting heater. "How're you doing?" Daniel asked, moving his hand from the gearshift to squeeze hers.

She shook her head numbly; then, at his worried glance, she forced herself to speak. "I'm fine. I got a bit of a shock, that's all. I shouldn't have freaked like that. I'm sorry."

"Don't be." His voice was grim. "Be angry, not sorry."

She didn't reply. They were almost at her street. She couldn't get the eerie voice of Iris's spirit control out of her head. "Beware the fall. Beware the fire. Believe. Believe." She shivered again and pressed her hands together. Oh, Arthur. She could feel tears threatening, but she grimly held them back.

Daniel parked the car and was around to open her door before her stiff hands could do more than fumble with the handle. He walked her to the front porch, took her purse from her, and rummaged in it for her key. He unlocked the door and conducted her inside. Within five minutes, there was a fire in the fireplace and a small glass of brandy in her hand.

Vaguely she wondered why he was making them comfortable here instead of hustling her off to his place. He had a drink, too, she noticed; he took a large swallow as he gulped down two small capsules she recognized as his allergy pills. He was obviously planning to stay.

They didn't speak. Kate nestled against Daniel, her face against the wool of his sweater, her feet tucked up under her as she sat on the sofa, staring into the fire. She was grateful for his presence, and for his silence. He seemed to sense that she couldn't talk about it yet. He didn't question her; he was simply there for her, strong, warm, and solid. He could be sensitive when he really tried.

She stroked his hand gently, knowing that he, too, must have been upset by the séance. It must have reminded him of his mother's sessions with the fake medium. How could she explain to him, though, that what had happened tonight was very different from that charade? There was nothing fake about Iris Carter, and if Kate had had any doubts about her mother's ability to communicate with the Other Side, those doubts had been banished tonight.

At some point, her eyelids began to feel heavy and her thoughts began to scatter. Daniel stroked her hair. His lips pressed undemandingly against the top of her head. Sleepily she listened to the steady, almost hypnotic rhythm of his heart as she sank more deeply into his arms.

* * *

She woke up in her own bed, naked and sweating with fear. She was falling. She hit the ground hard and felt pain everywhere. There were sirens and the mumbling sounds of people talking somewhere near her, urgently. She thought she could hear Jeff's voice, crying out in pain. There was a smell she recognized from her stay in the hospital, an acrid antiseptic smell. And Arthur was holding up a heart-shaped frame containing a wedding picture of her with Daniel, but it was burning in his hands. The silver in the frame glowed and began to melt over Arthur's fingers, which twisted and turned black.

"Ssh, babe. It's okay." Daniel's voice was thick with sleep but firm in its reassurance. He curled around her body, his own warm naked limbs surrounding her like a sensual cocoon. She moaned and rolled over onto her back, pulling him down onto her, cradling him between her thighs. Her brain was foggy; she felt scared, and then, in a bewildering flash of emotion, aroused. She searched for his mouth in the darkness.

"I need you," she whispered. It was true. She needed him so much. "Love me."

She thought she heard a faint sigh just before his lips closed over hers. Pleasure? Relief? She drank in the warmth of his mouth, sucking on his tongue, nipping his lower lip with her teeth. Between her legs she felt him spring to life. His eager response heightened her excitement, and she twisted and arched and tried to draw him inside her.

"You can't be ready so quickly." His hands moved gently on her breasts, drawing out the nipples and rolling them between finger and thumb. "Let me hold you for a while, my love."

But she was moving her body in a fever of restless agony, needing to affirm her existence—and his—in the most elemental way. "Now, please," she insisted. "Just love me!"

He must have heard the desperation in her voice, because he didn't make her wait. She heard him fumbling with a condom, and then he joined their bodies in a long, slow stroke while she writhed beneath him. Her nails raked the hard muscles in his back as they moved.

"Faster," she whispered, beginning to pant. Her skin was slick, burning. "Harder, Daniel, harder."

He groaned and did what she wanted, but before long, she knew it wasn't going to work for her. Instead of concentrating on her own feelings, she seemed to float above the bed, watching the two embracing bodies straining there, snatching at pleasure in a world of loneliness and pain. But pleasure wasn't enough, not for her. She needed something else. Something like what she'd had with her husband. She needed more.

The truth struck home to her—she had fallen in love with Daniel. Wild and passionate though he was, controlling and primitive and oh-so-different from Arthur, she loved him. For he was also gentle, thoughtful, and compassionate; he had proved that tonight. Furious though he had been with her mother and Graham, his first concern had been for her.

He cared for her, of that there could be no doubt. But how long would it last? He was here now, and that was good. But how would she cope when she lost him, when his too-hot fire burned itself out? He didn't love her in the way she had begun to love him. He would leave her, just as irrevocably as Arthur did.

"Beware the fire. Do not try to salvage your heart from the ashes." Somewhere on the Other Side, Arthur was watching out for her, warning her against further involvement with Daniel, the man of fire, the man who had once threatened to burn her. The man who had burned her already.

"Kate!" Daniel's voice was a hoarse gasp. He thrust one trembling hand into her hair, never ceasing the rhythm she'd demanded, the rhythm he now couldn't control. "Come with me."

It was an order she couldn't obey. Instead, she held him tighter and found his mouth in an attempt to heighten his pleasure as he fell off the world without her. But his body shook afterward, and she knew his pleasure was bittersweet.

"I'm sorry," she said when his breathing had finally returned to normal. She was still shaken by all the powerful emotions of the night. So much had happened. So many things realized, so many things confronted. "I lost my concentration."

He rolled over, pulling her to nestle on his shoulder. "I should have trusted my instincts. All I meant to do tonight was hold you and comfort you."

She ran her palm over his sweat-damp chest. She loved the feel of his smooth, strong muscles. "Why here? Why didn't you take me to your house?"

"You know the answer to that. I wanted you here, where he had you. King Arthur." He laughed without mirth. "He'd have to be king of something to exert such power from beyond the grave." His hand moved on her, cupping a breast almost fiercely. "Well, I defy him to disturb us in bed." He raised himself up on one elbow, his high-cheekboned face dark with feeling. "You're with me now, Kate. You're mine. You know that, don't you?"

Kate nodded, but turned her face away. She bit her lip until it hurt. She understood. Daniel was a sensual man. Sex was important to him. He was possessive, but the foundation of his possessiveness was not love; it was primal male need. She was his woman—for now. So he hated Arthur.

"Why I didn't see it coming, I can't imagine. A widow, a séance. I should have known what would happen. My only excuse is that I couldn't believe your own mother would do such a thing. That she would actually sink to tricking you that way."

"It wasn't a trick."

"Don't say that." With one finger he turned her face back to his, looking angrily down into her eyes. "It was a shock to you, I understand that. But you're much too intelligent to let yourself be sucked into that particular never-never land. Of course it was a trick. When you can think about it rationally, you'll realize."

She shook her head. "No. You're wrong. I know the truth for the first time in my life. Sir Godfrey Vernon is real. He has to be."

"What the hell do you mean?"

"He told me to believe. That was a code word between Arthur and me. We agreed long ago that whichever one of us died first should signal the other, if possible, from the Other Side by using the word 'believe.' Harry Houdini and his wife made the same pact. Like you, Houdini declared that all mediums were fakes, but if there were any way to escape from death with a message, he, the great escape artist, would do it."

"I know the story," Daniel interrupted. "He and his wife devised a private code and defied any medium to crack it. After he died lots of them tried, but they all failed. Nobody ever collected the ten-thousand-dollar reward."

"That's right. The word 'believe' was supposed to have been part of their encoded message. In honor of Houdini, Arthur and I also used it. My mother never knew. You're the first person I've ever told." Her eyes looked into the distance as she added, "So you see, it must be true: It really was Arthur who spoke to me tonight."

There was a chilling silence; then Daniel sat up in bed and switched on the light. Kate was startled by the anger in his eyes.

"Daniel?" she whispered as he rose from the bed, stalked over to the chair on the other side of the room, and grabbed his clothes. She ventured a look at the clock. It was three-thirty in the morning.

"What are you doing?"

"I'm leaving." He was throwing on his clothes, quickly and haphazardly. Her heart twisted inside her. Even if he didn't love her, she needed him beside her. Tonight of all nights, she needed him. "Daniel. Don't go. Please."

Dressed in jeans and an unbuttoned shirt, he turned to her, his body moving in jerks. There was a flush of anger on his cheekbones now, and his fingers clenched and unclenched at his sides.

"I'm sorry, but everybody has limits, and I've just reached mine. I warned you in the beginning. I told you I wouldn't compete for your attention with a fucking ghost."

"You're not—" she began, then stopped. She wanted to explain, but how could she? The beliefs they held about the world were very different. She wanted to tell him that it didn't matter whether or not Arthur had really spoken to her tonight. If anything, Arthur's presence on the Other Side brought it home to her with utter finality that he was dead. He was gone forever, and he would not be coming back. She had known that of course, she had known it. But it hadn't seemed entirely real to her until tonight. It had taken a ghost to make her believe that her husband was gone forever. He had told her goodbye.

But she, Kate, she was still here; she was alive. And she was in love with a vibrant, living, breathing man. She was in love with Daniel.

"I've tried to be patient," he thundered on, oblivious. "I've done my best to be understanding. I've even left your hellcat mother alone."

She could hear the rustle of cloth as he finished dressing. "What happened tonight was fraud, pure and simple and you're a naive little fool to think otherwise. Arthur could have told your mother your precious code word before he died, or you could have told her yourself—after the car accident, perhaps, when you were in shock. Maybe you raved it to some doctor or nurse, for godsake—yes, that's probably exactly what happened. You told somebody in the hospital, and that somebody informed your mother."

"You're wrong. I never told a soul."

"No, Kate, you're the one who's wrong about this. You woke up moaning that word on the first night we were together. Remember? 'Arthur told me to believe,' you announced. Some secret! Your mother's probably known it for years."

Flustered, she realized he was correct. But she still couldn't accept his primary contention. "Even if she knew, my mother would never deliberately hurt me in such a manner. She may not be the most conventional mother in the world, but she loves me. She would never try to trick me."

"No? Parents have been known to do worse things to their kids. She's been tricking people all her life. It's certainly clear where your acting talent comes from. 'Sir Godfrey Vernon' is a masterpiece, I admit. For a few moments there she nearly had me convinced."

He paced once across the room, and then came back to tower over her. "Use your brain, Kate. Your mother's getting old; she's probably afraid her so-called powers might fail her. Her own daughter has never totally believed in her abilities, and now, to make matters worse, you've gotten yourself involved with a professional skeptic—me. She's running scared."

"That's the most absurd thing I've ever heard. She's not afraid of you. She doesn't have the sense to be afraid of you."

"Absurd, my ass. Look at the results: You're on the hook, now, aren't you? You think she produced Arthur, raised him from the dead. A miracle: Hocus-pocus, you have your husband back."

"No. That's not the way it is."

"I've watched this process, Kate," he said roughly, forcing his hand through her hair and lifting her face up to his. "I saw my mother go through it, and I've researched it in countless other cases. It takes no psychic ability to predict what will happen next: You'll want to talk to Arthur again. You'll want to hear all about how it feels to be dead. You'll turn away from living because you'll be obsessed with the blasted world to come."

"That's not true. You don't understand." Her shoulders shook. His mocking words were hurting her deeply, but he wouldn't stop.

"Don't I? She's got you now. You're her heir." His fingers twisted into her long brown hair as he added, "She's going to take you and turn you into the witch I thought you were the night we met."

Kate felt sudden fury storm through her, and she fought to free herself. "Let go of me."

He released her immediately and bent to put on his shoes. Then he grabbed his jacket and headed for the door. At the threshold he stopped. "You're a beautiful, sensual woman, Kate Kingsley. It's criminal that you should choose to wall yourself up in a tomb."

"You don't even know how I really feel, what I'm really thinking—"

"No?" His glare was merciless. "I know you're not ready for a real flesh-and-blood relationship with a living man. Maybe you'll never be ready. Maybe you'll hang on to your dear, precious, perfect King Arthur for the rest of your life."

"Maybe I will," she retorted, goaded.

"Then I'm getting out, now, before I get hurt."

"Before you get hurt?" It was just as she had thought. He desired her, but he didn't love her. He could still turn around and walk out.

"Before I get hurt," he repeated bitterly. "Before you suck my soul out, witch, and bear me down with you to hell."

"That's what you're doing to me!"

But he had already left her, slamming the bedroom door so hard behind him that the house seemed to rock on its foundations.

Moments later, she heard the roar of his Porsche as he skidded away into the night.

CHAPTER SIXTEEN

Early the next morning, Kate was in the gym at the Cambridge Fitness Center, working out with weights. She counted aloud as she felt her sinews stretch and burn, burn and stretch. She worked steadily, almost grimly, using every variation she knew, until the sweat poured off her and her mind was blank.

Afterward she swam, her arms cleanly stroking through the water, her legs kicking hard and rhythmically. Twenty laps, thirty. She pushed herself, not stopping at the turns, not slowing her pace, but her body made no real protest. She was accustomed to the routine.

Since her childhood, Kate had loved to swim. In the pool, she didn't have to think. All she knew was the silky sensation of the water gliding over her slim, fit body and the sound of her heartbeat pounding in her chest.

When she heaved herself out of the pool after forty swift laps, her legs vibrated faintly, making it difficult to walk normally. To this, too, she was accustomed. She ducked into a hot shower, letting the needlelike spray soothe her body. Gradually she felt her heart slow, her muscles unkink, and her brain begin to work again.

Daniel, she thought, as she soaped her naked body. Her hands moved almost roughly over all the places he loved to touch. Daniel, she thought again as she toweled off and dressed, covered the body he desired but did not love in a pair of old jeans and a faded sweatshirt. In front of the full-length locker-room mirror, she dried her thick hair, dragging her brush through it, stroking it until it crackled and shone.

When she finished she automatically applied a little lip-gloss and smoothed her eyebrows into perfect arches, then stood back, almost curiously, to look at herself. Her hair was a rich dark curtain framing her oval face, bouncing and curling luxuriously against her shoulders. Her cheeks were flushed with health and exercise, and her green eyes were dark and huge.

Looking farther down, she noted that her body was fit and straight and strong. Despite everything she'd gone through—a dead husband coming back from the grave, a lover abandoning her—she looked as if she were still capable of taking on the world.

On a wild impulse, Kate tossed her head and laughed out loud. The sound rang out, bouncing off the locker-room walls, and she cast a quick look around to see if anyone was there to hear her and wonder if she was nuts. But it was early, and the place was apparently deserted. She giggled again at the thought of whooping it up alone in a locker room. She should be moping around weeping, but instead she was laughing. To hell with Daniel!

Then she was angry, and it felt terrific. She planted her fists on her hips in front of the mirror and stamped her feet. She threw her head back, whipping her hair around her shoulders, and then delivered a few short jabbing punches into the air. She moved across the room, kicking out first with one leg, then the other. She took an imaginary rapier in her hand and fenced with an invisible opponent. This reminded her of Jeff, who was seriously into fencing. It had been too long since she'd spent any quality time with her college friends. Toying with her imaginary opponent for a while, she moved in for the kill with a furious lunge. "Gotcha, you son of a bitch!" she cried. "Take that!"

"Hey, there, you all right?" a voice inquired.

Kate swung around to see a brown-haired woman whom she recognized as one of the other regulars at the gym. She was dressed in sweats and carrying a gym bag. Kate grinned at her, unembarrassed. They had chatted a few times while working out. Her name, if Kate remembered correctly, was Philippa, and she also lived nearby. "Just getting my aggressions out."

The other woman nodded understandingly. "Are you into fencing?"

"Not really. I have a friend who is, though."

"I used to fence," the woman said. "Competitions, even. It's been awhile since I've had time for it. Watching you reminded me that I miss it." Her eyes looked a little dreamy. "You know how it is when you're exercising hard and you go that place where everything's smooth and easy? Out of this world, almost." She shook her head and laughed. "Fencing takes me there, for some reason. No wonder I miss it!"

"I should introduce you to my friend Jeff. He says the same thing, and he's always complaining about not having a partner to fence with."

Philippa grinned. "As long as he's not the same guy who's got you all boiling mad."

"Nah, that's somebody else. You know the type. He wants my soul, but all he gives in return is his body."

"Isn't that just like a man."

"So what do I do?"

Philippa tilted her head to one side, considering. "How's this body he's offering? Nice?"

"Mmm. Very."

She looked deep into Kate's eyes, and then shook her head. "Dump him. There're plenty of nice bodies around. It's the beautiful souls that are rare."

Kate pondered Philippa's advice all the way home, getting angrier with each step she took. It occurred to her that she'd been down on herself since the beginning of her relationship with Daniel, believing herself not sophisticated enough, not passionate enough, not good enough for him. What a crock of bull, she told herself now.

So what if Daniel was attractive and sexy? So was she. So what if he could have any woman he wanted? How many of them were as sexy and smart, as good-natured, and as much fun to be with as she was? How many other women did he know who could come bouncing back after losing a beloved husband at a young age and be willing to give their heart again? It was difficult for him to make a commitment, was it? Well, to hell with him! If it was so damn difficult for him to love her, he was the loser, he the fool.

By the time Kate reached her own street, she had talked herself into a militantly good mood. But when she saw a distant figure sitting on the wicker bench on her front porch, her heart turned over. Had he come back to her?

When she got closer, however, she realized that the person on the porch was not Daniel, but her mother. Oh, heavens, her mother! She'd left her at Graham's last night and forgotten all about her this morning.

As Kate bounded up the porch stairs, Iris rose and opened her arms. "My dear," she said, hugging her. "I heard what happened. I'm so sorry. I knew it was an unstable period for you. I should have thought more carefully before going ahead with the sitting."

"I'm good," Kate assured her. She urged her mother inside and took her coat. "How long have you been waiting? I shouldn't have left you at Graham's. Were you okay there for the night?"

"I just got here a few minutes ago, dear. And Graham and I are old friends. We had a lovely chat over breakfast this morning. He's worried about you, you know."

"I know. Poor Graham."

"I sometimes wondered if he might be the one you would turn to when you finally stopped mourning Arthur. But Daniel is much more suitable. Where is he, anyway?"

"He's gone, Mother. He left me."

"Left you?"

"He walked out." She drew a deep breath. "He doesn't like competing with a ghost."

"Oh, dear," said Iris.

"He wasn't my type anyway. I suspected it from the start. He's a bad-tempered, thick-headed, arrogant know-it-all, and I never want to see him again."

Her mother's pale blue eyes regarded her in silence. Kate sensed immediately that Iris knew every word she'd just uttered was untrue. Oh, Daniel, she thought in misery. Couldn't you have given it just a little more time?

Her mother's fingers gently touched her cheek. "Don't worry. He'll be back."

"Is that a psychic prediction or a fond mother's reassurance?"

Iris smiled faintly. "A little of both, I think. Come into the kitchen, my dear. Let me fix you a nice cup of tea."

"I have only regular tea, you know. No exotic herbs and spices."

"That's quite all right."

A few minutes later, as she poured a cup of strong, scalding tea for Kate, Iris remarked, "We could brew him a love potion, of course, if you could just get him over here..."

"Mother!"

"I'm serious. There are certain herbs, you know, that—"

"I'm not in the mood for any more witchcraft today, please. Last night was bad enough."

There was a short silence. Her mother was absently patting Chester, who had crawled up into her lap and was purring loudly. Chester adored her mother, and missed her, no doubt. "What exactly did Arthur say?" Iris asked.

Kate put her head in her hands. "Daniel is adamant that Arthur said nothing at all. He insists that it was nothing more than a trick, and he's appalled that a mother could do something like that to her child."

"Do you believe him?"

"I don't know what to believe." Then, to counter the faintly hurt look that crossed Iris's face, she quickly added, "I know you would never purposely deceive anyone. But I can't help wondering what really happens to you when you go into a trance. Maybe Sir Godfrey Vernon is simply a creation of your unconscious mind. And maybe the things you know come to you telepathically rather than from some mysterious spirit who survives beyond the grave."

"There is uncertainty in all things," her mother said quietly. "I have often doubted the source of my power."

Kate was astonished. "You have?"

"Of course. Do you think I've never read the various scientific 'explanations' of what it is to be a medium? Do you imagine I've always accepted my lot without a murmur of protest? There was a time when I hated and fought my destiny. When I was about your age I wanted nothing more in life than to be normal, ordinary, and as free of psychic power as everybody else." She set Chester down on the floor and took her daughter's hands in hers. "But there are some things you can't change, darling, and it only breaks your heart and health to try. I can't change the fact that I see, hear, and know things that other people cannot see, hear, and know. And you can't change the fact that your husband is dead and that you're falling in love with another man."

Kate squeezed her mother's hands. "I know," she said softly.

"Nobody can verify what happens after death," her mother added. "Life is the only thing we're sure of. You have to love life, Kate."

"I've always believed that. I'm not mourning Arthur anymore."

"Aren't you, dear?"

The way her mother asked the question surprised Kate. What did she mean? Hadn't she proved she was finally over Arthur? She had spent the past few weeks obsessed with Daniel.

"I'm not sure that your new young man understands that, if it's true," her mother went on. "You have been in mourning for a very long time."

"I know I have. But I loved Arthur, Mom. He and I had known each other since we were little. He was always there, at my side. It's been really, really hard to face my life without him."

"I know that. But it really is time for you to move on."

"I am moving on. Or at least, I was moving on until Daniel flew into a rage and left me."

"It can't be easy for him, trying to forge a relationship with a woman who keeps looking back to her past."

Kate felt herself stiffen. Unless she was misinterpreting what she was hearing, her mother was doing something she rarely did:

she was criticizing her. Feeling defensive, she shot back, "I wasn't the one who called up my dead husband in front of Daniel."

"I know, sweetheart. Of course you weren't."

"Anyway, it's gotten pretty obvious that I'm not meant to be with Daniel. Arthur—if it was Arthur—was warning me against him last night."

Iris seemed puzzled. "Are you certain of that?"

"Pretty certain. 'Beware the fire.' Daniel is the fire. I've always thought of him that way, and you know the spirits always speak metaphorically. Besides, his middle name is Blaze."

Her mother shot her a somewhat arch look. "Is it indeed? Blaze." She seemed to mull this over for a bit before continuing, "It's a puzzle sometimes, what the spirits really mean. So don't presume too much. Even if that was Arthur's spirit who spoke to you last night, the dead don't know everything. In fact, they usually know disappointing little about this world."

Kate laughed shortly. That was certainly true. She couldn't remember ever getting good advice from a dead person, and she had met quite a few.

"They've moved on to a different reality," her mother went on, "They're no longer connected with what's happening to us here in the living world. The 'fire' might refer to something else entirely."

"Well, whatever it means, Daniel's gone, and he's not likely to come back. He doesn't love me, and he no longer wants to have anything to do with a freak who talks to ghosts. He hated that from the start." She dropped her mother's hands to rise and pace about the kitchen. "I wouldn't put it past him to come crusading against you now," she went on. "I was the only thing preventing him. He's been at me about interviewing you ever since I met him.

He wants to put you on *Facts and Fantasies* and make a laugh-ingstock out of you."

"Really?" Iris's eyes were speculative. "I still think it might be quite an interesting experience to be on YouTube."

Oh, dear God, thought Kate. Before Daniel had appeared, she was quite certain her mother had never even heard of YouTube. She spent the next fifteen minutes explaining to her mother ex-actly what sort of webcast D. B. Haggarty had in mind. And even then, she wasn't entirely sure she had sufficiently terrified Iris Carter.

CHAPTER SEVENTEEN

For the next week, Kate threw herself into her role at the theater with extraordinary passion. On stage she could forget herself. In the process of becoming somebody else, she could blank out her growing feelings of anger and loss. But as each day and each long, lonely night passed by, it became more difficult to maintain her balance in the face of Daniel's desertion.

Secretly she expected him to relent and call her. Surely his hot temper had cooled off by now. Didn't he care enough about her to call and ask if she was all right? Or at least to send a text? Wasn't he curious? Wasn't his lust for her on the rise again? Or had he already replaced her with a new sexual partner?

When the phone chimed early in the morning, nine days after the play's opening night, Kate's first thought was that Daniel was calling her at last. Still half asleep, she put the phone to her ear without checking to see who was calling. Her uncaffeinated eyes weren't working too well yet.

"Hello?"

"Kate, it's Stephen."

Stephen? Why was her old college friend phoning her at seven a.m.? That couldn't be good. She came more alert. His voice sounded odd. "Stephen? Is something wrong?"

"I don't want you to worry, but Jeff had an accident yesterday. He's in the hospital, but he's going to be fine."

"Oh my god, Stephen." Her heart had immediately gone into overdrive. "What kind of accident? How badly is he hurt? What happened?" Not Jeff, not Jeff. Ever since the accident that had killed Arthur, she had known how fragile life could be. In the space of a few minutes, or even seconds, you could lose everything. Tears came into her eyes. "Are you sure he's going to be okay? Have you spoken to an actual doctor?"

"I have, yes." Stephen's voice was calm, but Kate had the feeling that he was deliberately keeping it so. Trying not to alarm her. "I called the hospital and spoke to the guy in charge. Apparently, Jeff was working up on his roof repairing some damage left over from the hurricane, when he slipped and fell. He broke his leg and cracked some ribs. He was knocked out by the impact, which is why the hospital kept him overnight, but he's awake now, and they've done all the necessary tests and scans. Apart from a slight concussion, there's no brain damage or anything. They're going to send him home this afternoon."

Thank god! But with a broken leg and cracked ribs, he would be laid up for a while. "I'll go at once," she decided instantly. "Someone can play my part today, and tomorrow the theater will be dark, so I won't have to work. Jeff will need a ride home from the hospital, and he'll need care at home."

"I'm actually planning to go get him and drive him home. If you like, I can swing by and pick you up. We can go together."

"That would be awesome. I can be ready whenever you can get here. You're sure he's going to be okay?"

"I'm sure. Don't worry, Kate. Look at the plus side—we'll be able to tease him forever about falling off his own fucking roof."

She smiled weakly. Her heart was still pounding. She was immensely grateful that Stephen had offered to drive her out to the college town in southeastern Massachusetts where Jeff lived. She hated hospitals, and feared that as soon as she entered one she would have flashbacks to her own hellish experience after Arthur's death. Stephen would know that; he would understand.

"Are you okay?" he asked.

"I will be. Just a little shaken up."

"Is your new boyfriend there with you?"

"No. We aren't seeing each other right now."

"Taking a breather or is it over?"

"I'm not sure. It's probably over. He walked out on me one night after an argument, and I haven't heard a word from him since."

"What an asshole. Sorry to hear it. Everybody seems to be breaking up. Melanie and I have called it quits, too. Love sucks."

"Hey, I'm sorry, dude. Are you okay?" Privately she had wondered what he had ever seen in Melanie, whom she hadn't liked at all on the few brief occasions when she had met the woman. Actually, she had a pretty good idea what he had seen in her. She knew Stephen very well.

"I'm good. It was time. We turned out to be mismatched even in those few areas where I thought we were compatible."

"I am so not going to ask what you mean by that."

He chuckled. "Probably just as well. Can you be ready in about two hours?"

"Absolutely. Drive safely."

"Always."

It wasn't until after the call had ended that Kate remembered Sir Godfrey's freakish warning about someone being in danger of a fall.

* * *

Kate was anxious when Stephen shepherded her through the hospital corridors. She could smell that unmistakable medicinal odor that hurled her back to those bitter days when she had lain in a Boston hospital, aching and sick to her soul with grief, unable to get her mind around the fact that she would never see her husband again. Stephen and Jeff had visited her daily, sometimes together, sometimes separately, disrupting their own busy lives to be there for her. Nick had been there, too; he'd left an archaeological dig in the Yucatan to come home and offer his support. Her friends had cared for her, cheered her, and protected her, and she would never forget it.

Because she hadn't been able to face going home to her empty house after being discharged from the hospital, Jeff had taken her to his home in Rolling Meadows. She had lived there for several weeks, recovering her strength, learning to breathe again with the help of the kindness and love her friends showered upon her. When at last she felt able, the three guys—Jeff, Stephen, and Nick—had taken her back to her own house in Cambridge. They had taken turns staying with her for several more days until she stiffened her spine and ordered them out, trying to prove to them, and to herself, that she could live there alone.

She couldn't imagine how she would have made it through the aftermath of Arthur's death without her friends. Now, if Jeff needed her, she was going to be there for him, for as long as it took.

Kate had performances of *Macbeth* later in the week, but since her role was small, she had been able to turn it over to another member of the company. She had informed Paul Tiele that she would be taking several days off, and, although he had grumbled, he had assented when he heard the reason. No one in the company had forgotten Kate's own accident, and she was touched to see how kind they were when they heard that one of her friends was hurt.

Before they actually saw Jeff, she and Stephen talked to the doctor who was in charge of his case. When asked if they were relatives, Stephen shamelessly declared himself to be Jeff's brother. Jeff didn't have a brother, but his parents, who lived in Arizona, were planning to fly in, and they had encouraged Stephen to use whatever means necessary to get all the facts out of the doctors.

"He's fine now," the young physician assured them. "Besides the broken bones he's got a slight concussion, but all his head scans are clear. There was one odd thing, though. When I first saw him yesterday he was conscious, but confused about his identity."

"What do you mean?" Kate asked. "He had amnesia?"

"Yes, but it didn't last long. We sometimes see transient amnesia after a head injury. According to the paramedics, he was knocked out by the fall, but recovered consciousness in the ambulance. When he came to, he was disoriented; that is to say, he didn't know the date, where he was or who he was. After a few minutes, he was able to identify himself correctly by his first name. The reports say he spoke strangely, with a foreign accent. Apparently he kept raving about *la peste*, which, as you may know, means the plague in French."

Stephen and Kate stared at one another and shook their heads. "He was speaking French?"

"Quite fluently, they claim. Has he ever lived in France?"

"I think he was there for a few months doing research for his dissertation," Kate said. "He's a college professor and interested in languages. I don't think he's super fluent, but he certainly knows some French."

"Well, the paramedics may have been inaccurate about how fluent he was. When I first saw him in the ER, he was speaking English, but he couldn't remember his last name. He seemed confused and a little alarmed by all the machinery and monitors around him. He kept asking whether anyone at the monastery was left alive or if they had all died of the plague."

"The monastery?" Stephen said, looking as if he were trying not to crack a smile.

"He also demanded to know what we had done with his sword, his armor and his warhorse."

This was too much for Stephen. He began to laugh, and even the doctor looked as though he was about to join in. Kate felt like kicking them both. "It's not funny! He must have some sort of brain injury. Are you sure he doesn't have a hemorrhage or something awful like that?"

"We're sure," the doctor reassured her. "He snapped out of it within the hour and has been fine ever since. We checked everything out thoroughly, though, and observed him overnight just to be certain."

"He's an historian," Stephen said. "His major area of interest is the 14th century, when there were knights with swords and armor. The Black Death also wiped out nearly half of Europe during that period. That could be what he meant when referring to *la peste.*"

"That's true." Kate felt relieved. Something else occurred to her: "Jeff's also into renaissance faire re-enactments and stuff like that. He actually owns a couple of swords, and he's a fencer."

The physician nodded, "That goes a long way toward explaining it. Sometimes people are briefly disoriented after a head injury. It sounds as though he needed a little while to reorganize his memories and separate his knowledge of history from his experience of the present."

"But he's going to be okay now, right?"

"He'll be fine. Those broken bones will take some weeks to mend, though, so he'll have to take things easy."

When they were finally allowed into Jeff's hospital room, Kate was happy to find that he was less badly injured than she had imagined. They found him sitting on the edge of his bed, glaring at his leg cast, and obviously trying to figure out how to walk without assistance. When they first entered, he said without looking up, in an uncharacteristically snappish tone, "Well finally. I've been pressing my buzzer for ten minutes. I need to get moving. Why don't I have any crutches?"

"Jeff, it's us," Kate said.

He looked up. One side of his handsome face was purple with bruises, and besides the cast, there were various pieces of gauze covering what must be lacerations. His ribs were taped up, too. But he smiled widely, his eyes lighting up when he saw them. "Hullo, you two! Have you come to break me out of this place? The docs all say I'm fine, and I want to leave."

Kate hurried to his side and hugged him, careful not to squeeze too hard. Stephen wasn't far behind. They spoke simultaneously, with her saying, "How are you feeling? I've been so worried," while Stephen said, "Shit, dude, you look like you collided with a truck."

"I fell off my roof."

"I told you your jet pack wasn't ready for prime time yet, you idiot."

Jeff groaned. "And that, I suspect, is only the first in what will be an unending stream of jokes at my expense?"

"'Fraid so," Stephen said cheerfully, while Jeff, good-natured as always, laughed along with them.

It took a couple of hours of hanging around the hospital and badgering the staff before Jeff's discharge was written up and certified by the hospital bureaucracy. By the time he was finally wheeled out to Stephen's car and helped into the front seat, Kate could see that Jeff was tired and in considerable pain, although he tried to hide it. "I'm really sorry to put you both to all this trouble," he said as they drove out of the hospital parking lot. "You needn't have driven all this way. I have friends here in town who could have helped."

"But we're your best friends," Stephen countered, "so we get priority."

"You took care of me when I needed you," said Kate. "No way you're going to escape now without me taking care of you."

"You might change your mind when you see what a terrible patient I am. I hate feeling helpless."

"That's because you're a control freak," Stephen told him. "You like to solve everybody else's problems. Heaven forbid someone should have to help you solve your own."

"There's probably some truth to that," Jeff admitted.

"By the way," Stephen said casually, "You haven't added a horse to the various animals in your menagerie, have you?"

"A horse? No. I have two dogs and several cats, whom I hope my neighbor has been caring for, but no horse. Why?"

"The doctor said you were asking about your horse when you first woke up." He paused for a beat, and then added archly, "Your warhorse."

Jeff snorted. "Bullshit."

"I do not jest, milord. You also demanded that the louts bring you your sword, your armor, and your droit de seigneur maiden for the night."

Jeff arched a golden eyebrow and grinned. He must have decided to go along with the teasing. Kate had never totally grasped the finer points of male insultology, but she knew you had to give back as good as you got. "In that case, you'd better have all the items that I require ready and waiting for me at the castle, young squire, or it'll be the stocks for you."

"The sword and armor'll have to wait til you're out of your straps and casts, dude," said Stephen, laughing. "As for the warhorse, for the time being, my car'll have to do."

"And the maiden?"

"You're gonna have to find one of those on your own, mate, just like the rest of us louts."

CHAPTER EIGHTEEN

A few blocks away from the New Cambridge Repertory Theatre, Daniel Haggarty prowled the small park known for several centuries as the Cambridge Common. He had driven to Cambridge with the intent of going to see his favorite witch perform her role in the evening's performance of *Macbeth,* the play no member of her superstitious theater company would even name. After not seeing or speaking with her for over a week, he couldn't take it any longer. He had been tormented by his memories of her for virtually every minute of that time.

He had to see her from the audience, at least. He'd told himself that it needn't be anything more than that. The theater would be dark and crowded. As long as he kept to his seat, she wouldn't even know he was there. He could allow his eyes to drink their fill of her. Surely this would ease some of his anguish. He just wanted to see her, and hear her voice. Then he could quietly leave the theater and go home.

He had bought a ticket, but he was early, so he'd walked north until he'd reached the Common. He had managed to kill half an hour and he should probably head back. But who was he kidding? There was no way he was going to be able to sit there and observe her from afar. If he got anywhere near her, he knew he would be sucked into her gravity well. He would crash. He would burn up and explode.

He was beginning to think that witchcraft really existed. Ever since he had seen her pretending to tell fortunes at that party, he had been under Kate Kingsley's spell.

He couldn't remember ever having felt so ripped up over a love affair before. When he had walked out on her that night after her mother's appalling séance, he had been convinced that he was doing the right thing. Fond though he was of her, he had no hope of a future with Kate. They were too different. She believed in a lot of things that were, as far as he was concerned, utter bullshit.

The spiritualism her mother practiced was anathema to him. Not only did he despise it on a personal level, but he had also made it his profession to expose such charlatans for the frauds and schemers they were. It was one thing to spend a few hot nights with a woman who was suffering from unscientific delusions, but something entirely different to permit himself to want more: to imagine building a life together.

Unfortunately, that was exactly what he had been doing. He couldn't seem to stop envisioning the two of them together, laughing and exciting each other for the rest of their lives. Just like Macbeth, he'd been tempted by visions of a future that offered him so much more than he already had. Unlike the Scottish king, he wasn't lured by power or ambition, but by the idea—the delusion—of love.

There were several old Revolutionary War era cannons in the park, and as he stopped pacing to lean against one, he was assailed by a memory from his childhood. Before his parents had moved to Winchester, the three of them had lived on the first floor of a house near the Common. His father had been a graduate student at the Harvard Business School. They had brought him to play here when he'd had been a toddler, and he had loved to climb on the old cannons. Dimly, he remembered his parents running about the park with him and laughing. His mother, dark-haired with sparkling eyes, pretty and happy. His father, tall and husky, a bulwark against all the dangers of the big, noisy, busy world.

It had been so long since he had thought of his parents as young, vibrant and lively that it was a shock to realize that at the time they had played with him in the park, they must have been around the same age that he was now. Both had died far too early—his father of a heart attack in his early forties, and his mother of cancer a few years later.

His parents had been in love. It had shone radiantly in both their faces whenever they looked at one another. Even as a child, he had recognized this. The bond between them had been deep and strong.

But somewhere, somehow, something had gone wrong. His father had become obsessed with his demanding career. He had turned ambitious, driven, stressed. He'd also been a smoker who kept quitting, only to take up the habit again when under pressure. Disdaining doctors, he'd refused to be monitored for things like cholesterol and high blood pressure. His mother's laughter—so like Kate's—had gradually worn away, leaving her pale-faced and worried all the time.

But she had never stopped loving her husband, not even when death snatched him away. She had loved him so much that she had sought his spirit in the afterlife. If there was an afterlife, which Daniel, frankly, doubted. Towards the end, as she had lain dying of cancer, also far too young, she had told her only son that she didn't mind because she would soon be with her husband again. And so she had gone to him, leaving Daniel alone to fend for himself.

Kate looked a little like his young mother, he realized for the first time. The same dark hair and laughing eyes. After his dad's death, though, his mother's hair had dulled, grey coming into it prematurely. Her eyes had laughed no more.

Daniel pushed himself off the cannon, irritated by the memories. What was the point of loving someone so much, if it opened you up to such pain, such torment? That sort of misery wasn't for him. Much better to live as he had been living for years, engaging in short affairs that didn't lead to uncomfortable feelings of attachment. Until now, he had been adept at choosing for his lovers women who were independent and busy with their careers; women who enjoyed the exciting sex he could provide but weren't looking for anything more complicated than that.

Granted, these women had been getting younger recently; women his own age, he had found, were more likely to be seeking committed relationships and making plans for marriage and motherhood. Before he'd met Kate, he had briefly dated a 22 year old. She had listened to music by bands he'd never heard of and she'd worn weird clothes. Her thumbs were always texting rapidly on her smart phone. She'd gone down on him less than an hour after meeting him, and tweeted him goodbye a couple of weeks later because he'd objected to her blogging the full details of their sexual encounters for all her friends to scrutinize. He didn't consider himself particularly romantic, but he wanted more romance than that.

As he strode back down the street to the theater, he mused about how Kate had seemed perfect for him in so many ways. They were close in age, they liked many of the same pastimes, they never had any trouble finding interesting things to talk about, and her laughter had warmed his cold heart. They had both lost people close to them and grieved over the losses. That was a powerful bond between them, even though it wasn't something he cared to dwell too much upon.

He had always felt comfortable with Kate. More than just comfortable. When he was with her, the world had seemed to open like a blossom, revealing scents and colors and textures that had previously been unimaginable to him. The air itself had seemed fresher and more breathable. He remembered the first night they'd made love when, after tramping through the hurricane, cold and shivering and dodging falling branches, she had laughed, lifted her face to the rain, spread out her arms and started twirling. Damned if she hadn't ripped his heart out right then and there. "What a magical night," she had said. And it had been.

Their lovemaking was incredible. Once she had gotten over her thing about not having sex with anyone except the sainted Arthur, she had turned out to be deliciously ardent and responsive. She had no inhibitions and she loved to laugh, but she could be a little wild and unpredictable in bed, too. Once she had taken him deep into her mouth while at the same time digging her nails into his ass and slipping one finger—

Don't think about it! You're only making yourself more miserable, loser.

He'd been with plenty of women, many of them attractive and passionate, but no one had ever been quite as physically attuned to him as she was. If he had actually believed any of the nonsense astrologers spouted about planets lining up to put two people in conjunction with one another, he might have begun to suspect that he and Kate had been destined to meet and fall in love.

But of course, he didn't believe in that sort of idiocy.

But he missed her. Dammit, he missed her a lot!

The curtain was going up when he found his way to his seat in the theater. He felt his heart contract with anticipation as the play began. Any moment now. He would see her. He would hear her voice.

But he didn't. There they were, the three witches, but his witch wasn't on stage. Daniel did not recognize the actress who was speaking her lines. He felt as if he'd just been kicked down a flight of stairs. He actually hurt. Why wasn't she performing tonight? Where the hell was she?

At the next scene break, he left his seat and went around to the rear of the theater. The stagehands recognized him as a friend of Kate and let him in. It didn't take him long to find Graham, who wasn't due on stage yet. "Where is she?" he demanded.

What he got in return was a cold stare. "Why is that any business of yours?"

"Just tell me, dammit."

"If you had been in touch with her at all, you'd know where she is. All her other friends do. Knowing when someone is in trouble is one of the responsibilities of a friend."

His heart thudded. "What kind of trouble?"

Graham just sneered and turned away. For an instant, Daniel nearly grabbed him and flung him up against the wall. He was bigger and probably stronger than Graham, but it had been a long time since he'd felt a physical urge to hit somebody. With an effort, he controlled it. "Fine. I've behaved badly. I'm sorry. Tell me what kind of trouble she's in. Please."

Kate's fellow actor relented enough to say, "One of her friends was in an accident. She's taken some time off to be with him."

Daniel immediately pictured Kate's own terrible accident. He had found crash scene photos through his connection with a

friend who worked for the state police. He had wanted to understand the event that had so changed her life, and the scars it had
left on her mind and her body. He had seen the wrecked car. He
had seen Arthur's body, covered with a plastic sheet, lying on the
ground. He had seen Kate being removed from the wreckage, unconscious and bleeding, but alive.

If a friend of hers had suffered something similar, she must be
in agony, worrying and reliving her own experience. Which meant
that he, Daniel, couldn't have chosen a worse time to indulge in
his own relationship histrionics. He ought to be there, with her,
wherever she was, supporting her.

"Who? Where?" he asked Graham. "How badly injured is this
friend of hers?"

"You, like everybody else in the world, have a phone, correct?
Has it occurred to you to call her and find out? Or isn't she taking
your calls anymore?"

Daniel whirled and left the theater before he lost it completely
and slugged the guy. He didn't know if Kate was taking his calls.
He hadn't tried. He had known that if he'd given in to the impulse
to call her, he'd be lost.

Just as he'd known he'd be lost if he came to the theater tonight. Her pull on him was too strong.

He walked back to his car and sat in it. His cell phone was
burning in his palm. Staring at Kate's name and number in his
contact list, he could feel his heart pounding. He didn't seem to be
able to breathe properly. It was as if the air had turned thick and
heavy. What if she wouldn't take his call? Why should she, after
all? She had needed him, and he hadn't been there for her.

Had he ever been there for her? His gut twisted as he realized
that he'd spent the entire duration of their short relationship ob-

sessing about himself and his own feelings. The sexual desire for her that must, at all costs, be satisfied. His increasing need to possess her body, mind, and heart. He hadn't been able to tolerate the thought of her first marriage. He was jealous of a dead man. How crazy was that? Worse, he was, at times, resentful of her grief, because it reminded him, uncomfortably, of his own.

She had told him she loved him. Sometimes he thought he'd imagined that, but, no, it had been real. She had said it, and he'd brushed it off because he didn't trust or believe in love. And then he'd walked out on her, so consumed by his own pain that he'd refused to acknowledge hers. Now she was enduring a different kind of pain, and again he wasn't there to support her.

Why should she take a call from him now? He'd been nothing but a selfish jerk from the night they'd met to the night he'd left her weeping. He couldn't believe he hadn't realized this before now.

Damn. Was it too late to make amends? What if she wouldn't talk to him?

He pressed the screen to initiate the call. He might be a jerk, but he wasn't a coward.

He half-expected the call to go to voice mail, but it went through. A male voice answered. He didn't sound friendly. "This is Kate's phone."

"I'd like to speak to her, please."

"Why? What do you want?"

"Uh...who am I talking to?"

"This is Stephen Silkwood. Kate's asleep. Call back some other time."

Daniel's brain felt fuzzy. Stephen Silkwood, the mystery novelist. What the hell was he doing with Kate's phone, and how did he know she was asleep? Jealousy and confusion warred in him for a moment. Kate had told him Stephen was like a brother to her, but right now it felt as if the guy was a rival.

"Look," he said. "I'm a friend of Kate's. In fact—"

"I know who you are," the man on the other end interrupted. "Your name came up on the screen when the phone rang. I doubt she'll care to speak to you, but if you want to leave a message, I guess I could pass it on to her."

There were about a dozen questions he wanted to ask, but the one that came out was, "Is she all right?"

"Do you care?" countered Silkwood.

He swallowed. "Yes. I do. I went to the theater to see her tonight, and I was told that one of her friends had been injured in an accident. Was it you? Are you, uh, okay?"

There was a short silence on the other end. Daniel guessed that the other man was deciding what to tell him. At last he said, "It wasn't me; it was Jeff. You met him, digitally speaking, that night you and Kate logged into the game."

"I remember. The college professor. What happened to him?"

"He was cleaning out his gutters and fell off his roof."

Shit, thought Daniel. "How bad is it?"

Without answering directly, the other man continued, "I picked Kate up in Cambridge this morning and drove her out here. We collected Jeff from the hospital and brought him home, and now we're taking turns sitting with him."

"So he's going to recover? He's not seriously injured?"

"He'll live," Silkwood said shortly.

Daniel let out a deep breath that he hadn't realized he'd been holding. He felt absurdly grateful to the man on the other end of the phone, who had just cleared up several points that he'd been agonizing about. If this guy had already been released from the hospital, his injuries couldn't be too severe. Which was good, for Kate's sake as well as for Jeff.

"Thank you," he said feelingly. "I had no idea what was going on. Graham refused to give me any details."

"Graham the actor? From Kate's theater company? He can be a bit of a dick at times."

"You've got that right," Daniel said dryly. "So." He hesitated for a moment before saying, "You guys are good friends, so I'm sure Kate has told you about me. I'm guessing I'm in pretty deep shit at the moment?"

"Oh yeah. To hear Kate tell it, you're quite the heartbreaker. And since I've known her since we were both freshmen in college, I'm inclined to believe it. In fact, I've been thinking about kicking your sorry ass, and I'm sure that Jeff, when he recovers from his broken bones, will be glad to help."

Daniel found himself grinning. "It's gonna take two of you? Why don't you just send that torturer hero of yours–what's the guy's name? Bartholomew Giles?"

"Whoa. The boyfriend can read? I'm impressed."

"I've read a couple of your books. I liked them a lot."

"Thanks, but flattery won't get you off this particular hook. You really messed with her heart and mind, and that pisses me off. Why are you calling? If your thing with her is over and done with, I get that. It happens. Just leave her the hell alone and let her heal."

"It's not over. At least, I hope it's not. I screwed up. I'm kinda just realizing how much."

"In that case, I don't know, man. You've got a lot of ground to make up, but this is not the time. She was pretty shaken up about

Jeff's accident–understandably, considering what she went through three years ago. She doesn't need any pressure from you right now."

This was not what he wanted to hear, but it was hard to deny that it made sense. Of course Kate was upset, and of course she had turned for comfort to the friends she had relied on for years, rather than the short-term lover who had seduced and abandoned her. At least this Stephen seemed like a good guy. He was direct, open, and was protective of Kate. It was hard to find fault with that.

"Your friend, Jeff. How badly hurt is he?"

"He'll be fine. Broken leg, ribs. Mild concussion. He needs to take it easy for a while. But it was scary last night when I first got the news, because I didn't have any details. It took forever to get a doctor on the phone, but I waited until I knew something solid before calling Kate this morning. I didn't want to frighten her. It still freaked her out, though."

"How's she doing now?"

"Better. She finally went up to bed, and I haven't heard her stir, so I presume she's sleeping."

Daniel had a sharp yearning to be lying next to her. Damn. What a fool he had been. He needed to see her, to hold her, to make things right again. A possible plan occurred to him. "What about you? If you were up last night trying to pump his doctors for info, you must be exhausted yourself. Do you need help? I think Kate told me Jeff lived in southeastern Massachusetts somewhere? I could be there in a little over an hour."

Silence. Then, "You're kidding, right?"

"I'm serious. Look, you don't know me, but I'm not bad in a crisis. Hell, I even spent some time a few years ago as an embedded journalist with an army med unit in Afghanistan. In a pinch, I can, like, change dressings and stuff."

"Dude, please don't try to convince me that you have any interest in changing dressings. You want to see Kate."

"Fine. That's true. But that doesn't mean I wouldn't be willing to help. I'm not completely selfish."

Silkwood made a skeptical sound.

"Look. I fucked up. I need to fix it."

"That's laudable," said Stephen, "but, number one, Max is arriving any minute to take the night shift. You remember Max, the guy you accused of being a hacker? Number two, this is a private party. No offense, but you haven't exactly earned a place in the club yet."

Daniel didn't have a good answer to that. He'd known that Kate's friends had collectively pulled her out of a pit of depression after the death of her husband. He'd known, of course, that they gamed together, although he had begun to suspect that the gaming was less of a geek pastime and more of a way for these old friends to connect and keep in touch. Arthur must have been part of their club, too. Kate had told him that she'd gone to college with Arthur, Stephen, Jeff, and at least one other guy whose name he couldn't remember. But Max wasn't one of the original group; Kate had never actually met Max, who was privacy-obsessed and possibly the only real hard-core gamer.

These were her friends, her support group, her circle. They'd had their own bodies tattooed for her. This had to be a tight-knit group. They had the power to take Kate in and close ranks against him. It occurred to him for the first time that maybe these were the folks he ought to be worrying about instead of dear dead Arthur.

"How do I do that?" he asked. "Earn a place?" It was a difficult question for him to ask. Daniel was unaccustomed to being humble. He had always been confident in his own abilities. When he wanted something, he thought about it until he devised the most direct and efficient way to get it, and then he charged into action. He rarely failed. But this problem didn't seem to have an easy solution.

"I can't help you there," Silkwood said cheerfully. "It's up to Kate. Treat her right and someday you'll be welcome. Treat her badly and you'll stay on our shit list for good."

Okay, thought Daniel. He couldn't really quarrel with that, but he wished he could think of a shortcut.

"Oh, and that reminds me," Silkwood went on, "Kate's mom? I've known her since I was 18. She's a little peculiar, but we love her. Get your facts straight, man. I don't know what she is, exactly, because I don't believe in that crazy ghost shit myself, but she's never deliberately deceived anybody in her life. She's incapable of malice. She's like one of those holy innocents who sees the good in everybody, whether they deserve it or not. Kate and her mom are both pure gold."

Daniel resisted the urge to get into a debate about Iris Carter. Come to think of it, Stephen's was an interesting perspective, when you considered that he wrote meticulously researched historical novels that evinced a rather stark view of human nature. Silkwood's books were both rational and intellectual. They were also violent. His hero, Bartholomew Giles, had overseen the torture of more than one malefactor accused of witchcraft. If anybody knew all the gory details about burning witches at the stake, it was probably Stephen Silkwood.

But Daniel couldn't focus on that now. At the moment, Silk-wood was a roadblock preventing him from getting to Kate, and what he needed was a way to get past him. "Look, I appreciate your talking to me, and I'm particularly grateful with you for be-ing straight with me. But I'd appreciate it even more if you'd take the phone to Kate and let me speak to her directly."

"Not gonna happen," Silkwood's pleasant voice informed him. "What I will do is tell her you called. Whether she wants to call you back is entirely up to her."

Shit. Frustration had never been a feeling he coped with well. But Silkwood had been more affable that he'd had any right to expect. "Okay, thanks," he said, feeling at a bit of a loss. Should he drive out there? He didn't know the address, but it shouldn't be too hard to find in this super-connected world. Instinct warned him, though, that anything resembling stalker behavior would not go down well with this crew. He needed to talk to Kate. Would she even consider calling him back? What an idiot he'd been not to have contacted her before now.

"I hope your friend feels better soon," he said, hoping it didn't sound too lame. It wasn't as if he knew the guy. "Sounds like he's lucky to have his friends looking out for him."

"We all look out for each other. You should try it; it feels good." No sooner had Silkwood said this than he barked a self-deprecating laugh. "Christ, listen to me. Sorry 'bout that. I've fucked up my share of relationships, too. I just got dumped, as a matter of fact. Love's a bitch."

Unexpectedly, Daniel felt himself grinning. Dammit, he was beginning to like this guy.

"Gotta go; heard the doorbell. Probably Max. Take it easy, man."

"You, too. Thanks again."

"No problem," Stephen said, and closed the connection, leaving Daniel once more staring down at the phone in his hand.

CHAPTER NINETEEN

Kate woke with no memory of where she was. Disoriented, she opened her eyes to a strange room with unfamiliar furnishings that were barely perceivable in the darkness. The only light was coming from the hallway beyond a door that opened slowly inward, revealing a shadowy figure moving into the room.

Am I dreaming? she wondered, feeling her heart speed up as the strange figure approached her bed. Arthur? No. In the light from the now fully-open door, she could make out a tall man with gangly arms and legs whom she could swear she had never seen before. He was entirely clad in black, and the clearest thing she could see about him was his face, which was very pale. He turned his head slightly, and she noted that he had the longest hair she had ever seen on a man—thick wavy hair that flowed over his shoulders and down his back, darkly shining as a few strands of it caught the light. Good god, he didn't even look human!

She sat up with start, realizing as she did that the room was unfamiliar because she was in Jeff's house. She must have fallen asleep, leaving Stephen to watch over Jeff. But this wasn't Stephen.

As she moved, the uncanny figure froze. "Kate," he said. "You're awake. Sorry if I startled you."

"Who the hell are you?" she said, her brain still muzzy with sleep.

The apparition gave a low laugh. "Close your eyes, Sleeping Beauty, and listen to my voice." He came closer. "You should probably keep them closed, because if you ever actually see my face—cliché alert–I'm gonna have to kill you."

She knew the voice. Relief washed through her. "Nekrotic?"

He smiled and nodded. His grin was a flash of white in the dark. "Hullo, Kate. Nice to finally meet you at last."

She switched on the lamp beside the bed so she could see him better. His eyes, huge in his angular, fine-boned face, blinked several times as the light struck him. Unusual eyes—they were coppery brown with gleaming gold flecks. And his river of hair was even more remarkable. She wondered how long it had taken him to grow it.

So this was the mysterious Max. Despite his sexy voice, she'd half expected him to be unkempt and ugly, but he was handsome in an unearthly sort of way. Those strange amber eyes....that impossible hair...maybe he *was* a vampire.

She shook her head, trying to clear it. Don't be ridiculous, she ordered herself. Just because she'd grown up with ghosts didn't mean she had to start believing in vampires.

"Stephen asked me to wake you before I left," he said. "I've been here for a few hours, but I've got to hit the road soon."

She glanced at the window, where she could see no trace yet of the dawn. "Got to get back to your crypt before daybreak?"

His grin broadened. "Something like that."

She pulled the sheet up a little higher. No need to expose her neck. "I've been sleeping longer than I meant to. How's Jeff?"

"I just looked in on him, and he's resting peacefully. About an hour ago, he was awake and demanding his pain meds, which I administered. He cursed me in a colorful manner for not giving them to him sooner. He's not a very good patient, is he?"

"Nope. Jeff's usually the one taking care of everybody else. He doesn't like having his role reversed. Where's Stephen?"

"He was up until after midnight when he finally crashed. I think he was awake most of the night last night, too, so he's exhausted. We should let him sleep. Can you handle things for a few hours? I've really got to get back to work."

"Where do you even live? Max, I hardly know anything about you."

"I live in New Hampshire. But, hey, you know all the important stuff."

She wasn't so sure about that. She knew he was awesome at Hunt the Night City, and that he was some kind of computer genius. He could be fun and engaging online, although he tended to clam up and get awkward whenever they played with anybody new. As far as his real life was concerned, she knew almost nothing.

"All I know is that you don't get out much and you don't have a girlfriend–why is that, by the way? You're an intriguing-looking dude. I've never seen hair like that on anybody. Don't women want to run their hands through it? Wrap themselves in it?"

His amber eyes seemed to get larger; he actually seemed puzzled by the question. "It's just hair. And I'm too busy working to manage much of a social life. I keep weird hours, and besides," he smiled at her, "I'm shy."

"Not with us, you're not. I've chatted and gamed with you for over two years now, and I wouldn't call you shy."

"With people I don't know, I am. I never know what to say. Making small talk's not my forte. As for girlfriends," he shrugged, "I'm not a total loser. These things never seem to last, though. I'm a bit of a loner, and I value my privacy."

"No kidding! You're obsessive about it."

"We all have our idiosyncrasies. So. Are you gonna get up now?"

"Not while you're looming over me, looking as though you might be about to sample the vintage from my jugular."

Another big grin. "It's tempting. But I'll try to control myself." He backed up, seeming to melt into the darkness. "I'll let you get dressed and meet you downstairs." And he was gone.

Shaking her head at the strangeness that was Max, Kate rose and shivered into her clothes. Max had originally been a friend of Jeff and Nick—the three of them had gone to high school together. But Max had gone to a different college, and she hadn't encountered him until she'd started playing the online game. The excessive secrecy he maintained about his work suggested to her that he worked on classified government projects, but she didn't know enough about the computer industry to assess whether or not that was really the case. Now that she'd actually met him in person, though, she wondered. She had never seen a government type who looked like *that*.

She was about to descend to investigate Max a little more when she noticed her phone on the bedside table, with a note scribbled on yellow legal paper wrapped around it and secured with a rubber band. That was odd. She'd left her phone with Stephen when she'd come up to bed because he'd forgotten to charge his.

She unwrapped the note, which was written in Stephen's clear, even handwriting. As she read it, she forgot all about Max.

Kate,

You'll be up before I will, if there's any justice in this world, so we won't be able to talk before you check your calls. Thus this note. Please finish reading it before you do anything rash.

Your boyfriend called. I recognized his name as the call came in, so I answered. Sorry if I crossed a line, but I was feeling protective. And, I admit it, I was curious.

Kate stopped reading for a moment. Daniel had called! She wished her heart hadn't just leapt with joy, because, dammit, he didn't deserve it. It had been over a week since she'd heard from him, and he had walked out on her on a night when she really could have used his comfort and understanding.

She returned to Stephen's note:

He and I had a conversation. Here's what I learned about D. B. Haggarty, professional skeptic and iconoclast.

First, he wants you back. It's not over for him, after all.

Second, he went to the theater tonight to see you. Apparently, Graham told him enough about your absence to scare the shit out of him without clarifying any of the facts. Have I ever told you that I don't like Graham? Anyway, Daniel claims to have realized that he screwed up with you, big-time.

Third, he offered to come out here and help. Mentioned he'd been embedded with a medic unit or something in Afghanistan, which sounded kinda cool. If I wrote contemporary thrillers, I'd interview him for research purposes. Anyway, I refused; we don't need some stranger among us who hurt you, no matter how sorry he is about it. But I give the guy some credit for the offer, which sounded sincere.

That's pretty much it. It wasn't a lengthy conversation.

So, here comes my (unsolicited) advice, which you of course are free to ignore. Don't be in any hurry to take him back. Please note that I am not saying this because I disliked the guy. In fact, I didn't dislike him. He seemed OK to me. But in my experience, there's a big gap between the realization that one has fucked up and the understanding of how to not fuck up again. Your Daniel, I suspect, is just beginning that journey.

And you, dearest Kate, have your own issues to resolve. Namely that Arthur is never coming back, in any way, shape or form. Forgive me for saying it, but you haven't wanted to let him go, and your mom's weird profession really does not help.

What I, in my great wisdom (LOL) suggest is that you take this thing slow. This is your chance to renegotiate the terms of the relationship. Demand some proof that he's capable of change, and provide the same to him. Only after he's made some sort of show of faith should you consider taking him back. Otherwise this probably won't have a happy ending.

OK. I'm done. Please ignore the fact that my own girlfriend just dumped my ass last weekend, which calls my ability to give relationship advice into serious question.

I love ya, babe, and want you to be happy again.

S.

Kate smiled as she read the last sentence, and then wiped her leaky eyes. "I love you, too," she whispered.

CHAPTER TWENTY

When Kate didn't call him back first thing the next morning, Daniel stewed for a while, wondering if Silkwood had ever given her the message. Most likely, he decided, he had. He'd seemed like a decent guy.

Unfortunately, Kate had plenty of reasons for not returning his call. He knew that, but he also knew it was vital that he talk to her. If he could speak with her, there was some hope of winning her back.

Since it would be even better if he could see her in person, he did the research necessary to track her down. Although he couldn't remember Jeff's last name, there were only two Jeffs listed on Stephen Silkwood's Facebook friends list, which he could see because Silkwood was the friend of a friend (Kate). Only one of these matched a Jeff on Kate's friends list. It looked good—the guy's job was assistant professor of history at a small Massachusetts liberal arts college. To confirm that this Geoffrey Slayton was indeed his object, Daniel used his press contacts to check medical emergencies in the area and hospital admissions and discharges. That nailed it. Slayton's address and phone number were in the directory, and Google Maps kindly provided him with a street view of the old Victorian farmhouse in Rolling Meadows, MA. where he lived.

Exercising what he considered to be great self-control, Daniel did not immediately climb into his car and drive out there. He rejected the idea of sending flowers or a get-well fruit basket since he couldn't claim to know her injured friend. All it would prove was that he had stalker abilities.

Since he was stalking anyway, he did a search on Silkwood, which lit up the internet. Authors, it seemed, had all sorts of pages and websites referencing their works. Getting personal info on the guy was a little more difficult, but by no means impossible. With the help of a few public databases, he quickly tracked him down to an address on Cape Cod. His home, right on the beach, looked much more contemporary than Jeff Slayton's place. Higher real estate valuation, too. Silkwood's mystery novels must be selling pretty well.

Their friend Max proved to be more of a challenge. Kate, Stephen and Jeff were all on Facebook, but none of them listed a friend named Max. He tried running Max, Maxwell, Maximilian, Maxim as last names on their friends lists, but came up empty there, too. Remembering Max's in-game avatar, he did a search on the word Nekrotic and found several references to Hunt the Night City. Apparently, Nekrotic was the name of the vampire boss of one of the early raids in the first edition of the game. That was interesting. It struck Daniel as odd that Max was able to use a game boss's name for his avatar, since non-player character names in MMO storylines were usually off-limits to ordinary subscribers. Was it possible that Max was one of the game's developers?

Pursuing this line of thought for a while, he researched the gaming company that had initially created Hunt the Night City. Although the game was quite successful, the company that owned it was small and privately held, which limited the available information. But Daniel was never less than dogged when he was doing research. He eventually dug up the tidbit that one of the original founders of the company that had developed the game was a guy named Max Rambler. Daniel felt a little gleam of excitement when he discovered this, and he got more hits when he returned to Google with a first and last name.

Max Rambler, it seemed, was some sort of "software genius," or so several computer industry writers enthused. He had been the CEO of a software company in New Hampshire that employed a large number of people, but had stepped down from that job a couple of years ago, for "personal reasons." He was now said to be working on some mysterious under-the-radar technology, but the details were scant, and personal info on Rambler was non-existent. No biographical data, no photographs. No address or phone records anywhere in New Hampshire or Massachusetts or, indeed, anywhere in the northeast region of the country. But he couldn't live too far away, Stephen figured, if he had shown up last night in Rolling Meadows to help Jeff Slayton. There were no public records like a marriage license or a property sale, and he was glad to find that there was no police record. Nothing came up on any social media search. If Kate's Max and this software genius dude were one and the same, he had covered his digital tracks un-usually well.

Why? Daniel wondered. The war against public dissemination of people's personal information had pretty much been lost during the last decade. Why would anyone take such care to bury his identity so deeply?

When afternoon rolled in and Kate still hadn't called him back, Daniel lost interest in Kate's mysterious friend and picked up his phone again. He stared it at moodily, willing it to ring. It didn't. Damn. He didn't want to hassle her; he'd done enough of that al-ready. She'd return his call when she felt like talking to him.

But what if Silkwood hadn't passed on the message? Maybe she didn't know he'd been trying to reach her; maybe she didn't know he was sorry for letting her down.

Pulling up her number in his contacts list, he sat with his thumb poised over the phone, trying to figure out what he would say to her if she answered. And, worse, what the hell he would do if she didn't.

* * *

"I taught my last girlfriend to do Buddhist meditation so she could control these panic attacks she was having," Jeff was saying. "It worked, apparently, but the next thing I knew she had joined a Buddhist temple, where she met this really hot monk who wasn't into asceticism. I got dumped so she could practice Tantric sex with the guy."

"I remember her," said Stephen. "You had her on a strict meditation schedule and yoga exercise regime. You wouldn't even give her a day off."

"She needed the routine. She was very disorganized. I was just trying to help her get her shit together."

"The trouble with you is that you're domineering. But in a nice way, so your girlfriends don't notice it at first."

"I'm domineering? This is coming from the guy who could have been the model for Sir Stephen from *The Story of O?*"

"Please. I am way more easygoing than that dude. Melanie broke up with me because I didn't dominate her harshly enough."

"Seriously?"

"Yep. One of her relationship-ending complaints was that I didn't order her to blow my friends."

"She was up for that, and you didn't invite me over? What the hell kind of friend are you?"

"She wanted to party with a couple guys, with me hovering and directing the festivities while she pretended to be reluctant. There would have been whips involved."

"Dude," Jeff said with a sigh. "Why is your sex life so much more interesting than mine?"

"Was interesting," Stephen said morosely. "Now, not so much."

Kate smiled as she listened to her friends analyzing their recent relationship disasters. Although she was sure they were exaggerating, once they got going, they could be pretty damn funny.

It was Monday afternoon, and Jeff was already feeling much better. His headache had abated and the pain from the broken bones was apparently under control. "As long as I don't move or try to breathe, I feel fine."

Jeff's parents, who had retired a few years before to Arizona, were going to come and stay for a week or two. Kate adored his parents, whom she remembered very well from their college years and afterwards; they were a warm and loving couple who would do just about anything for their only son. Jeff had protested that he'd be fine on his own, but they had already booked their flight. Stephen was going to pick them up at the airport tomorrow morning.

"You know," Stephen was continuing, "It's Max's sex life that's really pathetic. No matter how barren things get for you and me, at least we occasionally get laid."

Kate broke in on them when she heard this. "Don't let Max fool you. I picked up some very sexy vibes from him last night. I'll bet he has more hookups than the two of you put together."

This caught their attention. Both Jeff and Stephen stared at her. Then Jeff scowled. "Did he come on to you?"

"No. Chill. He just —" she grinned "—hovered a bit."

Now Stephen was scowling as well. "Where did this hovering take place?"

"Over my bed in the middle of the night. When he woke me, I thought for a moment that I was back in my mother's house, and that vampires had chased out the ghosts."

Stephen laughed. "He is pretty freakish. Undead? Maybe. They say your hair keeps growing after death, and by that reckoning, I make him about 500 years gone."

Jeff scoffed. "Will you guys stop with the vampires, please? I'll bet you've been sampling my pain medication."

"How are you feeling?" Kate asked instantly.

"Not too bad. How are *you* feeling?"

Uh-oh. Both her friends were now directing their attention toward her, which was nowhere near as amusing as when they were haranguing each other. "I'm fine," she lied.

More raised eyebrows. "So?" said Stephen. "Did you call him back yet?"

The subject of Daniel had been avoided by them all, except for the thank-you she had offered to Stephen when she'd first seen him this morning. "I really appreciate your advice," she'd told him. "I might even follow it."

"No," she said now. "But it's kinda hard not to."

Jeff, who hadn't spoken on the phone to Daniel and had no sympathy whatsoever for him, said, "You can resist. We'll help you. We'll stick to you like human nicotine patches. If the temptation grows too great, tell us and we'll stop you."

"With what?" she smirked. "Stephen's whips?"

Stephen's green eyes were twinkling. "That's a better offer than I've had in quite a while."

"Shut up," she laughed.

"Well, hey, I won't stop you calling him," Stephen said. "I just think you ought to make him reflect on his mistakes for a while. He's not a dick; he's just messed up."

"I'm busy reflecting on my own mistakes," Kate said. Indeed, that was pretty much what she'd been doing all day since she'd read Stephen's note. "You're right, Stephen, that I haven't been able to let go of Arthur."

The guys exchanged a look. If she was interpreting it correctly, Jeff agreed with Stephen about this. That was a surprise. Jeff had never said anything along those lines. "Wait. Do you both think that?"

They exchanged another glance, and then both looked at her, nodding.

"It has been three years," Jeff said gently.

"Daniel's the first man you've had sex with in all that time," said Stephen. "You like him a lot, if I understand you correctly, but one of the first things you do with the guy is take him to a séance where your mom starts channeling Arthur's ghost. Even if he hadn't been all anti-spiritualism, how do you suppose the average new boyfriend is gonna feel about that?"

"The séance wasn't my idea. I tried to stop it. It was Graham making mischief; he doesn't like Daniel."

"Graham's an ass," said Jeff.

"Graham wants to nail you," said Stephen. "You knew that, right? He's a player, and it irritates the hell out of him that he's never had the chance to play with you."

"Wow," Kate said. "You guys are harsh."

"And you, dear heart, are a bit like your mom in that you tend to see the good in people and avoid looking at the bad."

"Good thing, too," added Stephen, "or she'd never have put up with us all these years."

"I'm not sure I want to put up with you now. What is this, an intervention?"

"Maybe it should be," said Jeff. "Tell me this. Have you cleaned out Arthur's office yet, or is it still exactly the way he left it on the day he died?"

"I've been meaning to."

"You've been saying that for the past two and a half years," said Jeff.

"What does Daniel think about Arthur's office?" asked Stephen.

She didn't reply. Of course he hated it. She hadn't forgotten that Daniel had referred to the room as a mausoleum. But, seriously, she hadn't expected her friends to get on her case this much. Her mother, she realized guiltily, had done the same.

"I don't get this. Arthur was your friend, too."

"Yes, he was," Jeff said. "And we loved him. But he's gone and he's never coming back. Nobody, not even your mom, can change that."

"I know that. I *know* it! I'm not crazy." She was beginning to feel upset. Then, in a flash, something occurred to her, something she had never considered before. Stumbling a bit for the words to express it, she said, "Look. This isn't just about me. It's about you guys, too. Don't look so skeptical. I mean it."

"Yup," Stephen said.

"Sure you do," said Jeff.

She scowled at their disbelieving expressions. "Look, I'll tell you one of the reasons I haven't changed Arthur's study. It's because when we play the game or chat on videophone, that's where

I am, surrounded by Arthur's stuff. That's where my computer is. So when you see me in his office, you know that I'm respecting my husband's memory and trying to keep him with us. Even though he's gone. You can always see his picture, which is always right there on my desk beside me." She paused. "You do see what I mean, don't you?"

The guys were looking at her attentively, but they both seemed a bit confused. They didn't get it. They didn't understand what she was trying to tell them.

"I keep everything the same as it used to be because Arthur was an essential part of us. Part of the circle of friends that we formed in college. I'm preserving it not just for me, but for you guys, too. I don't want you to think I'm forgetting Arthur, or that I'm disloyal to him. I don't want to lose our circle. Don't you see?" Her voice felt choked up. "Right now it's all I've got."

"Babe, you've not gonna lose us," Stephen said. "We're still here. Look at us."

"If anything proves that, this weekend surely does," added Jeff. "You've both been here for me, taking care of me. We're still tight. Our circle isn't broken."

"But it could be." She felt a little teary, but so far she had managed to keep the moisture from overflowing. "Arthur's gone, and Nick hardly ever hangs out with us anymore."

"Nick's having internet connection issues on his dig. But he sent me email a couple hours ago. He says hi to you both, called me a klutz, and wrote something in Turkish that I'm guessing means get well soon."

"Well, tell him to come home. He's been gone too long this time." She turned accusingly to Stephen. "You said in your note that when Daniel offered to come and help, you told him no because we didn't want some stranger joining us. Well, he isn't a stranger to me. Why can't he join us?"

Jeff looked questioningly at Stephen. He apparently hadn't heard about Daniel's offer.

"Actually, what I told him was that he would have to earn a place among us. That isn't easy, but it shouldn't be, should it?" Stephen countered. "It's not impossible, either. Max wasn't part of the original group. I hadn't even met him in person until last night, and neither had you. But you can't say that Max isn't part of our circle."

"Didn't you go high school with Max?" she asked Jeff.

"I did, for a while at least. So did Nick. We were all at St. Crispin's in New Hampshire. But Max was a phantom even then, and he was off the radar for years, geeking out or something. We didn't really get close again until we started playing the game."

"Our circle *can* expand, you know," Stephen said. "We all make new friends from time to time, and that, surely, is a good thing."

"Kate," Jeff said, "Were you worried that we'd think less of you if you wanted to bring someone other than Arthur into our group?"

"I guess," she said miserably. "I don't know. I realize it might not make a lot of sense, but things are changing and people are changing, and nothing's the way it used to be anymore. I thought my marriage was going to be forever. Even after Arthur died, I never expected to fall in love again. I thought that when I died, my spirit and his would be together for all eternity. But now, I don't know what I think." She paused to collect herself before adding, "I really fell for Daniel, which is why this separation has been so hard. But, at the same time, I'm terrified of losing you guys. And

Daniel's such a whirlwind. He doesn't even play Hunt the Night City....oh god, I'm so messed up."

"No, Kate," said Stephen dryly, "trust me, you're not. Melanie, my ex, the kinky orgy queen, is messed up. I'm pretty twisted myself, with the whips and all. Max thinks he's a vampire, and as for Jeff, he just took a dive off his roof. You, in comparison, are only mildly confused."

She began to laugh. Laughter and sobs got all mixed together as she kissed Stephen and hugged Jeff, and thanked the powers that be for giving her such friends.

The laughing and hugging was still going on when Kate's phone chimed. When she looked at the screen, the heat in her cheeks rose. "It's him," she said, and with a quick smile at her friends, she fled the room, phone in hand.

Stephen looked at Jeff, who was frowning. "Looks like New Guy might get her back, after all."

Jeff's scowl deepened. "I don't think I like him."

"He's okay. Give the guy a chance. I think he really cares about her."

Jeff shifted uncomfortably, obviously in pain. "I just hope this Daniel character treats her right. She deserves some happiness."

"Well, if he doesn't, I've got whips."

Jeff grinned. "And I've got one helluva nasty roof."

CHAPTER TWENTY-ONE

Kate answered her phone on the stairs as she ran up to the room she was using at Jeff's house. "Just a sec," she said, closing the door and crossing to the bed. She sat down, ordered herself to be calm, and put the device to her ear. "Daniel?"

"Kate." She heard him exhale. It was as if his breath flowed into her over the airwaves, warming her right down to her toes. "I was afraid you weren't going to take my call. You didn't call me back. Did you get my message?" Before she could reply he added, "I'm so sorry, Kate. Are you okay?"

"I'm fine." Her voice sounded a bit unsteady. Gripping the phone harder, she tried to calm herself. "Nothing happened to me; it was my friend Jeff who was injured."

"I know. Your other friend told me all about it. Is he, Jeff I mean, feeling better?"

It seemed so odd to her that he should even ask about Jeff, whom he didn't know and couldn't possibly care about, that she fumbled for a moment. "He's—thank you for asking—he's in a lot of pain, but being brave about it. He broke some bones. His leg, his ribs. We're not supposed to make him laugh, but that's hard because Stephen's always joking around."

"I liked him. Stephen, I mean. He was decent to me when he really didn't have to be."

"He's a good guy. They all are."

"Yeah, I can see that."

There was an awkward silence. She was about to break it when Daniel said in a rougher voice, "Dammit, Kate! I can't stop thinking about you. I'm sorry for being such a jerk. I want to make it up to you. Just tell me, please, what can I do to mend things between us?"

Even though her heart leapt to hear him say this, she felt gunshy. "I'm not sure. I mean, thank you for saying so, but I'm a little overwhelmed right now. I was glad when I heard you had called, but I'm kind of messed up. There's a lot of stuff I need to figure out."

"I get that. I just—" He paused and she heard him swallow. "I don't want to lose you."

She wasn't sure what to say. She didn't want to lose him, either, but she didn't think she'd be able to endure it if they got back together and he stormed out on her again.

"I thought I could just walk away," he continued, "but that was really selfish, and anyway, I turned out to be wrong. I didn't realize how hard I'd fallen for you. I guess it's not easy for me to acknowledge feelings like that. It's probably, you know, that guy thing? That avoiding intimacy thing? I think I have that thing."

It was strange to hear him struggling to describe his feelings. It was sweet, actually. Previously, the only strong emotions he had expressed to her were those centered upon sex, possessiveness, and anger at the various deceptions practiced upon the world by unscrupulous con artists.

Okay, maybe that was a little unfair. She recalled the night he had told her about the deaths of his parents—he had been really sad then, and she had caught a glimpse of what had probably been a lonely life, particularly during his teenage years. She had seen it again the day he had told her about his mom's obsession with spiritualism. But he rarely showed that vulnerable side. No doubt it felt safer not to.

Now she sensed that he was trying now to repair the damage, even if he wasn't quite sure how. She found herself smiling at the phone, and wishing she could hug him and assure him that there were probably lots of folks who had that "avoiding intimacy thing."

"I'm trying to overcome it," he added. "Oh hell, I'm not very good at this."

"No, I get what you're saying. Anyway, it wasn't just you. I screwed up too. I'm just beginning to understand how tightly I've been holding onto Arthur, and how reluctant I've been to accept the finality of his death. I threw him in your face constantly, even though I didn't mean to do it. I'm sorry for making you feel as if you had to compete with a dead man. That wasn't fair to you at all."

Now it was his turn to sound surprised. "No, Kate, it's all good. I knew you were a widow, and I knew you'd loved your husband and that you weren't over him yet. You were honest with me about that. I just didn't want to accept it."

"I guess we both made mistakes."

"I kept thinking that all I was to you was a first step. A way out of your solitude, maybe, but just a temporary way station on the road to something else."

"I thought I was temporary to you, too. That you'd be all passionate and intense for a while, and then lose interest."

He gave a short laugh. "When are you coming home? I need to see you. I need–" he cut himself off for a moment, and then continued, "I *hope* you will allow me to apologize to you in person. It must have been frightening to learn your friend was in an accident, and to have to go to the hospital. I know you hate hospitals. I'm sorry that you had to face that without me."

Wow, he was being so nice. But he was still Scorpio, and still equipped with that sharp, lashing tail. She remembered Stephen's advice about this being a crucial point in their relationship. A chance to renegotiate some of the terms of their interaction. So far it had been all sex and passion, but it they were to continue, it needed to be something more.

"I want to see you, too. I think I need some time, though, to understand my own feelings, and to fathom where we go from here. If there's a path forward for us, we have to figure out how to find it."

"There is a path forward for us." He sounded more like his old confident self. "Don't doubt that, not even for an instant."

"I can't help doubting it, considering how differently we view the world."

"I'm willing to expand my horizons, if you are."

She would love to believe that, but she wasn't convinced. "Show me. Or rather, let's show each other."

"All right," he said slowly. "How? Do you have something in mind?"

"I don't," she admitted. "Surprise me."

"Surprise you?" He sounded doubtful. "I don't think I'm very good at surprising people. Can we get together and talk about this? When will you be back in Cambridge?"

"In a day or two. Jeff's parents are flying in to stay with him for a while, and I have to get back to work. I don't want to lose my part in the Scottish play. But I don't think we should get together, not yet. I don't want to rush into anything."

There was a brief silence, and then he said, "Are you afraid we'll get lost in the sex again?"

There was something about the husky way he said it that brought all those sexy feelings rushing back. Memories of their hot magic nights assaulted her. Blazing nights. It could be like that again. It could probably be like that immediately if she said yes to him. Not saying yes was like resisting the sucking of the tide.

"I am afraid of that, yes. Sex makes us forget our differences. But when we crawl out of bed, my mother is still going to be a psychic who has mysterious powers that I can't account for and that you won't acknowledge. I love her, Daniel. I don't think I can be with someone who loathes her. That's a deal-breaker for me."

He was silent. At last he said, "I hear you. I'll need to think about that. I'm honestly not sure how far my horizons can stretch."

"I'm not asking you to accept psychic phenomena or spiritualism or ghosts or mediums. But I wish you could look beyond those things and see my mom for the warm, sweet lady that she really is. Maybe she's crazy in some sense; I don't know. But I do know that she loves me and that she would never deliberately hurt or deceive me. If you could bring yourself to accept that, it would really help a lot."

"I guess I can try," he said, sounding a lot less confident than he had sounded a few minutes ago.

"That's all I'm asking," she said, knowing, even as she said it, that she was asking a lot.

After his call with Kate ended, Daniel remained lost in thought for a long time. Finally, sighing heavily, he flipped open the cover of his laptop and clicked the folder entitled "Iris Carter." He had refused to let himself think about Kate's mother ever since the night of the séance when she'd conjured Arthur's "ghost." Now, it seemed, he was going to have to figure out a way to deal with her. A freakin' medium. Of all the possible women in the world, he had somehow had the incredibly bad luck of falling for Kate, a medium's daughter. The gods must be laughing.

CHAPTER TWENTY-TWO

It sure looks like the archetypal haunted house, was Daniel's wry assessment the first time he mounted the front porch of Iris Carter's Victorian home in Cambridge. Although the building appeared to be freshly painted and well maintained, its odd little cupolas and turrets, with narrow windows and wispy curtains, conveyed a spooky air that would be even more dramatic at night.

He didn't want to be here. His interest in interviewing Iris Carter had vanished after the night of the séance. If it hadn't been for his desire to find a way back to Kate, he would have been happy never to encounter the old scam artist again.

He hadn't called to tell her he would be stopping by. She might have refused to see him. It would be safer just to show up. He rang the doorbell, but didn't hear anything echoing inside, so he rapped sharply on the front door. About a minute went by with no response. He was about to knock again when the door began slowly to open. She took her time about it. The big door actually creaked.

"So," said the petite woman who stood gazing owlishly at him on the threshold, "Kate's Daniel, isn't it? What a surprise. I had no idea you were coming today. Or—" the expression on her face altered, and she looked frightened. "Has something happened to my daughter? Please don't tell me you're here with bad news."

For a moment, he was confused, then it struck him that when Kate had been in that accident with Arthur, her mother must have received notification about the tragedy from someone—

probably the police. She must have grieved over losing her son-in-law, but even worse, she must have feared that her daughter would die, too. He had never thought about the accident from the point of view of Kate's mom before. But he was old enough to have several friends who were married with kids, so he knew that there was nothing worse for a parent than the fear that their children might die before them.

So instead of beginning his conversation with Iris on a confrontational note, he found himself taking her arm to support her as he assured her that her daughter was fine. Which just went to show, he thought, as he accompanied Kate's mother through the front hall and into the "parlor," as she called the living room, that she couldn't be all that psychic. Nothing terrible had happened to Kate. Unless...for an irrational moment anxiety swept through him. What if something *had* happened to her?

Angry with himself, he shook off the fear. Kate was fine. He had exchanged texts with her just a few hours ago. Although he hadn't seen her yet, they had been communicating.

"So, Daniel," said the old witch, sounding much more composed now that she was seated comfortably on a chintz sofa that looked as though it had been designed during the reign of Queen Victoria, "How can I help you?"

Although he had prepared a little speech for this occasion, it had flown right out of his head. All he could see was this sweet-looking old lady putting on her preposterous show on the night of Graham's party, committing her heartless fraud with her own daughter as the object. Anger flared in him again, and for a few seconds he couldn't say a thing.

"You look annoyed," she noted.

"It doesn't take psychic ability to see that."

"Indeed it doesn't. You don't like me. That has been plain since the moment we met. Do you always judge people before getting to know them?"

"I don't like liars and frauds. I despise people who deceive others and take advantage of their grief. And I particularly hate people who play nasty games with their own children."

"Then you and I have something in common. I don't like such people any more than you do," she said calmly.

He nearly got up and left right then. The woman was in denial. She was probably going to claim that she didn't remember what had happened during that fraudulent séance. That was common—the medium pretended to have no conscious connection with the "entity" she channeled. Their bodies were possessed by some spirit from the Great Beyond, so how could they be held responsible for anything the "entity" said or did?

Such incredible bullshit! It still amazed him that there were people who actually bought into this sort of scam.

But he couldn't walk out. Not yet. What would he say to Kate if he couldn't come to some sort of understanding with her mother? He was supposed to be widening his horizons, dammit.

"Would you like a cup of tea?" Iris Carter asked.

What I'd really like is a slug of whiskey, he thought.

"Or perhaps something stronger?" she added with a slight smile.

"No. I'm only here because Kate says that my not being able to tolerate you is a deal-breaker for her. Plus, one of her college friends insisted that I was wrong about you."

A line formed in the middle of her forehead. It looked just like the tiny line that appeared in the same spot when Kate was worried. For some reason, this touched him. He wanted to see Kate's lively face again, with her all playful and passionate emotions darting across her features. He yearned to stroke her luxuriant hair and kiss her soft, sweet lips.

"Kate shouldn't be thinking about me right now," said Iris. "It's you she needs, not me."

This surprised him. He had thought that the séance had been Iris Carter's way of getting rid of him.

"She has been grieving for Arthur for far too long. He was a lovely man, and it's sad that he passed so young, but I had never expected her to marry him. I thought, in fact, when she met those college friends of hers–Stephen, in particular–that she would fall in love with him and leave Arthur behind. Or, if not Stephen, Jeff, who has, I imagine, always been a little in love with her. Either of them would have been a better match for her than Arthur, sweet though that boy was."

Whoa. Daniel's possessive streak was aroused. Silkwood had said something about going through a break-up, which meant he was available. He had no idea about broken-legged Jeff, but women had fallen for invalids before. "What about Max, is he in the running too?"

Iris looked puzzled. "Who is Max?"

"Good question. No one seems to know. Tell me, do you chat with vampires as well as ghosts?"

Kate's mother blinked at him from behind her small wire-rimmed glasses. "Don't be silly. There are no such things as vampires."

Daniel laughed. "Well, that's a relief."

"At least," she added, tilting her head to one side as if considering, "I haven't met any. Perhaps they simply aren't attracted to me in the same way that spirits are."

He rolled his eyes.

Iris rose to her feet. "I'm still not sure why you're here, young man, but it's 4 pm, which is time for my afternoon tea. Please excuse me for a few minutes while I prepare it. You're most welcome to take a cup with me, or something else if you prefer. Are you hungry? I have some delicious shortbread tea biscuits."

A little bemused, he followed her through the front hall and dining room to the kitchen at the back of the house. It was a large room, and the late afternoon sun was pouring in the tall double-paned windows. The kitchen had probably been renovated once or twice, but it still seemed old-fashioned, with an aged refrigerator and a somewhat battered gas stove. Everything seemed in working order, though.

He noted that the refrigerator door was decorated with cuttings, clippings, and photographs. Moving closer, he realized they were all pictures of Kate, and that she was a child in many of them, with a huge smile and laughing eyes. Enchanted, he looked from picture to picture–Kate on her first day of kindergarten, Kate graduating from sixth grade, Kate in leotards in a ballet recital, Kate twirling in a short skater's skirt on an ice rink, Kate in costume performing on stage, Kate lolling in the grass with her arms around three boys who looked like those friends of hers from college. There were also a couple of professional glamour shots and one very sexy photo from lingerie commercial.

What he did not see was a single picture of Kate with her dead husband.

Iris noticed him examining the photos, but made no comment. He asked awkwardly if he could help her with the tea, but she waved him to sit down at the kitchen table while she put the kettle on. She opened one of the cupboards and removed a teacup for herself and a couple of small plates. She poured some milk into a pitcher and placed it, with a sugar bowl, on the table. The shortbread was next – several pieces arranged neatly on a plate. "I can make coffee for you if you don't care for tea," she offered.

"No thanks."

"In that case," she placed a bottle on the table in front of him. He checked out the label. Single malt Scotch. A superb brand. She handed him a crystal glass. "Please help yourself. I have ice."

He poured some, admiring the rich amber color. "No need. I take it neat."

The kettle whistled, and a couple of minutes later she was seated opposite him at the table, sipping her tea and delicately helping herself to a piece of shortbread. If she was at all rattled by his presence, she didn't show it.

"Why did you think your daughter wouldn't end up married to her high school boyfriend? From everything I've heard about the late lamented Arthur, he was the perfect man."

"Well, we often think that about the dead, don't we? Especially when they die young. Not that he wasn't a very special boy. He was kind and loving. He would have done a lot of good in the world, I think, had he lived." Her eyes took on a distant expression. "If he had been born in an earlier era, though, I think he might have become a monk. He was the quiet, contemplative sort. Kate, on the other hand, is vibrant and full of life. She is fiery, Daniel. Like you."

"And that's a good thing?" he asked warily.

"It can be. Not, of course, if you direct your passions into fighting instead of loving. You, I think, are stubborn and strong-willed, correct? Something of a loner? Very persistent, of course.

You wouldn't be here, would you, if you were not determined to solve whatever problems exist between the two of you."

"I'm not sure if you're trying to read my mind or psychoanalyze me, Mrs. Carter."

"Call me Iris, please. I was never Mrs. Carter, anyway. I have never been married."

Daniel was startled by this statement. He had presumed that she was a widow, like her daughter, but it struck him now that nothing in his research about her had ever mentioned a husband. He blurted out the question that immediately rose to mind: "So who was Kate's father?"

Her eyes glinted mischievously behind her glasses. "I'm not entirely sure."

He half expected her to make some ludicrous claim about virgin births or congress with a demon, but instead she went on, "There were three men in my life at the time. It could have been any one of them. It was, I'm afraid, a rather boisterous and unsettled period for me."

Daniel's mouth dropped open. He hardened his jaw, trying not to look like an idiot. He found it impossible to imagine the prim white-haired little woman sitting opposite him engaging in a wild erotic romp with three different men.

"They were all lovely, intelligent men," she went on. "I was deeply in love with one of them, but he, like you, had a difficult time accepting my psychic abilities." Her well-lined face grew wistful and her eyes looked a little misty. "I understood that, of course. He was a physicist, so naturally he was bemused when I saw spirits hovering in the corners of our bedroom. I was devastated when he broke up with me, and I'm afraid I had a bit of a fling with another dear friend who was there to offer comfort. A few days later, an old lover of mine happened to be in town, and, well, you know what can sometimes happen with old lovers. I wasn't in the best frame of mind at the time, as perhaps you can imagine."

She was silent for a few seconds, while Daniel absorbed this. Again, he had never considered what Iris's personal life must have been like. If he, a rational man, was having trouble coping with the fact that his lover's mother was delusional, how much harder must it have been for Iris's own lovers. In some ways, he realized, she must regard her "gift" as something of a curse.

"Anyway," she continued, "the father of my child could have been any of them. I didn't tell them, of course. There was no point, since I wasn't sure who it was, and besides, I didn't want to be a burden. Marriage to someone like me would be a difficult proposition for almost any man."

He felt something closely akin to pity for her. That was something he hadn't expected to feel. "You didn't consider terminating the pregnancy?"

"I considered everything. But I delayed, and at some point, I felt Kate's spirit move within me, which brought me great joy. From then on I knew the pregnancy was meant to be."

"Does she know about this?" he choked out.

"Of course. She had every right to know. I told her when I judged that she was old enough to understand."

"Hasn't she ever wondered who her father is? She could still find out. There is DNA testing nowadays."

"She is okay with not knowing, but you're welcome to discuss it with her if you wish. We did look the three of them up on the internet a few years ago. They were all married with families of their own. She felt, and I agree, that it would be wrong to cause confusion in their lives after so many years, especially since, for two of them, the confusion would be unwarranted."

Wow. This entire conversation was not going at all the way he had expected.

"I always believed that my daughter was happy with our life together, strange though it was at times. But perhaps one of the reasons she settled down at such a young age was that she felt the need for a larger family. Not only did she marry, which I have never done, but she also created her own extended family with her college friends, who became surrogate brothers to her."

"Maybe she needed something real in a world that was constantly being invaded by specters," he said caustically.

Iris didn't respond to this. Instead she said, "The important thing now is my daughter's future. Are you in love with her?"

"I want her back," he said, looking back at those photographs on the refrigerator. His lovely, bright-eyed Kate—even as a child she had been aglow with energy and laughter. He hadn't given Iris the answer she'd been seeking, but hell, he was the interviewer here, not this crazy woman. She didn't seem so crazy today, though. Neither had she been smooth, glib or defensive, the way frauds usually were when confronted. She was actually kinda sweet. Or maybe the Scotch was mellowing him out a bit. "We've only known each other for a few weeks, so it's a bit early to speak about love."

She had spoken about it, he remembered. The moment came back to him vividly and he felt a tightening in his groin. Although he had never used that word with Kate himself, it was impossible to deny that he had felt something real, something deep, something powerful from almost the first moment he had seen her.

Dammit, Kate. I need you.

Iris was looking at him, her head tilted slightly to one side. He got the sense that she could read his body as well as his mind. He felt his cheeks grow warm.

"I believe in a lot of strange things," she said gently, "including love at first sight. It's in the blood, it's in the bone. Maybe scientists can't explain it yet, just as they can't explain the odd turns that come over me at times, the feeling that the walls are breaking between the worlds and that things are leaking through from some other reality. But science is moving rapidly—biology and neuroscience, in particular. We understand many things now that were mysteries to us when I was young. Perhaps in your lifetime there will be a rational explanation for love. And for people like me."

At least she knew that the current explanations were irrational.

"I don't expect you to believe in what I do, Daniel, but I do hope you can believe in love. When I saw you together with Kate that night, the two of you felt paired to me. Well and truly mated. I was never conscious of anything similar when she was with Arthur. There was an aura around you, a glow."

He rolled his eyes, but something deep inside him thrilled to her words.

"She, I think, is in love with you," Iris went on. Her voice seemed to grow strong and more authoritative as she spoke. "Love is a special kind of magic. Whether or not you believe in it, when it reaches inside you and seizes you by the heart, there is nothing you can do but hang on tight and hope you turn out to be one of the fortunate ones whom love blesses. For love can also curse." She paused and smiled at him in a kindly fashion as she went on, "Whether you are blessed or cursed by love depends on the strength and the quality of the heart inside you. Is it loyal? Is it benevolent? Does it swell with valor, compassion and truth?" She glanced down at what remained of her tea, and then stared him directly in the eye. "What of your heart, Daniel? Can you share it with my daughter? Can you love her? Will you nurture, honor, and protect her for the rest of her days?"

He wanted to laugh at her. He wanted to get up from this creaky old table in this ancient house and get the hell away from this witchy woman with her beguiling tongue and her quaint old-fashioned virtues like valor and loyalty and honor. He wanted to tell her to mind her own damn business.

But he did not.

Surprising himself, he said to her, "Yes, I think so." And then, more firmly: "Yes."

Iris Carter beamed at him. "I thought so. As soon as I met you, I knew."

Again he wanted to laugh, but he couldn't. He was astonished by his own words, but he did not want to take them back.

"So," she said, still smiling. "A few weeks ago you said something about interviewing me for your YouTube broadcast? I've been considering it. Shall we return to the parlor and discuss the matter? Oh, and bring the bottle. You look as if you need it. Another glass, too, I think. I could use a wee dram, myself."

CHAPTER TWENTY-THREE

When she got home from Jeff's, Kate embarked on a project of redecorating Arthur's study. She cleared the desk of Arthur's things and decided what to keep and what to donate to various charitable organizations. She threw away a lot of old scraps that were now pointless to save. She went through the bookcase, giving away any volumes she didn't intend to read. Arthur's papers, his degrees, even his photographs had been neatly stashed in cartons, and she lugged most of those boxes up to the attic. Then she rented a wallpaper stripper and spent several hours poring over paint charts and drapery patterns, selecting bright and lively colors.

It was the first time she had attempted to do any work on the house by herself; she and Arthur had always done everything together. It was a bit intimidating at first, but her confidence soon grew. She began to feel a strong sense of pride and independence as her efforts took shape.

Each dawn, after crawling alone out of an empty bed and climbing into her swimsuit and jeans in the early morning light, Kate stumbled out, half-asleep, to walk to the fitness club. The days were getting shorter now. It was torture getting up, but she always felt better after exercising.

One morning she overslept, so she pushed herself even harder than usual at the gym. She swam for an hour rather than her usual forty-five minutes. She lost count of the number of laps. It didn't matter if she ached all over; she wanted to ache today. It was

Halloween, and she had no one to share it with and nothing to celebrate.

She had not forgotten that Halloween was also Daniel's birthday. She sent him a cute e-card. She still hadn't seen him, but they'd been exchanging texts and email. He hadn't called her again, though, and he seemed more distant than he had sounded when they'd spoken on the phone. She had asked him to accept her mother, but maybe that had been too much to demand of him. Maybe if he hadn't lost his own mother the way he had, it might have been a more reasonable request.

She had lost weight. Millicent, the head costumer at New Cambridge Rep, had complained only yesterday that Kate's costumes no longer fit properly and would have to be taken in. Her appetite just wasn't the same now that there was no Daniel to enjoy huge, hearty meals with.

After her swim, she dressed quickly, grabbed her gym bag, and walked out into the sun. As always, she cast a quick glance at the spot where Daniel had lounged beside his car on the morning he'd ambushed her. She still half expected to find the witch-hunter stalking her again. But there was no Porsche, no Daniel. After scowling at the empty parking space, she jogged all the way home.

The phone began ringing as she unlocked her front door. She bent down to pat Chester, who came to the door to welcome her home, then pulled the phone out of her pocket and answered it.

"Kate? Darling, is that you?" Her mother's voice crackled as if the connection were breaking up. "Happy Halloween, dear."

"Thanks, Mom. Same to you. How are you?"

"As well as can be expected, dear, considering that it's a busy time of the year for my friends in the spirit world."

Right, she thought.

"Do you have a cold, darling?" her mother went on. "Your voice sounds huskier than usual. This is still a very unstable period for you, according to all the indications. I hope you're taking good care of yourself."

"I'm fine," Kate assured her. "What are you up to today?"

"Well, darling, I was trying to prepare some treats for the children who'll be coming around tonight, but it's difficult with these video people hanging about. One gets a little tired of having to look nice for the camera. I was quite shy the first time they stuck that microphone at me. I could hardly answer the questions. But after a while, I relaxed and felt quite my old self again."

"Mother! What video people?" Kate could feel her blood pressure soar. "Please don't tell me Daniel Haggarty is there with his microphones and cameras?"

"Yes, he's right here, darling. Would you like to speak to him?"

"Oh, dear God! I certainly would."

"I'll hand him my phone."

"Hey," said Daniel a few moments later. "How's it going?"

"What are you doing in my mother's house?"

"I'm interviewing her. I'm finally doing that program on spiritualism. Thanks for the birthday card, by the way. I was pretty sure you wouldn't forget, with my being a Scorpio and all."

"Happy birthday," she snarled. "You promised me, Daniel, and I have not given you permission to interview my mother. I thought you were trying to change..." She sputtered to a halt, and added, "Oh, what's the use? I should have known I was asking the impossible."

"I've got some really interesting recordings," he went on in a pleasant, conversational tone. "And since your mother gave me her permission, I've broken no promises."

Kate was speechless.

"She's a charming woman, and so entertaining on camera. And her history! Imagine how excited our viewers will be when they hear that she's a reincarnation of Merlin the Magician."

"Shut up. She'll hear you."

"She likes me," he said, unconcerned.

She *liked* him? Only the fact that her woolly-brained mother was at D. B. Haggarty's mercy prevented her from cursing him soundly. Or maybe bursting into tears–she wasn't sure which. "Listen, Daniel. If you insist on sharpening your claws on somebody, let it be me. My mother's almost seventy years old. Does it make you feel powerful, setting up an old lady for ridicule?"

"The material I've got is really good," he answered in the same maddeningly polite tone. "I'll show it to you soon. How about tonight? I should have the stuff edited by this evening. It'll be rough, but you'll be able to get the idea. Why don't I stop by your place after the play? We could have a little birthday celebration, followed by, you know, a celebration of another type."

She understood what he was demanding. Her face flushed, and her stomach muscles tightened, sending a warm flood of feeling up into her breasts and out along her limbs. She could hardly believe it. After everything that had happened between them, Daniel was going to blackmail her with her mother's interview. And her traitorous body appeared to be at least a little bit receptive!

She forced her voice into a normal register. "Let me get this straight. Despite all that talk about how you were going to try to widen your horizons, what you're really offering is to trade those recordings for a night in bed with me?"

She thought she heard him swallow. "A night? No, babe, I think the stakes should be a little higher than that. The material

I've got so far is terrific. I'd want more than a single night. A lot more."

A lot more? What exactly did he mean by that? She had to draw a deep breath and clear her throat before she could answer. "You left me. You're the one who walked out of my bedroom and out of my life. I took a big chance on you, and I lost. There's no way I'm going to give myself into your not-very-reliable keeping again."

There followed a silence she couldn't interpret; then he said slowly, "I miss you, Kate. I can't work, I can't sleep. Ghosts or no ghosts, I want you back."

"Can we leave the ghosts out of it? We're talking about you and me, and whether there's a way forward for us. I deserve something better than the way you've treated me. And my mom deserves a lot better, even if you still can't see that. I told you, attacking my mother is a deal-breaker for me."

"And I heard you," he said, sounding absolutely serious for the first time since he had taken the phone. "Trust me. Can you do that? Meet me tonight, and all will be explained. I swear it. You won't be sorry."

Something about his husky voice made her anger fade, shift, and transform into something else. He was working his dark, sexy magic again. Memories of their nights together assailed her, sending arrows of sexual arousal shooting through her. She had missed him so much. Ever since they'd spoken on the phone when she'd been at Jeff's, she had hoped they might somehow manage to patch things up. "Is my mother listening to this conversation?"

"No. She went into the kitchen to brew me a cup of tea."

Tea. That was her mother's solution to everything. A nice cup of tea.

"I still can't believe you'd do this to her, Daniel."

"To you, Kate. I'm doing it to you." His voice caressed her roughly in a way that reminded her of the night they had met, she and the witch-hunter. Trust me, he had said. He added, "You did tell me to surprise you."

And suddenly, hope flared. Was he playing some sort of game? Was he teasing her, as she had teased him when she'd allowed him to believe she was a professional psychic? Her heart lightened, although she wasn't quite sure why.

"It will be okay," he added, his voice low but intense. "I promise. Please trust me, Kate."

Although it made no sense–surely there couldn't be anything okay about Daniel interviewing her mother–Kate felt herself relax. It might be crazy, but she believed him. "I'll see you later, then," she said, adding mischievously, "give my mother my love."

"I'd rather keep it for myself," he said, and ended the call.

Pondering his words, Kate wandered around the first floor of her house, absently picking up the latest things knocked over by Chester's ravaging tail. Did he mean that? Could she trust him? Warning herself not to get too optimistic, she tried to stifle the wild excitement she was feeling. She forced herself to remember him as he had been on the night they had met: dark, brooding, satanic. The Scorpio brooder. What she really ought to do tonight, she told herself, was not come home at all.

CHAPTER TWENTY-FOUR

Kate was late leaving the theater that night. After the play, the cast decided to celebrate Halloween in the greenroom with a party. She had a bit more to drink than she was accustomed to, and before long she was giggling at everything everybody said, funny or not. It got late, and most of the cast members left, but Kate and Graham were still there, chatting merrily. Kate went to get herself another cup of punch and stirred the bowl, murmuring an incantation from Act IV: 'And now about the cauldron sing/ Like elves and fairies in a ring/Enchanting all that you put in.'"

Graham smirked, saying, "It's a good thing Paul isn't still here to hear you. You'd better do the exorcism before you leave."

"What nonsense. I'm not superstitious."

"Nevertheless, you don't want any disasters to befall you. Your stars are in a somewhat precarious position today anyway."

"Meaning what?"

"Misfortune, followed by great happiness," he intoned.

"You're full of it, Graham, you know that?"

"The stars don't lie."

"Maybe not, but I don't think you're the ultimate authority on the stars."

"Do the exorcism, for heaven's sake. 'There are more things in heaven and earth, Horatio...'"

"How come it's okay to quote from *Hamlet* and not from *Macbeth*... Whoops!"

"Oh, hell," Graham moaned. "Naming the play, too. You're calling double doom upon yourself, Ms. Kingsley."

Remembering what awaited her at home, Kate decided to do the exorcism after all. The last thing she needed was more misfortune where Daniel was concerned.

Resolutely, she opened the door to the corridor so she could knock thrice and reenter. Instead, she took one look and slammed it shut again.

"What's the matter?" Graham asked.

Getting a grip on herself, Kate opened the door once again. There on the threshold stood D. Blaze Haggarty, lounging against the doorjamb in the same insolent manner he'd adopted on the night they'd met. He was dressed all in black, looking like a ruffian in his leather bomber jacket and a pair of skintight jeans. A very hot and sexy ruffian.

Kate swallowed and continued her reckless quotations. "'By the pricking of my thumbs/Something wicked this way comes.' Hi, Daniel. You want some Halloween treats?"

"You're late," was the lazy reply.

"What are you doing here?" Graham demanded, charging over to where Kate and Daniel stood, staring each other down, at the greenroom door.

Daniel ignored him, gazing only at Kate. "I got sick of sitting around on your front porch, witch. What's the matter—afraid to come home?"

"Terrified," she said, raising her eyebrows in mock fear.

Daniel glanced from her eyes to the punch cup in her hand. "Have you been drinking?"

"Just a little. It's Halloween. We've been having a party. I'm sorry I kept you waiting, Haggarty." She bowed deeply, as if to a monarch. "Pray forgive your humble servant. Oh, and happy birthday once again."

Graham turned to Kate. "What do you mean, kept him waiting? Surely you hadn't agreed to see him again?"

Kate stared at her erstwhile lover and knew with an elated heart that she would see him again and again, whenever he wanted her. So much for her resolutions. He had only to look at her and she craved his touch.

She drank in the sight of his crisp black hair, slightly ruffled from the wind, his broad, strong shoulders and long, muscular legs. The tight jeans molded to his thighs in a manner that did little to conceal his blatant masculinity. She stared at his hands, long-fingered and sensitive, his deep velvet-blue eyes, his aggressive thrust of a nose, his sensually curving mouth. She fixed her gaze on that mouth, remembering. She could hardly breathe with her consciousness of the sheer physical presence of this male who had taken her to bed and shared that beautiful body with her.

"Yes, actually, I had," she answered Graham, her eyes locked with Daniel's. She could not fail to note the gleam of satisfaction behind his thick lashes. He was smiling confidently, in the manner of a man who knows he's going to get exactly what he wants.

"Are you off your head? I thought you were starting to get yourself together after the way this guy walked out on you—"

"Hamilton," Daniel interrupted, looking at Graham for the first time. "Do me a favor and don't interfere in what doesn't concern you."

Kate was conscious of Graham bristling beside her, and she automatically put her hand over one of his. Daniel's eyes narrowed to slits. "You two alone here?"

"Don't start," she warned. "You've forfeited the right to be possessive. You left me. I could be sleeping with every man in the cast, and with all my college friends, too, and it wouldn't be any of your damn business."

A muscle worked in Daniel's jaw, but before he could say anything more on the subject, Kate moved over to the table where the punch bowl was. "We have cake. It's not birthday cake, but close enough. Want some? It's delicious." She helped herself to another piece, stuffing it into her mouth and licking chocolate frosting off her fingers with great zest.

Daniel grinned as he watched her eat, looking relaxed for the first time since he'd walked in. "Bring me home a piece. I'll eat it later. I've got other appetites to satisfy first."

Kate laughed a little nervously while Graham scowled. "Use your brain, Kate. The guy makes you miserable for ages—you lose weight, you flub your lines—"

"I never flub my lines!"

"You mope around here like a kitten that's lost its mother, all because you're hopelessly in love with this bastard who blows you away in bed but doesn't give two pins for you out of the sack. And then the moment he strolls back into your life with an appetite to satisfy, you fall into his arms?"

Kate turned on him, furious with him for betraying to Daniel how wretched she'd been feeling. "For pity's sake, Graham. You don't know anything about it. Will you please shut up?"

Daniel had gone curiously still. "Is that true? You're hopelessly in love with me?"

"Don't be ridiculous. Graham's being dramatic, as usual."

Daniel moved easily across the room toward her, trapping her in front of the table, his gaze drifting over her casual jeans, her high-heeled boots, and loose top. His attention shifted to her face, dwelling overly long on her eyes, which she knew were underscored by shadows. "You have lost weight. In fact, you look like hell," he added with a Scorpio's blatant honesty.

"Thanks a lot."

"Aren't you sleeping?" Daniel asked more gently. "Are you still having nightmares about Arthur?"

"Any nightmares I have are about you, Blaze," she said, trying to put as much bite in the name as she could manage.

Daniel quirked his eyebrows and smiled. He jerked her coat down from the hanger behind the table and held it out for her. As she thrust her arms into the sleeves, he pulled it closed across her chest, not touching her skin, but making her burn as if he had. "We'll have to do something about that. Come on. Let's go."

Kate slipped out of the circle of his arms to nod to Graham, who had just shot Daniel a careful, reassessing look. To her surprise, he had nothing more to say. Maybe he could sense it, too, this powerful magnetism flowing between Daniel and her. "Thanks for the cake and the party and all. It's okay, Graham. Really."

"Take care of yourself, luv," he said, kissing her cheek.

It wasn't until she had settled into the warmth of Daniel's Porsche that Kate recalled she had never actually completed the exorcism.

* * *

Daniel stood beside her on the front porch as she manipulated her door key, one of his arms braced against the doorjamb over her head. When the lock gave, Kate turned to him, scrunching back against the door. "I trust you remember what I said on the phone. If I invite you in, it's only because we have to talk things over."

He pushed the door open with the flat of his hand. "I'm not making any promises. We'll talk and then—"

"You never make any promises, do you? Or if you do, you're careful to tack on an escape clause, as you did with the promise about my mother. Which reminds me, where's my mother's interview?"

He entered beside her and switched on the front hall light. Chester was right there, meowing a welcome to Kate and rubbing his ample body against her legs. He lifted his head and cast a hostile look at Daniel. Daniel stuck out his tongue at him. "It's safe on a data stick. I'm holding that data hostage until I see whether or not you're going to live up to your end of the bargain."

"We didn't make any blasted bargain."

"Stop sputtering. We're off to a great start, aren't we? Kate and Daniel, loving adversaries."

"Adversaries, yes. Loving, no." She snapped off her coat.

"Loving," he repeated. He snagged her wrist and pulled her into his arms. Her breath came out in a tiny "uumph" as she crashed against his chest. Then her breathing all but stopped as he dipped his head and kissed her.

It began all over again—the bursting colors, the melting bones. His lips were firm and warm, his tongue gently arousing as it slipped past her teeth to stimulate the inside of her mouth. She yielded, obeying the special command of his body to hers; she opened to him, pressing her breasts against his hard chest, arching her head back as his mouth left her lips and pressed fluttery kisses along the curve of her throat.

I love you, I love you, beat the rhythms of her blood as his hands adored her, sliding over muscles that shifted and shivered to the pleasure of hardness meeting softness, male meeting female. She sighed with pleasure. It had been so long, and she needed him so much.

When his fingers closed fiercely over her breasts, she pressed against him, reveling in the feeling that this was right, that she was home, that in his arms was where she was meant to be. "I love you, Daniel," she murmured, then froze as she realized she had said it aloud.

"I love you too," he returned, his mouth coming back to tenderly kiss her cheeks, her forehead, the tip of her nose. "I've been in hell, missing you."

"Dammit! Don't do this to me." She pushed hard with the palms of her hands against the buttery texture of his leather jacket. "Don't break my heart again."

His hands imprisoned her wrists, pulling her arms around him. When he let her go, her arms stayed there, clasped behind his neck. "I won't," he said. He lifted her from the waist, forcing her legs around him, too, then carried her into the living room and set her down on the sofa. Dropping to the floor, he knelt between her thighs, caressing her breasts with tender, beguiling fingers. "I promise."

She whimpered in an anguish of desire. Her blood was dancing for him, but she had to have it out with him now, before her ability to think and reason completely melted. "How can I believe you? You're all passion and intensity again, just as you were at the start. Couldn't you get anybody else? Are you so eager for a woman that you'll venture into a witch's bed?"

His hands moved up to cup her face. "I don't want anybody else. Since the moment I first laid eyes on you, Kate Kingsley, all other women have ceased to exist for me. I'll never want anybody but you."

Did he mean that? "Look, Blaze, I'm not foolish enough to listen to passionate declarations from a man who hasn't had sex lately. It's like going shopping when you're hungry: Everything in the store looks delicious, but when you get home, you're stuck with a bagful of junk food."

Daniel threw back his head and laughed. Glaring at him, Kate tried to untangle herself, but despite his hilarity, he held her fast. "A bagful of junk food? Is that what you think you are to me? Listen to me, woman. I love you. If you don't believe it from a man who hasn't had sex for almost three weeks, get your damn clothes off and give me some sex so I can repeat it to you afterward."

Kate stopped squirming to blink her eyes at him. "Don't keep saying that. Don't say I love you unless you really mean it."

"Don't you love me, too?"

She blinked even harder as her eyes misted over. "I thought it was unrequited."

He shook his head solemnly, but there was a smile on his lips. "Some mind reader you are. It's requited. Very much so."

"I never claimed to be a mind reader, dammit. Why didn't you tell me? I told you."

"I remember," he said with a chuckle. "But I didn't know whether or not to believe you. You were under a certain amount of pressure when you said it." He moved his hips against her to indicate the sort of pressure he meant. "People say all sorts of thing in the heat of the moment."

"Which is why I told you that I don't want to have sex again before we resolve all these—"

"Ssh," he cut in. "We're having sex."

"You're such a controlling, domineering—"

He was laughing openly now. "Hey. Concentrate on my good points. I'm honest, remember. And constant. When I make a friend, the tie endures for life. You're the friend of my heart, Kate. You're the groove my erratic heart line has finally settled into. I love you. I never want to be with anyone but you."

Kate longed to believe him but couldn't quite. "When you walked out on me, you said you were going 'before you got hurt.'"

"Bravado. Did you really think I wasn't hurting? I figured I was just the first guy you'd allowed into the empty half of your bed after a long, sexless drought." He paused, and then added, "I didn't want to be the first guy. I wanted to be the only guy."

"If you felt that way, why didn't you tell me?"

"I tried to. Even after our first night together, I knew we had something different, something rare. I started to tell you that. But you stopped me. You didn't want to hear it."

"We hardly knew each other then. I didn't want you to say something you might regret."

"I'm not claiming that I loved you right from the start. But I felt something powerful, and then it just kinda grew without my noticing it." He hesitated, and then added, "Loving someone scares me, I guess. It's still a bit hard for me to admit that I'm willing to take the risk of opening myself up to love."

Wow, Kate thought. It sounded as though he really meant it. Deep inside her, a seed of joy was growing.

"And it was a risk," he went on. "I thought you were still hung up on Arthur. I was afraid you'd shoot me down."

"I was still hung up on Arthur. Or at least, I was still hung up on all the memories of my life with him. I'm really sorry about that. It can't have been easy for you to see that I still had all Arthur's things over the house."

He shook his head slowly, his beautiful eyes leaking pain. "That was hard, but it was the séance that really terrified me. All I could think of was my mother. When she began communing with the supposed ghost of my father, she turned away from the real world. I was right there, but it was him she wanted, him she went to, leaving me alone in the world at the age of sixteen. That's too young, Kate. I wasn't as tough then as I am now."

She cradled his dark head against her breasts. "Oh, Daniel, I'm not like your mother. I'm young, I'm alive, and I'm not obsessed with the blasted world to come." Her voice was intense as she leaned her face closer to his. "We're here now. We're together. That's what it's all about, isn't it? Being alive?"

"Yes, my love. That's what it's all about." He lifted his head and kissed her hard. "And it's what first attracted me to you: your liveliness, your laughter. You seemed the last person in the world who'd be mixed up in the dark, depressing world of spiritualism."

"I'm not mixed up in it."

"I know. I understand that now, thanks in part to your mother."

"My mother? What's my mother got to do with it?"

He just smiled, his eyes gleaming with mischief.

"I want to see that interview."

"Later." His hands slipped into her hair and held her head still. "Your mother told me you were in love with me, and damned if Graham didn't confirm it a little while ago at the theater. Then there were your eyes." His hands lightly brushed her cheeks, and her eyes closed while his fingers stroked them. "Your eyes told me the truth. Some actress! A few cups of punch, and you no longer hide your heart."

Kate began to laugh with sheer delight. She pushed him away as he tried to pin her to the sofa. She jumped to her feet and seized his hand. "Wait. Come with me. I have something to show you."

She led him into the room that had been Arthur's study and flicked the switch for the overhead light. There was a flash as the bulb blew. "Dammit," she said. "There's no other light in here."

"Here," he said, going back into the living room to pick up a thick homemade candle from the mantelpiece. He lit it with a fireplace match. "Romantic." He grinned. "Now, what's this you have to show me? I suggest you hurry up about it. I haven't had sex for ages, and I might turn into a werewolf if I don't get it soon."

"Vampire."

"Whatever."

She took the candle and set it on Arthur's old desk. The light was dim, but it illuminated the study enough for Daniel to see that she was redecorating. The beige wallpaper had been stripped off, and the walls painted a bright shade of yellow. She was painting the woodwork white; that part of the job she hadn't finished yet. There was still a faint odor of paint in the air.

"I haven't quite finished," she explained, waving her hand at the cans of paint and turpentine in the corner near one of the few boxes that she hadn't yet taken up to the attic. "But when I do, this study will be mine, not Arthur's. I ought to have done it long ago."

Daniel slid an arm around her waist. From the desk, he picked up the one photograph that was left, the wedding picture in the heart-shaped frame.

"I'm keeping that," she said softly. "It will always be important to me."

He stared at it without any trace of the jealousy that had once burned in him. He set it carefully down. "You're the woman you are partly because of Arthur. For that I can be grateful to him." He kissed her. "I love you, Kate. I love you."

Their mouths melded sweetly for an instant, then turned abruptly hot. He crushed her against him, groaning. "I can't wait." He moved his hands up under her jersey to capture her breasts. "I'm going to take you right here."

"Daniel—"

"Don't argue."

"I wasn't arguing," she assured him, forcing the jacket off his shoulders with hands that trembled. He pushed her away to remove her top, tossing it on the floor, and then pulled her back to kiss her. Their heads rocked from side to side as their tongues danced against each other. She unbuttoned his shirt. He unclasped her bra. The pile of clothing on the carpet grew.

"Dear God, but I've missed this," he said as he gently weighed her breasts in his palms. His thumbs whispered over the nipples now hard with desire. Every time he touched her, her stomach muscles tightened, and when his head dipped to take one swollen bud into his warm mouth, she felt urgent contractions deep inside her.

"Daniel," she sighed. Her fingers went clumsily to his belt, and his attacked hers. "This is inefficient." She laughed as their hands were tempted to tease each other through their jeans, their mouths to cling, their chests to rub maddeningly together.

"You're right," he agreed, stepping back. A yard apart, they finished undressing, their eyes intent upon each other. Kate could feel her heart beating in her throat; her skin was warm with the flush of love and desire.

When at last they were naked, Daniel held out his arms, and she ran into them. He stroked her gently from head to thigh, and then pushed her down to the floor, spreading her legs apart with his strong thighs. "Now, witch, practice your magic." His mouth covered hers, and he took her.

Kate wrapped her legs around her lover's driving body and gave herself up to his violent rhythm. As the tension in her lower body grew, the clarity of her mind seemed to increase, and she felt his love, knew it for a true thing. And in her imagination she heard her mother's wise words once again: "Life is the only thing we're sure of. You have to love life."

"You're my life, Daniel." She didn't expect an answer; she thought he was beyond words. But she got one.

"You're my soul, Kate," he replied.

* * *

A few minutes later, as they lay sprawled and spent on the rug, Kate looked over Daniel's shoulder to see two gleaming eyes staring at her in the dim light. Chester was standing in the doorway, watching them curiously. "Look," she said, tugging on a lock of Daniel's hair until he lifted his heavy head from the hollow between her neck and shoulder. "A voyeur."

Daniel started when he saw the eyes. "Not a ghost, I hope?"

Kate giggled. "It's Chester."

Daniel scowled at Chester, who was disdainfully regarding the two naked bodies entwined on the floor as if to say, good grief, now I've seen everything.

"Get out of here, you wretched beast," said Daniel. "Go find your own female." He made a playfully threatening gesture toward Chester, who immediately leaped up on the desk for a better viewing angle. His tail twitched as he balanced there, knocking over the wedding portrait in its heavy frame. It fell against the candle, which rolled backward off the far side of the desk. Moments later, there was a loud hiss and a flash of orange flame.

"Oh, my God!" Daniel was on his feet.

"The paint!" Kate cried at the same moment. And they both stared in a moment of frozen shock as fire engulfed the open jar of turpentine and, immediately thereafter, one of the few cartons she hadn't yet lugged upstairs.

"Do you have a fire extinguisher?"

"On the wall in the kitchen."

He ran to get it, ordering her out of the study as he went. She paid no heed. The draperies were starting to catch. Coughing from the acrid smoke that was beginning to fill the room, she struggled to jerk them down to the floor.

"Stand back," Daniel ordered from behind her. He had the fire extinguisher in his arms, and as soon as she moved, he turned it on full blast.

Moments later the fire was out, but they were both coughing from the smoke. Daniel dropped the extinguisher and threw open a window. "Let's get out of here. The fumes are probably lethal."

But Kate was gazing down at the blackened, foam-coated mess that was all that remained of a carton of Arthur's old books and papers. Misfortune, she thought vaguely, recalling Graham's words. "Dear God," she said aloud, "I should have done the exorcism."

"What are you talking about?"

She hardly heard him. Sparkling amid the mess was the one thing she had wanted to save: the silver-framed wedding photograph. Without thinking, she reached down and grabbed the heart-shaped frame. It was white hot, and she cried out and dropped it, then stood staring numbly at her hand. The photograph had turned black.

Muttering his full repertoire of imprecations, Daniel seized Kate and carried her bodily out of the room, slamming the study door closed after them. He took her into the kitchen and thrust her hand under cold water.

"Idiot! 'Do not try to salvage your heart from the ashes—the heat is too strong—it will burn you,'" he snarled at her.

"Dear God," she whispered, forgetting the pain. "So that's what he meant."

CHAPTER TWENTY-FIVE

Later, when her hand had been bandaged and the house venti-
lated to clear it of smoke, Kate and Daniel climbed, exhausted,
into bed, took one rueful look at each other, and burst into laughter.

"I don't know what's so damn funny," he protested even as he
continued to laugh.

"I don't either." She held up her bandaged hand. "When you
threatened to burn me, it never occurred to me that you meant it
literally!"

"I didn't mean it literally, dammit. And who would have
thought that Sir Godfrey Vernon did either? 'Beware the fire'—
really!"

"I thought you were the fire I was supposed to be wary of, Mr.
Daniel Blaze Haggarty," she confessed. "I thought 'Don't try to
salvage your heart from the ashes' meant there was no hope you'd
ever truly love me."

"That's the trouble with prophecy: We unenlightened mortals
misinterpret it all the time. Either that or the 'spirits' deliberately
mislead us, just to cause mischief."

"Um, speaking of mischief, Chester has really done it this time.
I'm probably going to have to repaint the study again."

Daniel promptly sneezed. "That damn cat. Where is he anyway?"

"The last I saw of him he was skulking under the dining table, looking guilty as the dickens." She handed him a tissue from the box on the bedside table and added, "I've been thinking... much as I hate to do it, I've decided to give Chester back to my mother. He's comfortable with her, and she adores him."

"No, sweetheart, don't do that. I know you love the beast. I can tolerate him."

"I love you more. And besides," she added as he sneezed again, "look at the energy you're wasting. I can think of a better use for all that physical power."

He raised his eyebrows and leered at her over the Kleenex. "Hmm, so can I."

"Speaking of my mother—" she began.

Her phone chimed.

"That's her. You see? Telepathy."

"How do you know?"

"I know." She answered the call without even glancing at the screen. "Hello, Mom."

"Kate?" said Iris in an agitated voice. "Are you all right? I had a terrible dream about a fire."

"I'm fine. We put it out before it did any real damage," Kate assured her. She had pressed the speaker on the device so Daniel could hear the conversation, too. When her mother mentioned the fire, he raised his eyebrows in amazement.

"What happened to your hand?"

"It's nothing. I burned it a little, that's all."

"Oh, dear. I have a special homemade cream for burns. You should come right over and let me tend it, Kate."

"Mother, it's not that bad, and besides, we're in bed."

"Is Daniel there with you? Let me talk to him."

Kate raised her eyebrows at the ceiling. "She wants to talk to you."

"I heard," he said, calmly taking the phone in his big hand. "Hi, Iris."

Iris?

"Is my daughter all right?" Iris asked. She was speaking loudly enough for Kate to hear her. "You were supposed to take care of her, Daniel."

"She's okay. She loves me, Iris."

"Well, of course. I told you so, didn't I? Was she very angry when she heard that we'd lied about the interview?"

A hot flush spread over Daniel's cheekbones. "Well, uh—"

"What do you mean, you lied?" Kate demanded, snatching the phone back.

"Kate? Didn't he tell you? Daniel didn't interview me after all. He told me his show was too crass for a lovely lady like me. Such a flatterer, Kate. You really mustn't let the sweet things he says go to your head."

"Oh, there's no danger of that," she assured her mother, looking daggers into her lover's eyes. "He didn't interview you, huh? Then what was on those video files?"

"What video files?" asked her mother.

"What video files?" added Daniel innocently, his blue eyes twinkling at her. "I haven't seen any video, have you?"

"You rotten, scheming louse! You tricked me."

Daniel grabbed the phone again. "Don't worry, Iris. That 'rotten, scheming louse' was meant for me, not you. I think I'm about to become the victim of a little mild domestic violence. Ow! She's clawing me!"

"Be nice to Daniel, Kate," her mother ordered. "He loves you."

"He's a rat!"

"No, darling, it was my idea. I told him you would do anything to keep me off YouTube. I really don't know why though. I still think it would be great fun to be interviewed."

Kate groaned, and Daniel laughed into her eyes. "Hey, Iris, do you want your cat back? Kate will need a new home for Chester when we move in together."

"Who says we're moving in together? Do you honestly think I want to live with a ruthless, underhanded Scorpio like you?"

"She's going to marry you one day, Daniel," Iris said happily. "I've known that for some time. And as for Chester, I'd already planned to take him. Kate, are you there? Did I ever tell you that Angelique knew Chester in one of her former lives? His name was Blackie, and it's rumored that it was a careless swat of his tail that started the Great Fire of London."

Kate took the phone back. "And you still want him?"

"Don't worry, sweetheart. He's allowed only one fire per incarnation. He's harmless from now on."

Kate laughed. "Good night, Mom. I'll talk to you soon."

"Good night, dear. I love you both."

"We love you, too," Daniel said just before Kate switched off the phone.

There was a belligerent silence. "Okay," she said finally. "Give."

"There aren't any recordings," he said meekly. "I couldn't do it. I went there the first time because I'd told you I'd try to learn to tolerate her, but I didn't have much hope. At first, I felt hostile, but she didn't take it personally. She started chatting about this and that, and before I knew it I was just sitting there, listening to her, thinking that maybe it wasn't going to be as hard as I'd expected to expand my horizons." He paused, reaching out to skim a finger along her cheek. "Your mom was charming. Very warm, very sweet, just as you'd told me. I forgot about my program. I just wanted to hear more about her and her lovely daughter. She told me all about your favorite bicycle and your dolls and the tree you used to climb in the backyard, and the next time I went there, she—"

"The next time you went there?"

"I've been to see her three times this week. Before I knew what was happening, we'd gotten to be friends. She kept telling me to call you, but you had asked for some time, and I didn't want to push too hard. Then I remembered that you'd asked me to surprise you, so I came up with tonight's plan."

"Some surprise! You made me really angry. I thought everything I'd said to you about my mother had just gone zooming over your head."

"Well, I told you I wasn't much good with surprises," he said, grinning mischievously at her. "Anyway, you could have called me."

"I was kinda afraid to. I thought I'd asked too much when I'd insisted that you accept my flaky mother."

"So we were both miserable, neither willing to make the first move? Don't let's ever do that again, Kate. In the future, let's sit down together and talk it out."

"If we can stop sniping at each other long enough. I never fought with Arthur, you know."

"How dull." He reached for her, fitting her snugly against him. "I like a good fight now and then." His mouth took hers, moving sensuously, exciting her. "It'll liven up our life together."

"You really want to move in together, Daniel? You want to live with a medium's daughter?"

"I hunt witches, remember?" His hands took possession of her body. "And when I capture them, I absolutely refuse to let them go."

"But what about your program debunking spiritualists?"

"I thought I might leave the poor suckers alone. One of my associates has come up with some great material on political corruption that ought to keep us busy for quite a while."

Kate was speechless.

"Anyway, I saw a couple of pretty weird things at your mother's place. Once the sugar bowl actually got up and walked across the table to me."

"What?"

"Yeah. Then my teaspoon heaved itself up and dipped into the bowl, putting just the right amount of sugar in my tea."

"You're kidding. Aren't you?"

His eyes were perfectly solemn. "Would I try to fool a medium's daughter?"

Chuckling, she kissed his throat. She could feel his pulse accelerate beneath her exploring lips. "My mother said you were changing. Loosening up and becoming more open-minded."

"Your mother's really something," he admitted, shaking his head in awe. "'Beware the fire.' Maybe there's something to this psychic stuff after all."

"And don't forget the prediction that someone was in danger of a fall. That must have been Jeff, falling off his roof while he was trying to clean his gutters."

"Whoa. I hadn't thought of that." He tilted his head to the side and added, "Or it could have been directed at me. Beware the fall into love. The jolt to my system didn't quite send me to the hospital, but it has certainly shaken me right down to my foundations."

Kate grinned at him. "See? I knew you'd come around eventually. Scorpios are very mystical, you know. They have a deep philosophical curiosity about the mysteries of the universe."

He pushed her back on the pillow and leaned over her, supporting his body on one elbow. He blew a dark strand of hair out of her eyes and trailed one finger lightly over her lips. "Yeah? Do they also have a deep philosophical curiosity about the way witches make love?"

"I thought you'd solved that particular mystery long ago."

"The mystery of you—your heart, your soul, your magic, your beauty—that's one I don't think I'll ever be able to solve."

"You could interview me."

"Hmm. Like this?" His hands slipped over her soft flesh, molding her curves while she arched under his touch. Her breasts, her belly, her thighs, all warmed for him as he stroked them.

"Ah... oooh... I don't think YouTube would allow quite so personal an interview."

"Don't worry. I'll keep this particular video for my own private collection."

She engaged in a little caressing herself, thrilling to the feel of hard bone and muscle beneath supple, love-dampened skin. "You're a primitive, predatory male, Blaze."

"And you love it."

"I love it," she admitted. "Interview me some more."

"I will. But don't call me Blaze."

"Why not? What's gonna happen if I keep calling you Blaze, Blaze?"

He gave a villainous laugh and showed her. She kept laughing, but the sounds quickly changed to soft moans of pleasure as he parted her thighs and slid between to take her down that long, slow road to fulfillment once again.

* * *

Kate dreamed of Arthur one more time that night. She thought she saw him standing at the end of the bed, smiling a benediction upon the couple there entwined. In his hand was a silver-framed photograph of Kate in a wedding gown. The bridegroom at her side was Daniel.

Arthur gave her the picture, then turned, waved cheerfully, and disappeared.

Rolling over, Kate cuddled to Daniel, who gathered her close. For the rest of the night they slept dreamlessly, peacefully, safely cradled in each other's arms.

AUTHOR'S NOTE

Blazing Nights is the first of several novels in the *Night Games* series. It will be followed by *Wicked Nights*, Max's story. For more information about the next release, please sign up for my newsletter at http://eepurl.com/yB2x5

I love to hear from my readers. You can contact me at: lindabarlow@lindabarlow.com.

You are also invited to connect with me on my Facebook author page at www.facebook.com/LindaBarlowAuthor or on Twitter at www.twitter.com/LindaBarlow.

If you enjoyed this book, please consider telling your friends about it. I'd also really appreciate it if you wrote a review and posted it online at your favorite book discussion forum.

Other recent releases by Linda Barlow: *Fires of Destiny*.

ACKNOWLEDGMENTS

I am deeply indebted to my wonderful lover and partner Curt Monash for all the support he has given me during my writing of this book. He has served as my consultant, my fact checker, and my incomparable copy-editor (who patiently read the manuscript several times, hunting down errors). I love you, sweetheart.

ABOUT THE AUTHOR

Linda Barlow is the author of 15 novels, with more on the way. She lives in New England with her mysterious partner (who sleeps during the day, which has often made her wonder if he's a vampire) and their equally enigmatic and nocturnal cat.

Linda has written in various genres, including family sagas, historical and contemporary romance, romantic suspense, and general mainstream fiction. Publishers have included Doubleday, Dell, Penguin, Warner Books, Hachette, New American Library/Signet, Berkley/Putnam, Silhouette and Harlequin.

She's proud to have earned a few awards over the years, including the Rita from Romance Writers of America for *Leaves of Fortune;* New Historical Novelist of the Year from *Romantic Times* for *Fires of Destiny,* and a Career Achievement award from *Romantic Times* for her contemporary novels.

www.ingramcontent.com/pod-product-compliance
Lightning Source LLC
Chambersburg PA
CBHW030020180626
46810CB00001B/129